BREAKDOWN
EMP TERROR SERIES: BOOK 1

by J.R. Tate

CHAPTER ONE

"Authorities are urging caution - a credible threat has been released toward the United States. The threat level has been raised to the red level and there have been increased security measures at all international airports and security checkpoints at the borders. We are asking the public to stay alert and if something or someone seems suspicious please call your local police station or dial 911."

Jake Shepherd sat down in front of the television, his microwave dinner steaming in front of him. He was only halfway listening to the news - it was the same old thing over and over again. A terrorist group had bombed someone, there was a shooting here, a stabbing there, and another sex trafficking network uncovered where most people would least expect it.

Grabbing the remote, he flipped through the channels. It was as if each news station was run by the same people, only different reporters pasted on screen to prove individuality of the networks. Multitasking, he dipped his fork into the corner section of the meal, cringing when the utensil wouldn't push through the hard top layer of the refried beans. Damn it, he had overcooked it again. His phone buzzed on the coffee table beside him and he grabbed it, answering it immediately.

"Hello?"

"Hey, Jake. It's me. They're having me stay until at least midnight. Apparently, there was a huge wreck on the interstate and we are bombarded in the ER for the foreseeable future."

"I figured it'd be a late night," Jake replied, forcing the fork to stab through the ruined beans.

"Why is that?"

"They already asked you to stay a couple of hours late. Seems like every time that happens, it ends up being a complete double shift." He tried to hide his frustration but it was hard. "I'm just starting to forget what my wife looks like, you know?" Jake stifled a laugh and attempted to cut through the enchilada that was buried in some kind of cheese sauce. He could already feel the reflux in his chest.

"Don't be silly. And don't forget to pick up Dylan from soccer practice. He should be done in about thirty minutes."

"I won't forget, Alice. I promise. I'm just going to finish up this fine enchilada dinner and I'll head to the soccer fields. Don't you worry about us."

There was a short pause in the conversation and the background noise seemed to be getting louder. "Oh lord, I regret ever buying those. Look, I gotta go. They're bringing in a wave of patients and there's a few who are critical. I love you, hon."

"I love you, too."

Jake ended the call and put the phone on the table, diverting his attention to the TV. CNN was also focused on the terror threat and he gave up, turning everything off and sitting in silence. The real news would be complete peace across the nation. Now that would be something to tune into.

The house was dark, the only light illuminating the living room was the lamp on the end table next to him. The second hand on the clock ticked and he tried to shove the negativity aside. Alice was a damn good nurse. Her commitment to the job was admirable. With their busy jobs, their schedules never seemed to mesh well and the one night off together for the week was thwarted due to a massive pileup on the highway.

Jake gave up on the enchiladas. Even if he under-cooked the food, the beans would be too hard, the enchiladas like leather, and he'd rather just get some takeout on the way home from getting Dylan. Their son would have no objection to grabbing a greasy hamburger after a hard day of workouts. The kid never denied junk food.

Glancing at his watch, he decided to head to the soccer fields. They weren't far from the highway where the wreck had occurred so the chances of a traffic jam were likely. Grabbing his hat, Jake stepped out on the porch, taking in the humid summer evening, the air warm and thick, hinting at possible rain later on. As expected, the traffic was backed up and moving slow, and his normal ten-minute drive took almost twenty. Dylan was standing with a few teammates as Jake pulled up and fist bumped all three of them as he jogged to the truck.

"Hey, kiddo. How was practice?"

Dylan threw his duffel bag in the backseat and climbed in the passenger side, the edges of his scruffy hair wet with sweat. For some reason, all of the boys on his junior varsity team were sporting 1970's style haircuts, his son included.

"Lots of running. I think coach was pissed that we lost last night."

"It's good for you. Mom's working late. How about we stop off at that burger joint on the way home? I bet you're starving."

***

"Did you see the news tonight?" Alice slid in beside Jake, her warm body pressed up against him in their bed.

"I vaguely listened. What'd I miss?" Jake reached for her hand, intertwining his fingers in hers. Despite her long hours of work, her palms were as smooth as silk and her touch reminded him of how much he missed their time together. They both had great careers but sometimes, it wasn't worth it.

"They raised the terror threat up to red again. That's the most elevated level." She spoke with her eyes closed but her fingers tightened around his, strengthening the embrace. She had made it home around twelve-thirty, which was earlier than he had expected.

"Yeah, but it's at that level almost every other week, isn't it?"

"I figured you'd know better than most, being a pilot and all. Don't they encourage y'all to pay attention to those kinds of things?"

Jake rolled over on his side, hugging her from behind. Her body nestled into his and for a second, neither of them spoke. He hadn't seen her in several days and the last thing he wanted to talk about was another potential threat to the country. The days after September Eleventh made them all wake up, and unfortunately, complacency was beginning to settle back in, and he was guilty of becoming numb to everything along with the rest of the nation.

"I do keep an eye on it, Alice. But what can I do? If we stop flying, the terrorists win. They want us to sit around fretting. That's why they dish out the threats."

"What time do you need to be at the airport tomorrow?" Her voice was low, muffled up next to the pillow. She'd be asleep in a few minutes. It was taking every bit of energy she had just to stay awake and chat with him.

"First flight is at ten AM. I'm on the Dallas to Seattle run tomorrow."

"Oh, good. At least we can have coffee together." Alice glanced over her shoulder at him, popping one eye open long enough to say, "Please be careful. I know flying is the safest way to travel but you know I worry. You're a damn good pilot…" She opened her mouth like she was about to say something else but nestled back into the pillow.

"And you're a damn good nurse. Get some sleep, babe. We'll have breakfast together tomorrow. Good night."

She responded with a low murmur that was likely her half-asleep version of "good night". It was close enough for Jake and he switched the lamp off, settling into the complete darkness that overtook the room. Terror threat red level. They'd definitely talk about it in briefing at work. It was a shame that was becoming a normal topic on their daily agendas.

The next morning, Jake was up early. Alice's worry about the terror threat passed onto him like she was sharing some contagious sickness that spread through touch. He had been a commercial pilot for twenty years - and despite his experience on the job, a twinge of excitement and nerves always coursed through him on mornings before he had scheduled flights. The adrenaline rush is what kept him doing it - the feel of the airplane as it sped down the runway, the inertia on his body as he pulled the yoke back for take-off. And the landing - there was nothing like knowing he got the passengers safely to and from their destinations. The skid of the tires on the asphalt, the flaps set to slow the plane down, and the hum of the landing gear as it edged out from the bottom of the plane.

Jake loved to fly and it all started when his father had taken him up in his small Cessna. He was just a private pilot but that is what heightened Jake's interest in turning it into a career. Being in the military also provided in his life path. And then things like terrorism had to come in, shadowing the industry and making everyone just a bit more guarded, including himself. But as he had said before - if they lived in fear to go on with their normal, everyday lives, the terrorist won, and it was no way to live.

Alice would be up soon and he gathered a carton of eggs, orange juice, and some bacon out of the refrigerator. The coffee was brewing next to the stove and he pulled a loaf of bread from the pantry. A good breakfast would do her some good after the long shift she had put in yesterday. Dylan would need to get up soon as well - the soccer team had to be at school early on Thursday mornings for weight training. He also made a mental note to call Sophie before his flight - she was off to college in Boston and he felt like he hadn't talked to his daughter in ages.

"What's the occasion?" Alice came down the stairs, rubbing a towel through her wet hair. Her bathrobe clung to her, accentuating her curves, and Jake wished they could have a little time to themselves. Yawning, she went straight for the coffee, pouring a large mug. "Yum, strong just like I like it."

"Good. Do you want fried or scrambled eggs?" Jake held up the spatula, turning the slices of bacon that were now drenched in grease. Alice was always health conscious and was careful about the food she ate, but she grabbed a crunchy strip off of the plate and nibbled on it with no objection.

"Scrambled will be just fine. Thanks, hon."

"You doing okay?" Jake finished the eggs and popped a couple of pieces of bread in the toaster.

"I'm good. I could just use a day off, you know?"

"You and me both. A day off together. Dylan could go stay at a friend's house or something. We could, you know…" His eyebrows danced as he insinuated something he was sure she'd easily catch onto.

"Doesn't look possible in the foreseeable future." Alice bit into her toast, a small glob of jelly smearing on her top lip. "I'm working another twelve today. And you know what that means. It'll turn into a repeat of yesterday. How many legs to Seattle are you doing?"

"Up to Seattle, down to Oakland, stop in Vegas, and then back to Dallas. I won't be home until late, anyway. Sometimes the leg from Vegas to Dallas gets canceled, so I might be spending the night there. I'll let you know what the flight schedule looks like. I've been keeping an eye on the weather. Looks pretty clear everywhere I'm flying." He made his own plate and they both sat in silence a few seconds before he spoke up again. "I'm going to call Sophie on my way in. Have you heard from her lately?"

Alice nodded and wiped her mouth with a napkin. "She texted me yesterday. A picture of her and a friend at some sporting event."

"A guy friend or a girl friend?" Jake asked, his stomach wrenching at the thought. It was one thing he had to accept - Sophie was living half way across the country and she was a pretty girl, hell bent on establishing her independence. One day she would bring someone home to meet the family. And Jake wasn't ready.

"It was a girl, Jake. I think her roommate."

"Oh, thank God." Jake went to say something else but stopped himself when Dylan padded into the kitchen, his dark hair sticking up in every direction, one eye closed as he rummaged for the milk. "Good morning, sleepy head. You better move faster. You're running late for weight training."

He mumbled something incoherent and Jake winked at Alice. "I'll take him to school on the way to the airport. You take a few minutes extra for yourself." Patting Dylan on the shoulder, Jake said, "Catch a ride with Randy or Rudy, or whatever his name is this afternoon. Neither of us will be home until after practice."

"You mean Ricky?" Dylan laughed and drank the rest of the milk straight out of the carton.

"Ricky, Randy, Rudy... same difference. Let's get moving." Leaning toward Alice, Jake pecked her on the lips. "Have a good day, babe. Love you."

"Love you, too. Text me every time you land."

It was standard procedure and important to Alice that they communicate regularly. There seemed to be a bit more sense of urgency today than usual, and Jake wasn't going to deny her peace of mind. If it were reversed and she was the pilot, he'd expect the same thing from her.

CHAPTER TWO

After dropping Dylan off at practice, Jake merged onto the freeway, headed to Dallas Love Field. He was thankful he worked for an airplane carrier that flew out of the smaller of the two Dallas airports. Dallas-Fort Worth International was a nice place but flights seemed to leave and arrive on time better at Love Field. Rush hour traffic was starting to pick up, and though the flow of traffic was still moving, it was slowing significantly and soon would be to a complete stop. He glanced at the clock on the dashboard. He still had some time to get there - he wasn't scheduled to fly for another hour and a half.

He connected his phone through the bluetooth feature and dialed Sophie's number. It rang several times and went to voicemail. That seemed to be standard procedure lately with her. She was a busy girl and Jake had to assume she was in class and couldn't talk.

Turning the radio on, he was able to catch a talk show based out of the Dallas area. His main focus was on the traffic and he was vaguely listening to whatever they felt like talking about. But the mention of the terror threat level pulled him from his focus and he gripped the steering wheel tighter than normal. Why was this bugging him? With the way the world was going, leaving it at the highest level was probably the best practice. And with airport security, he didn't have much to worry about. But poor Alice - she was a sitting duck at the hospital. Being an ER nurse allowed her to see so many various issues and sometimes, the safety around her was lacking.

"Do you really think this new threat is credible?"

"It must be for the government to heighten security."

"But usually, aren't the serious terrorists not going to let their intentions be known? To blindside us with no warning or threat? It's almost like a bomb threat - why warn people if your main intention is to kill as many people as possible?"

Jake listened as the two DJs argued about it. It was amusing and also informative to hear two different sides - Jake was on the woman's side. Why broadcast your intentions? But they still couldn't take any threat lightly.

"The moment we brush any threat under the rug is the moment we get attacked like that Tuesday morning in September."

"So, what does the threat entail? Airports? Bridges? Tunnels? For the government to even announce it to the citizens means it must be pretty serious."

"I don't think they've released that much information. Authorities are just asking us to be on the lookout."

Traffic picked up a bit and slowed again - people in Dallas had no idea what the concept of merging meant and Jake gripped the steering wheel tighter, shifting his weight in his seat. His exit for Love Field was coming up soon so he made sure to get in the far right lane. The airport was only about ten miles away from where he lived but it took well over forty-five minutes to make the trek - he knew better than to leave right when rush hour started but taking Dylan to school put him right in the middle of it. He was glad to take their son to school - he didn't want to pawn it off on Alice after she had to work a double. It was either her sitting in traffic or him, and with as edgy as she had been lately, he preferred to be the one going through it.

Finally, a break in cars and he made his exit. There was a special parking area for pilots and he flashed his ID to the person working the gate. He knew the man's face but never could remember his name - he was always smiling and had been doing it nearly as long as Jake had been flying. Waving at him, the gate swung upward and Jake pulled into his usual parking space. He wondered who his co-pilot would be for the day. He got along with most of the people who worked with him, including the flight attendants who really had the hard jobs of dealing with cranky passengers.

He joined his co-pilot in the briefing room - His name was Colin Durham and Jake had flown with him before. He had plenty of flight time experience but he was still young. As his maturity developed, he became a better pilot every day. Jake nodded at him as he opened his flight bag - it was time for their pre-flight preparations, which would include a meteorological briefing, route selection, flight plan preparations, and a physical inspection of the aircraft that they'd be using for the day.

"Good morning, Captain Shepherd and Pilot Durham."

"Good morning, Mr. Hogan." Jake shook their superior's hand. He was a former captain, pilot, and now he worked as the pilot supervisor for the company. He held a leather binder that he opened, which contained their information for the day.

"I'm sure you're both aware of the security level."

"Yes, sir."

"Be on alert. Fly your route. Make sure you communicate with your flight deck staff on security measures. Certain knocks to enter the cockpit, no passengers forming a line at the front of the cabin, and if anyone seems like a threat, make sure the proper procedures take place to remove them from the aircraft."

It was the normal checklist they always went through, with heavy importance being placed on clear communication with their flight attendants. They were their eyes behind the door and would notify them of anything suspicious happening while in flight.

Jake and Colin went out to their aircraft. It was the first flight of the day for the airplane and the crew was already filling it with jet fuel, completing the pre-flight check, and maintenance was looking over the brake system, cooling system, and engines.

The luggage cart was also there, already loading people's suitcases and belongings into the belly of the plane. From that alone, Jake could tell that it would be a full flight. He nodded toward the three flight attendants who were already on the plane, stocking up the snacks and beverages for everyone.

"Good morning, Captain Shepherd!"

A female flight attendant greeted him - her name was Becky, and she seemed to be on the same schedule as Jake. The other two attendants were familiar, each one welcoming them on board with a smile. They introduced themselves as Nelly and Bryan, both appearing enthusiastic. Nestling into the cockpit, Jake put on his headset and communicated with the ground crew, going over their list of checks they had to ensure were functioning properly before they could even consider pushing back from the gate.

"How do three short knocks sound for entrance to the cockpit?" Becky poked her head inside, her dark hair bulled back in a bun, her makeup almost perfect.

"Sounds good to me. Three short knocks," Jake clarified.

"Three short knocks," Colin confirmed with a nod of his head.

"We'll call if we need to use the restroom or anything." Jake stopped Becky before she exited. "I'm sure they went over the security threat to y'all this morning."

"They did. We'll be paying close attention."

Jake had the pre-flight tasks down well. After twenty years of the same thing, with minor alterations as the years passed, he could do it in his sleep. But it also meant he had to try extra hard not to get too complacent. If they skipped just one check it could prove detrimental for the equipment of the plane, as well as the possible danger the passengers could bring with them inside the cabin.

They left the cockpit open as the passengers began to board. Jake would catch glimpses of them as they waited in the aisles - the frustrating part about being a passenger was fighting for overhead bin space as well as cramping into the closed in seats. With his company, they didn't have first class and it was open seating, which meant there was always competition for window and aisle seats. People patiently waited as others in front of them got situated - it was always what took the longest when getting off the ground and off to their destination, and unfortunately, a necessary evil.

Becky closed the cockpit door, reiterating their plan of three short knocks if one of them needed to open it. It was about time to be towed out onto the runway. The sound of the flight attendants going through the seat belt, flotation device, and oxygen mask routine could be heard through the door. Jake had heard it so much that he could spout it off himself. The ground crew motioned for the tow to push the plane back from the jet-way.

Queuing the overhead microphone, Jake spoke to the passengers in the cabin. "Good morning. We are headed to rainy Seattle today, so if that is not your destination, I suggest you flag a flight attendant down to get off. We're looking at a little under a four hour flight time with sunny skies for most of the flight. Current weather in Seattle is cloudy and a cool fifty degrees. We'll come back on overhead as we get close and if we anticipate any turbulence. Please relax and enjoy the flight."

"Flight two-twenty eight, you are clear for take off."

The air traffic controller's tinny voice vibrated in Jake's ears. They turned the corner and taxied to their designated runway. There was one plane in front of them and after it was gone, they'd be up next to go. Jake gripped the yoke tightly - he felt the sweat form on his palm and glanced over at Colin. His co-pilot appeared calm and collected but any seasoned pilot would tell you that deep inside, right before take off, adrenaline is pumping, heart beats are racing, and the excitement is why the majority of them stayed in the business.

"Flight two-twenty eight, you're clear for departure."

Jake allowed Colin to accelerate the plane, the inertia strong as they sped fast enough to get the plane to lift off of the ground. Pulling back on the yoke, the landing gear was no longer touching the asphalt. The aircraft gained altitude and there was nothing before them but complete blue skies.

"Pulling up landing gear. Landing gear is up," Colin said and Jake confirmed it.

"It's a beautiful day to fly, isn't it?" Jake took a deep breath. "How many people can wake up every day and get the rush we get just from going to work?"

Colin flashed Jake a smile. "Hot damn, I love it!"

***

Alice was thankful that the start of her shift had started slowly. She had time to catch up on her charting and even had a second to enjoy another cup of coffee. The ruckus from the night before appeared to have been taken care of - many of the patients were already in private rooms on different floors, some were sent to ICU, but there was no clear evidence that a major wreck had even happened. She wouldn't dare say it out loud - one mention of a calm shift and all hell would break loose. She kept it to herself - life as an emergency room nurse meant that things changed by the second.

"Good morning, Alice. Thank you for staying late last night." Rose smiled, though there was a hint of exhaustion behind her dark eyes.

"I was the charge nurse last night. How would it have looked if I bailed on everyone?" Alice asked, watching as her coworker and fellow charge nurse got a bottle of water from the refrigerator and tossed one to her.

"How'd Jake take it?" Rose sat across from her, glancing up at the TV and back to Alice.

"As best as he could, I guess. Jake's not one to raise a fuss when it comes to the job. I mean, look at his career. How many flight cancellations and delays that hindered him from getting home have I had to deal with?"

"That's true," Rose replied, her tone flat. "It takes a special person to be married to a pilot. But then again, it takes a special person to be married to an ER nurse, too. How in the hell has your marriage lasted?"

Alice felt her cheeks heat up. Talking about her love life was not exactly what she wanted to do. She drank the water and tossed the bottle into the recycle bin. "This, coming from someone who has been divorced twice." Alice nudged Rose. If they weren't good friends she would've never brought up the touchy topic, but Rose would be the first to make jokes about her failed marriages.

"Exactly, which is why I'm asking you how you've made it work! I guess if I had a husband who looked like Jake, I'd do everything in my power to not let him go. Holy hell, Alice! The man is sexy."

"He is, isn't he?" Alice laughed and noted the time on her watch. It'd be time to make rounds and she needed to check the radio - she couldn't miss report if an ambulance was bringing someone in.

"Combat pilot in the Air Force and everything. I don't think I would've stayed late last night if it meant getting home to him." Rose smirked and nudged her.

Alice stood up and adjusted the stethoscope that rested on her shoulders. "You really need to get laid, Rose. I gotta go do rounds. Maybe you oughta think about doing the same, huh?"

She didn't allow Rose to respond - her friend was right. Jake was gorgeous and she found herself daydreaming about his green eyes, his dark and crazy hair, and how hot he looked in that Air Force uniform all those years ago. She was a lucky girl, which in turn made her wish they really did have more time to spend with each other. When they both had a night off together, whenever that may be, she was going to take full advantage of her time alone with him.

Aside from a few walk-ins for flu-like symptoms, things were quiet. Alice double checked on the other nurses - there were three others working the emergency room with her, including Rose. Today was the perfect day to be understaffed, though she anticipated a big call at any second. Then it would be all hands on deck.

Checking her watch again, she remembered Jake's flight plan for the day. If flights were running on time, he had just taken off for Seattle. She wished she was on that flight - cool and rainy Seattle sounded amazing at the moment.

CHAPTER THREE

Jake relaxed once they got the airplane up to altitude. They were flying at about forty-five thousand feet, ground speed of five-hundred and fifteen miles per hour, and the sky remained calm and clear in front of them. He allowed Colin to take the controls - he needed the practice and Jake wanted to enjoy the view around them. It was just under a four hour flight, which was on the long side for domestic transport, but nothing compared to the flights he had to take when he was in the military.

"What's the longest flight you've ever taken?" Jake asked, breaking the silence in the cockpit. The low hiss from the engines made it where they had to talk a little louder but each man was used to the sounds coming from the airplane.

Colin pondered the question for a moment, clicking his tongue against the top of his mouth. "I've had to fly to Europe. Across the Atlantic."

"I used to do that run quite a bit. That's a long one. Makes this flight look very short."

"What about you? What's the longest you have done?"

"Europe as well. But it was just the connection. We continued on to Saudi Arabia and the Middle East. Back when I was in the Air Force they had me flying all over the damn place. But it was for the best - it gave me enough flight hours to score this job."

"Is that why you decided to be a pilot? Since you did it in the military?"

"Yes and no. I used to fly with my dad as a kid."

Colin nodded and looked out of the side window. "Same here. My dad flew for American Airlines since I could remember."

"Oh yeah? How's he feel about you flying for a competing airline?" Laughing, Jake made sure to imply that it was a joke. He had flown with Colin before but didn't know him well enough to gauge his sense of humor.

"He gave me hard time at first but now he enjoys having a son he can relate to. My mom hates when we get together and start talking about airplanes and flying. Though she knows more than she lets on - she was a flight attendant about the same amount of time my dad flew. That's how they met each other."

Jake enjoyed the conversation. He had flown with other pilots who rarely said much of anything, making the flights seem much longer than they really were. Colin seemed to have a bright future in front of him. He was calm but aware, self-assured, and willing to take the controls to gain the experience needed to eventually become a captain.

Jake heard three knocks on the door and opened up the cockpit - Becky was standing in the threshold, offering each of them a steaming cup of coffee and a small bag of cookies to go with it. He wasn't hungry just yet after the breakfast he had prepared for him and Alice but they'd be nice to snack on halfway through the flight.

"Thanks, Becky. You're a lifesaver."

"I can grab y'all some cream and sugar if you like."

"Black is fine. Thanks again. How's it going in the cabin?" Jake asked, craning his head to look over his shoulder. From the angle he was sitting at, he couldn't see a lot of the passengers, but the few he saw were already snoozing.

"Quiet. Everyone is reading, playing on their tablets, or sleeping."

"Perfect flight," Colin said, chiming in on their conversation for the first time.

"Yeah but also makes time crawl. I'll check on you boys in a little bit."

The cockpit door slammed behind Becky, leaving the two pilots back to their task at hand - they were cruising even higher now, at about forty-eight thousand feet. Jake increased their speed to five hundred and twenty miles per hour - they had only hit a few minor patches of turbulence so he also turned off the fasten seat belt sign, granting the passengers a chance to get up for the restroom, to stretch their legs, or if they needed to grab something from the overhead bins.

"We might make it to Seattle before schedule," Colin said, checking their flight path.

As soon as he spoke, the plane hit a large pocket of air, making it shimmy and jump up several feet before plummeting into a free fall for about five seconds. The large bout of turbulence made Jake's stomach fall with it, as if he were on a huge dip in a roller coaster at an amusement park. All of the navigation tools shut off, leaving black screens where the systems once guided them. The plane plummeted again, only this time Jake was unable to pull the yoke up to get it to level out.

"What the f…" He cut himself off as he flipped the switch to the system off and on, but got no response. Speaking into his headset, he said, "Mayday, mayday, this is flight two twenty-eight flying to Seattle out of Dallas Love Field. Mayday, we have lost all programs, navigation systems, and it's hard keeping this plane in the air. We are descending quickly!"

The mayday call went out, only to be replaced by a large amount of static that was deafening in Jake's headphones. Looking over at Colin, the younger pilot's eyes were wide, his hands gripping his yoke so tight that his knuckles were turning white.

"Holy shit, we can't check anything! The computers went black. There's no one on the radio!" Jake tried to stay calm but without any of their systems working, there was no way to control the plane that was controlled almost completely by technology that left them falling rapidly toward the ground.

"All three flight computers are out," Colin said, his voice shaking as he looked out the side window. "We've dropped at least fifteen thousand feet. It's hard to say without our systems up."

Jake looked out of his side window and Colin was right - the ground was getting closer and with their rapid descent, the plane's engines whined and whistled from the abrupt change in altitude.

"How can we not tell our altitude? That's not part of the flight computers." Jake inquired out loud, though Colin likely didn't know the answer to it.

The engines sputtered until they completely crashed, leaving the plane in an all out free fall. Jake had to self-motivate - he had been through hundreds of training exercises with gliders. He knew how to guide a plane to safety. He even had a couple of crash landings when he was in the military, but none of them included a large commercial jet with hundreds of passengers in the cabin fearing for their lives. The oxygen masks were likely down as the cabin pressure was completely shot from the sudden plunge in altitude.

"Mayday!" Colin yelled into the headset but it was a lost cause - any communication with the ground was hindered along with the systems inside the airplane.

What had happened? Jake speculated lightning but there were no storms on the radar - it could be a weather phenomenon where there is lightning with no storm to go along with it but it was an unlikely scenario. Had the plane been tampered with? There was no way they had missed a system outage during their walk through before the flight. And a nationwide system outage usually didn't down a plane - it usually just hindered ground control at the airports.

Jake was running out of time. The engines were shot and as he tried to pull the plane up to glide, the yoke felt as if he were maneuvering it through thick mud. It was like he was controlling a vehicle without power steering, only this was on a much larger scale.

Out of desperation, Jake tried to start the engines back up to no avail. They were dead and though he knew they didn't stand a chance in functioning enough to allow a safe landing, he tried anyway.

"Jesus, it's like we're flying with dead weight on our back," Jake said, still attempting to glide the plane as best as he could.

The ground was getting closer, the speed of their fall was getting faster, and a crash landing was imminent. He tried to open the cockpit door but there was no way he could do that and maintain the slight control he actually did have. He pushed the button to signal for a flight attendant. It was a lost cause but he had to try - maybe some of their systems were still working. With the angle of the plane flying downward, the chance that Becky or one of the others being able to get to a standing position to get to them was impossible and it would just put them in more danger.

It was going to be a hard landing. Jake estimated that they were somewhere over New Mexico, Colorado, or maybe even into Utah. They weren't too far into their flight and regardless of what state it was, they were over mountainous terrain that would make their landing even more difficult.

"Assume crash positions!" Jake yelled over the loud rumble of the plane as it shot through the morning air, slicing through it like a sharpened knife through a tomato. He wasn't sure what else he should do. He pulled on the yoke again, holding it so tight that his hands and palms ached. The nose of the airplane pulled up just a tad and he hoped it was enough to help slide the plane on its belly. They were going way too fast for a soft and gentle landing. When they hit the plane would slide for a long time until it made impact with an object to stop it completely. Since they were in hilly terrain with trees, maybe it'd happen quicker than he thought. He didn't have time to think about it. They were just a few feet away from making contact with the ground.

Gritting his teeth, Jake did the only thing he could think to do - he held onto the yoke and closed his eyes, thinking about the things that mattered most in life - Alice, Sophie, and Dylan. The plane hit hard, jolting him upward, his seat belt tightening over his chest to keep him in his seat. Crunching and grinding sounds of metal being destroyed were the last things Jake heard before everything went black.

***

Alice's calm day in the emergency room was driving her crazy. Her twelve-hour shift was starting to feel like a double just by how time was dragging. She was caught up charting, making rounds, and checking on the other nurses to make sure they didn't need help with anything. Glancing at her pedometer watch, she was shocked that she had already hit her ten thousand step goal despite the lack of work needing to be done.

Smiling at the clerk, Alice glanced up at the clock. "Dare I say it?"

The younger woman grinned in return and Alice noticed her name tag - Jocelyn. ER clerks came and went like patients did so she wasn't familiar with her, just that she always had a smile on her face and was willing to do anything the nurses and doctors asked of her.

"You know the rules, Alice." Jocelyn wagged her finger at her. "But you don't have to say it for me to know. And you're right."

Alice patted the counter in front of Jocelyn and walked down the hallway, glancing behind the curtain at a patient waiting for their doctor to come in so they could transfer to an actual room. Looking up at the TV, she stopped in her tracks when she saw the news story - the crawler mentioned a possible plane crash but the information was sketchy. Hurrying down to the break room, she quickly turned the channel to the first news station she could find, ignoring the people who were watching the soap opera.

No one said anything as they were all pulled into the story - Alice felt a lump form in her throat, her pulse thumping in her temples as she waited for the anchor to report more information.

"At this time it isn't clear if the plane has actually crashed, just that it went off of radar about fifteen minutes ago. Air traffic controllers have not been able to make contact with them but they do report that a possible mayday was sent out just seconds before all systems crashed."

"Do they have a flight number?" Alice asked out loud as if they could hear her through the TV. Looking over her shoulder, she bit her lip when she saw the sympathetic looks from her fellow co-workers. They knew her husband was a pilot. Hundreds of flights went across the country daily - the chances that it was Jake's flight were slim, though very possible considering where the loss of communication had happened.

"Again, we are reporting about flight two twenty-eight, direct service from Dallas Love Field to Seattle-Tacoma International. The plane has gone off the radar, no communication is being made with the flight crew, and there may have been a possible mayday alert sent out just seconds before they disappeared."

Dallas Love Field to Seattle? That's exactly what Jake was doing. Alice felt the room begin to spin and she took a few steps back, sitting on the lounge sofa behind her. Pulling her phone from her pocket, she checked the flight information that Jake always gave her so she could track him for instances just like this. Scanning through her messages, the numbers two and twenty-eight flashed right at her, confirming that the news story was about the airplane her husband was on. This couldn't be true! Flying was the safest way to get around.

She dropped her phone and it hit the floor, the case breaking into two pieces. Everything was moving in slow motion and she looked up at the TV again, only she wasn't comprehending anything that was being said. No! Jake's flight was fine! This was a mistake!

"Oh my God, Alice, that isn't Jake's…" Rose cut herself off as she picked Alice's phone off of the floor. Sitting beside her, she put her arm around Alice's shoulders and pulled her in for a side hug. "They don't have much information right now, hon. You know how the media is. Pure speculation for ratings."

Alice didn't want to be coddled. Rose was a good friend but now was not the time to smother her. Standing, she smoothed her hands down her hair and took a deep breath, pacing in front of the TV. What did a person do in this situation? Did she call the airline? Did she let Dylan and Sophie know that their dad had disappeared off of radar? No one could ever prepare for a situation like this to happen. No one even wanted to think about it.

Licking her lips, Alice felt the urge to drink some water. Just as she was about to say something, the lights in the emergency room flickered several times and then completely shut off, leaving them all standing in the dark. The emergency lights didn't even come on like they usually did. The hospital had generators and everyone stood by, waiting for the machines to kick on and bring life back to their work area.

CHAPTER FOUR

"Hey, Sophie, can I borrow your notes from psych class this morning?"

"Where the heck were you, Danny?" Sophie pulled out a spiral notebook and a pen, ready for her next class to start. Normally, she would tell a freeloader to hit the road, but she liked Danny. He was the first boy to pay attention to her for longer than the time it took to play a football game - back in high school, it was the same old thing. The boys loved watching the cheerleaders jump around with their shapely legs, their spirit, and their caked on makeup. Now at college, all of that crap was over. Danny didn't even know she had been a cheerleader.

"I worked late last night so I couldn't exactly get out of bed this morning. Come on, Sophie. I'll pay you!"

"Worked late or stayed up late drinking? One isn't exactly a job."

"It is if you work in a bar."

Sophie shook her head and rummaged through her book bag, pulling the spiral designated for her psychology notes. "I'll need them back tonight. No exceptions. I'll see you at the game, right?"

"Yep! I'll make sure to bring them with me."

"You better or I'll charge you interest."

"So you do want me to pay you?" Danny asked, his grin making a pang of butterflies shoot through

Sophie's stomach. Before she could answer, the professor stepped up to the podium and began the lecture for the day. The flirting would have to wait and even though they had stopped talking, Sophie couldn't get her heart rate down. It was good and bad - she always swore to never be the pushover girl to impress a guy, and here she was, allowing a slacker student to borrow her notes. This would be the last time, she swore.

Mentally pulling herself from Danny, she tried to focus on what Professor Baughman was talking about. It was college algebra, not her strong suit, so she had to really pay attention to what was going on. Her parents would kill her if she flunked a class.

Her phone vibrated in her pocket and she pulled it out, noticing a text message from Brooke, her dorm roommate. Her heart skipped a beat at the question that flashed on the screen:

"Your dad is a pilot, right?"

Sophie made sure the professor wasn't looking her way. The last thing she needed was to get caught playing on her phone in front of Danny. Teachers frowned on it and she didn't need the embarrassment.

Feeling like the coast was clear, she texted back: *"Yes, y?"*

A few seconds passed before the phone buzzed again with Brooke's response:

"Plane crash. Flight from Dallas. U might wanna check out the news."

There were hundreds of flights that left from Dallas every day. What were the chances that it would be her dad? Sophie slid the phone back in her pocket. The professor had moved to her area of the classroom and she almost got caught with it out. Taking a deep breath, she jotted down what he had written on the white board, though none of it made sense. It was like she was learning another language, and now she had the distraction of a plane crash out of Dallas on her mind. She couldn't sit still - her leg bounced up and down in anticipation as she thought about everything clouding her busy mind.

She glanced at her watch - Damn it! There was still an hour left in the lecture. She couldn't sit here wondering for another hour! Gathering her belongings, she hurried out of the classroom, ducking everyone's glances as she disrupted their mental focus. She didn't even look back to see Danny's reaction - she didn't care at that point. She needed to try and get hold of her mom for clarification. The fact that she didn't have any calls or messages from her made Sophie believe that the crash didn't involve her father.

Pulling her cell phone out again, she sat on a nearby bench and dialed her mom's number. She'd call her dad but if he really was on a flight, he wouldn't be able to answer anyway. The other line cut to a tinny message that said, *"Your call cannot be completed as dialed. Please hang up and try again."* What? The voice sent a chill down Sophie's spine and she hit the red button screen on the screen to hang up. Looking around her, life was moving along normally. People were hurrying to and from class, it was a beautiful day, and inside she felt like she was imploding. She tried to call again, this time the tinny voice said, *"All circuits are busy. Goodbye."*

She tried her father's phone - same story. She also tried her little brother Dylan's phone and got the same result.

"Your call cannot be completed as dialed. Please hang up and try again. All circuits are busy. Goodbye."

"Sophie, why'd you leave class? Is everything okay?" Danny stood in front of her, pulling her from her panic. His eyes widened when she made eye contact with him. "You look like you've seen a ghost! You're sweating!" Reaching out, he touched her brow, his fingertips smooth on her skin.

"I need to get to a TV. I need to see what's going on."

"What do you mean? What's wrong?"

Sophie stood up and pulled her backpack on, hurrying toward the student union building. There would be TV's in there where she could catch some news. She didn't even wait for Danny but could feel him matching her step for step. Once inside, she spotted a flat-screen on the wall and there were several people crowded around, everyone fixated on the news story. She read the headline at the bottom, highlighting the story:

"Major power outages spanning from the west coast to the Midwest"

"There have been multiple plane crashes, power outages, and loss of communication that spans from Los Angeles all the way to Chicago. Sources say that it is working its way eastward, knocking out everything in its path."

"What is it?" Another news anchor asked.

"We aren't clear on that, as we can't make contact with anyone in the affected areas at the moment."

"Is it safe to say that it will happen here as well?"

"If it continues, whatever it may be, the pattern shows that within the next hour, the entire United States will be crippled."

Sophie felt claustrophobic and needed fresh air. She was also scared to walk away from the news coverage in fear of missing something. Backing away, she had to push through the crowd that had formed behind her. This had to be a nightmare. She'd wake up eventually in her dorm room, laughing to herself at the crazy dreams she always seemed to have. Or in this case, nightmare.

"Your family is in Dallas, right?" Danny asked, his mouth set in a hard line.

"Yes. And my dad's a pilot. And they mentioned…"

"Plane crashes," Danny finished her sentence with the shake of his head. "That doesn't mean his plane was one of them. Was he scheduled to work today?"

"I don't know." Sophie shrugged and went outside. The air in the student union building was stagnant and she couldn't breathe. "I don't keep up with his schedule." It came out harsher than she had wanted it to and cringed. "I'm sorry. That was rude, Danny."

"No, it's okay. Have you tried to call? My family is in Abilene. I should try to contact them too."

"I couldn't get through." She held her cell phone out. "I tried my dad, mom, and my little brother. Nothing." Her voice shook and warmth gathered in the corners of her eyes. "A nationwide power outage? Have you ever heard of such a thing?"

"I've read about possibilities but it was all conspiracy theories. EMP's, terrorists and war, all things we probably shouldn't talk about right now."

Sophie nodded in agreement. "I need to find out if my parents are okay. If I could just get a call to go through and hear one of their voices, I'd calm down a little bit."

She tried to call one more time and got the same damn result! She almost threw the phone down but resisted the urge. It was her most precious commodity at the moment - and if the power outage spread toward the east coast like the news was speculating it would soon be completely useless.

"The power is out!" Someone opened the swinging door that led into the student union building. "The power is out! Get inside!"

Sophie didn't know why but she followed suit, being herded inside like they were livestock. Just as she stepped through the threshold, a loud explosion rumbled nearby, shaking the building they were in like an earthquake. The electricity flickered and came on for a split second before it shut down again. What had exploded? Most importantly - how much danger were they in at the moment. The building was so crowded she couldn't move and was getting pushed further and further away from the exit. One big bomb and they'd all be dead, taken out in one fell swoop. A sense of dread settled in the pit of her stomach and she tried to think of a better plan to get out of harm's way. She hated how she went straight to doom's day and war but unfortunately, it was the world they lived in.

"Sophie, stay close to me. I don't want to get separated!" Danny yelled and grabbed her arm, his grip tight on her bicep. He was right - the last thing she wanted to happen right now was to be alone.

"What the hell is happening, Danny? We need to get out of this crowd!" She had to raise her voice - with the number of people rushing to get inside, the chatter of others predicting what was going on was deafening. "We need to get out of here!" She couldn't panic. Panicking would make things worse. As they edged deeper into the building and farther away from the exits, it got darker. It was daytime, the sun was out, but it was dark inside, heightening Sophie's fears.

"Just stay with me. We'll get it figured out." Danny's voice of reason was what she needed to pull her back in and calm her down. His hand on her arm helped her realize she wasn't alone in the darkness and in the crowd. She had a friend with her and he was okay. At least she knew that much, even if she had no idea what the status of her family was.

"There's a basement in this building. Let's try and get to it." It was the safest place Sophie could think to be, especially if planes were dropping out of the sky and things were exploding. The challenge was getting through the crowd. No one was willing to move and everyone was panicking. "Come on, Danny! We're almost there!"

CHAPTER FIVE

The first thing Jake felt was pain. It was hard opening his eyes as if there were weights on his eyelids. Forcing them open, he let out a deep groan when he turned his head to the side. His vision was blurry - everything around him was enveloped in fog. He had no idea where he was, nor could he recall what had happened to put him in so much pain. Was he dead? What a stupid thought to have - dead people didn't feel pain, and he was hurting bad enough that if death came for him, he'd welcome it.

Blinking, Jake tried to clear the blurriness but it got worse. He attempted to sit up but something was restraining him, right across his chest. Lifting his arm made him lose his breath - the small task that people did daily turned into an unimaginable challenge. Pain radiated down his side, all the way to his toes. From the harsh discomfort, he had to estimate that he was severely hurt, and with the fog in his brain, could he possibly have a head injury? That would explain his lack of memory - he still couldn't recall where he was or why he was hurting so bad.

The restraint across his chest felt like a seat belt and he traced his hand down to where it was buckled. Unfastening it, he was able to move a bit more freely, but he regretted even trying when the pain came on so bad that he almost passed out. Leaning back, he took a deep breath and closed his eyes. The strong taste of metallic was thick on his tongue and he winced at the flavor. Nausea hit him hard and he gagged, dry heaving several times before stomach acid finally came up, burning his esophagus and throat.

Jake knew he had to move. If he stayed where he was, his body might get used to it and his injuries could get worse. Or maybe not - moving could heighten whatever problems he had and do more damage than good. Injured spine? The last thing he needed to do was paralyze himself.

Preparing himself for the agony he was about to face, he sat up, freeing himself from whatever he was leaning back on. He had never felt such discomfort and he had to take a moment to catch his breath. The metallic taste came back, replacing the acidic liquid he had just thrown up. Sweat poured from his brow and he wiped it away just as it began to sting his eyes.

His vision still wasn't one hundred percent but he was able to get a good look around him. A torn up instrument panel lay before him. An airplane yoke was still intact, between his legs. Was he in a plane crash? Looking up, the top part of the cockpit was completely gone and he was surrounded by a large blanket of trees overhead. What remained of the cockpit - the crushed up instrument panel, pilot chairs, and yoke were torn to shreds. And then it dawned on Jake - how was his co-pilot?

Painfully angling his body to face to his right, he reached out, touching the man's arm and he didn't respond. Was he dead? Jake placed his middle and index finger on his wrist to check for a pulse. It took him a moment to find it but when he did, he yelled out. It was weak but there was one, which meant there was a chance to save the man's life.

His memory did fail him again - who had he been flying with? The blood covering his co-pilot's face didn't help aid in him being able to tell who it was. Lifting his leg away from the floorboard of the cockpit, he moved where he could face the injured person even better. More searing pain beamed through Jake and he clenched his jaw, let out a groan, and pushed forward.

"Colin?" Jake whispered it at first, getting a closer look at not only his co-pilot but his friend as well. "Colin?" He raised his voice this time. "Holy shit! Colin, wake up!" He jolted Colin with his loud voice and his eyelids fluttered. "Colin, can you hear me?"

Colin muttered something but didn't open his eyes. It was a positive result but Jake would feel a lot better if Colin would wake up and prove he was alert.

"Open your eyes, Colin! Come on! Can you open your eyes?"

Colin's eyes fluttered open for a moment but he was unable to focus on Jake. They shut again and he moaned and Jake shook him again. The threat of exacerbating an injury was present but the important thing was making sure he was alive.

"Open your eyes and look at me, Colin!"

Colin responded again, this time holding them open longer, focusing on Jake. He couldn't pinpoint it, but it seemed like Colin recognized him and fought against going back to sleep. "Jake?" It was a low whisper but he definitely said his name.

"Yes, it's me. It's Jake. Can you stay awake for me?"

It was taking the little energy Jake had left to make sure Colin was okay. His head throbbed and the flavor of blood in his mouth came back. He had no idea where he was injured but it was safe to assume that he was better off than Colin.

"We need to get you help, Colin."

"You too." Colin forced a smile, his words coming out in short pants.

It didn't occur to Jake until that second that they were hauling a full flight, which meant there were almost two hundred souls on board. Were there any survivors? The fact that they had made it through was nothing short of a miracle.

His eyes scanned the instrument panel. Spotting the radio, he went ahead and queued it just to try. They were lucky enough to make it through the crash. Maybe luck was on their side and the radio was working.

"This is Captain Shepherd, transmitting from flight two twenty-eight out of Love Field. Can anyone hear me? Does anyone copy?" He released the button on the radio and nothing happened. Not even static like it usually did after a transmittal across the airwaves. "Anyone copy?" He slammed the microphone down and cursed. "Shit! The radio is smashed up just like the rest of the plane."

"Don't get too worked up." Colin paused between breaths, closing his eyes as he spoke. He had a small glimmer of a smile on his face but he was pale and in pain. "You don't look so good, Jake."

"I can say the same thing about you, Colin."

Jake took a second to look around the area again. They were in the middle of a heavily wooded area. The cabin behind them was torn up but some of it was still intact - trees had done their part in completely splitting the wings in half. Once he was able to get up and walk around, he'd get a better look around. The most important thing was searching for survivors. With the damage around them, Jake had to assume there would be some casualties. He was scared to estimate how many they'd have on their hands.

"So, what do we do now?" Colin asked, leaning back on what remained of his chair.

"You need to rest. And I need to move to the cabin and find out who is still alive."

Attempting to stand, Jake crashed right back down into his seat. It was like a huge man was sitting on his shoulders. Rescue efforts were going to be a lot harder than anticipated but he had to try. Regardless of his level of injury, sitting around was just going to kill them slowly, and that was not an option. He needed a count for when the rescue crew located them. Giving them a good idea of the task before them would hopefully allow for things to move faster. If people were in as bad of shape as he and Colin, every second mattered.

***

The generators kicked on not long after the electricity went off. Alice was still in a total state of shock after what she had witnessed on the news. Did Jake's flight really crash? They didn't have much information but apparently, they had enough to report the flight number and the plane's destination, all of it pretty much confirming it was probably Jake's aircraft. There were no reports on survivors or casualties so no news was good news. She wanted to curl up in a ball and disappear. She wanted answers. And when she tried to dial out on her cell phone again, her phone had gone completely dead. She couldn't even get it to turn on to make just one more phone call!

"Alice, what do we do? The generators are up but we've got limited access to machinery. Some things are running thanks to the back up power but it isn't much."

Alice's flight or fight response kicked in and she tried to push the distraction of the news story out of her mind. After all, they hadn't even mentioned what airline it was. Lots of airlines flew out of Dallas and went to Seattle. While it was the flight number he was on, other carriers used the same numbers, though it wasn't likely. It was still keeping some shred of hope that it wasn't him. She needed to get information. She needed to call the airline and find out if it was Jake's plane. There was a special number she could call for families for occasions just like this.

Going to a land-line phone, she tried to dial out but it wouldn't work either. Not even a damn dial tone! Damn it! What was keeping her from finding out information on her husband? She needed to leave! She couldn't be here and focus on her work with the possibility of his plane crashing lingering over her head.

"I need to go," Alice whispered.

Rose looked up, shaking her head. "I wouldn't go out there. They're saying it's a nightmare. Street lights out, traffic jams, the whole thing."

"But it's Jake, Rose. I need to make sure…"

Dr. Wallace cut her sentence off. "We need all staff at the nurse's station, immediately! We are in a state of emergency and I need everyone ready to go!"

Alice hurried toward the nurse's station, clipboard in hand with the safety procedures on it. They had been through thousands of drills for occasions like this, but despite their training, her staff seemed panicked, everyone standing at the nurse's station waiting for orders. Clutching the plastic clipboard, Alice glanced down, her nerves not allowing her to even read anything. To hell with protocol - the people who wrote them out had never been down in the trenches, dealing with real life.

"Everyone go make your rounds. We only have a few patients in the ER but make sure all equipment is working. The generators are on but we still need to make sure."

"What caused the outage?" The ward clerk's eyes were as wide as saucers, her voice stammering as she looked around, unsure of what to do.

"We don't know but we need to prepare the ER for an influx of patients. It could be this power grid. It could spread wider than that. We don't know any details but right now our priority is taking care of our current patients and preparing for more that might come in." Dr. Wallace clenched his jaw as he spoke - a dead giveaway that this was bothering him. It went further than a simple power outage. Something was going on. Alice tried to remain as calm as possible and to her chagrin, her staff did as they were told, dispersing down the hallways to perform their tasks at hand.

"Alice, they're saying it is at least citywide." Rose sped past her, glancing over her shoulder as she ducked behind a patient's curtain.

"Citywide?" Alice spoke out loud though no one was in earshot. "How in the hell…" she cut herself off and went to a TV. It turned on but nothing was transmitting over the airwaves. It was all dead air, a snowy picture all that could be seen on every channel she tried. She was hoping to at least catch more news about the plane crash but there was nothing. Nothing at all, and she felt like she was in a blurry haze of a nightmare that she couldn't wake up from.

"We need all hands on deck, Alice - I think there was a wreck nearby when the traffic lights went out. There are some medics out at the ambulance bay with some people on gurneys."

Alice clicked the TV off and jogged to the ambulance entrance. She was expecting to see several ambulances lined up, their red and blue lights flashing, but that wasn't the case. Two medics were standing at the door with two gurneys, a patient on each one. Why were they on foot? Alice didn't have time to ask questions as they opened the doors to allow them entrance.

The medic began spouting off stats and Alice led them to the closest vacant room to where they were. One patient was a five-year-old child with a chest wound that was bleeding profusely. He was awake and alert but it seemed like his body was going into shock. The other patient appeared to be a man in his early thirties but he wasn't as lucky as the boy.

"Patient is unconscious with a weak and thready pulse. Approximately thirty-three years of age with an apparent head wound and an injury to his side."

The medic handed off the patient to the emergency room staff. Dr. Wallace began with the unconscious patient, motioning to Rose to cut his clothes off. The injury to his side was worse than they had anticipated - the gash ran from under his arm to his belly button, deep enough that they could see tissue. Blood poured from it and if they didn't put a stop to it soon, he'd bleed to death.

What in the hell had happened? Alice couldn't piece any of it together - the power outage that they were guessing was citywide, and most of all, why in the hell did the medics show up on foot with two stretchers? The child was in the way and frantic as he watched Dr. Wallace and Rose work on the adult, so she, with the help of the medics, wheeled him down the hallway to the next room.

Forcing a smile, Alice snapped on a pair of gloves and cleaned out the wound. It wasn't deep but they would need to do a scan to make sure he didn't have any internal injuries that might not be apparent to the naked eye.

"Can I ask y'all something?" She glanced at the medics and back to the child.

"Sure."

"Where is your ambulance and why on earth did you come here on foot?"

Both medics glanced at each other, neither men wanting to appear scared but their faces were a dead giveaway that they had witnessed something they had never experienced before. Alice documented the child's stats on a piece of paper and realized in all of the commotion that she hadn't gotten his information.

"Can you tell me your name, sweetie?" She poised the pen, ready to write, watching the medics as she also waited for their answer. What in the heck had they seen to make them clam up so bad?

"My name is Davey."

"Davey? That's a good name. Was that your dad?"

"Yes."

"I'm going to have a nice girl come and sit with you for a second while I go take care of something out there, okay? I will be right back and if you need anything, let her know." Alice exited the exam room and motioned for the ward clerk. "Sit with him for a second. I can't treat him until I get parent's consent and his father is in the next room, unconscious and he probably won't make it. We need to see if we can find his mother or a next of kin who can give the okay."

The medics followed her out into the hallway, both wide-eyed and still unwilling to talk.

"What gives, guys? What is going on?" She snapped her gloves off and threw them in a nearby trashcan, resting her hands on her hips as she waited.

"We responded to a wreck before the power went out. On our way here the ambulance just died. Just completely died and we had to coast to a stop. Traffic lights are out and all of the traffic on the freeway died along with it. I've never seen anything like it."

Alice took note of the medic's name on his lapel - Gary, and his partner's name was Bryan. "What do you mean, it just died?"

"Just what he said," Bryan replied. "Everything just shut off. People were going sixty miles per hour on the freeway and their cars just went crazy. There are a lot of accidents - lots of people running into each other from losing control. We were close enough to the hospital to run these two over. Now we gotta get back out there. There are tons of people stranded and hurt and there's no way to get them here in a timely manner. I've never seen such chaos."

Alice still couldn't comprehend what Bryan and Gary were telling her. It was almost like they were up to a really bad joke that wasn't going over well. She didn't have time to question them - now was not the time to try and discredit them.

"It sounds like we've got our work cut out for us today. Sorry to keep you waiting. Bring them in and we'll take who we can. As long as our generators stay up and running, we can do as much as we can."

It was going to be a long day. And she hadn't even had a chance to think about the plane crash. Just as she was about to lose her cool and panic about Jake, three more patients arrived at the entrance to the ER. There was no time to even process a second of what was transpiring - a blessing and a curse - and all Alice wanted to do was go home and make sure all of her family was okay. She needed to make arrangements with someone to get Dylan from school. He was supposed to ride with a friend but she'd feel better if she could get him herself. Would the phones be working by then?

With the patients piling up, there wouldn't be any chance of taking a breath, much less pausing to think about the chaotic world outside the hospital walls. At that moment, her duty was to take care of the injured, though the panic and worry of her entire family's safety would nag her until she heard from all of them.

CHAPTER SIX

It was taking too long for Jake to grasp his bearings. Any time he tried to move, the world spun and the vertigo was so strong that he couldn't stand up. He tried not to panic but when he got a better look at Colin, he noticed that his co-pilot's leg was pinned against the instrument panel and side of the airplane. Blood soaked his pants and down his leg. Despite the dizziness, Jake forced himself to push through the discomfort - there were hundreds of other people that would likely need help and he couldn't let his small injury keep him from helping.

"Can you move your leg?" he asked Colin, his breath out of control, partly from an adrenaline rush, and partly because of the pain he was feeling.

Colin gritted his teeth and tried to shift his leg free but it wouldn't budge. Groaning out in pain, he shook his head and closed his eyes. "No. It's jammed in there pretty good."

"Shit." Jake mashed the heel of his hand in his eye, rubbing it. Sweat stung his eyelids and he leaned forward, attempting to help Colin. "C'mon, on the count of three let's try again… one… two… three!" On three, he pulled but as Colin had already stated, the leg was stuck. More blood came from underneath the panel, saturating his pants. "We should probably hold off on moving it anymore. I don't want you to lose any more blood."

Jake didn't say it out loud, but he feared that Colin's injury could be life-threatening - what if the impact had nicked the artery in his leg? Would he already have bled out? Jake wasn't a medical person like his wife. She would know the answer without even hesitating.

Thinking about Alice prompted Jake to dig in his pocket for his cell phone. He had turned it off in flight so the battery should be full enough to make calls. Why hadn't he thought of it sooner? He could call 911, though he had no idea where they had crashed since the flight monitoring system had crashed but air traffic control would be able to give a good estimate based off of where they went off the radar.

Too much time had already passed and Jake was pissed that it wasn't the first thing he tried to do. His brain was foggy and his head ached - his inability to focus could easily be blamed on a head injury but none of that mattered. He needed to get Colin free and he also needed to check on everyone in the cabin. Becky hadn't come to the cockpit to check on them, nor had any of the other flight attendants. Jake surmised that he wouldn't like what he'd find out but he had to check - and hopefully, help was already on the way.

Jake pushed the power button on his cell phone and nothing happened. Sometimes it took it a second to power on but it wouldn't respond. Attempting to turn it on again, it still wouldn't work. Maybe the impact from the crash completely rattled it but it was literally unscathed. He tried one more time, unwilling to completely give up but he got the same response.

"Colin, where is your cell phone?"

"In my pocket." Colin motioned with his head to his right pocket. He tried to move to get it but he groaned out in pain, jarring his pinned leg.

"Sit still. I can get it if you want." Jake leaned over him, digging into his pocket. Pulling the phone out, he tried to turn it on and got the same result as he did with his. "Son of a bitch, your phone isn't working either!" He clutched his phone in his hand, and if he squeezed any tighter the device might have been crushed. He didn't need to do that. Maybe they'd eventually be usable and he'd lose a good resource due to his temper.

"They won't turn on?" Colin asked, keeping his eyes on his leg.

"No. Neither one will. And no one is responding on the radio. I don't know what the hell is going on."

Jake kicked his legs out of the side of the cockpit. With most of it destroyed in the crash, it didn't have a roof and the left side wall was gone. Sliding out, before he braced for the fall to the ground he glanced over at Colin. "I'll be right back. I'm going to look around for other survivors and get an idea of what everything looks like. Holler for me if you need anything. I'll just be back in the cabin."

It would have been easier to go through the cockpit door that led right down the aisle to the fuselage but it was completely obstructed by a tree that had fallen on the plane, narrowly missing both Jake and Colin. One second sooner or later and they would've been smashed by the trunk. The fall to the ground wasn't as high as usual, as the nose of the plane had hit the ground and was buried about three feet under. It was still hard on Jake - his injured body being jolted as he hit the ground below. Tucking and rolling, he was thankful there was green shrubbery underneath that padded the fall.

His head throbbed and it felt like his brain was sloshing inside of his skull. It took him a few seconds to get over the vertigo - like an ear infection times a thousand. Standing, he ran his hands down the front of his shirt, patting away some of the dust on his clothing. He got his first real look at the damage, his breath catching in his throat. Both wings were gone, cut off almost right where they connected with the body of the plane. The cabin's roof had been ripped off and crumpled toward the tail, mangled like a crumpled piece of paper. If anyone was standing up, they probably were no longer alive.

Suitcases scattered near the baggage compartments - blue, red, pink, and black stood out against the ground. Jake stepped forward, shielding his eyes from the beams of sunlight that cascaded through the trees - he was much more sensitive to light than usual, which was another strike against him when it came to a possible concussion. He probably shouldn't have been moving around and his body warned him, sending another wave of nausea through him.

Leaning against a tree, his body lurched forward but only small bouts of acid came up - the dry heaving made his pulse pound and he had to stay against the tree to prevent himself from falling over. This was taking too long - all he wanted to do was see if there were any survivors. By the looks of the plane, he and Colin were very lucky - if there was anyone left alive in the cabin, it was nothing short of a miracle. The fact that the plane hadn't completely crumpled on impact was another miracle but it was also helpful that Jake and Colin had glided it in. It could've been worse. It also could've been better. And it shouldn't have happened at all.

"Anyone up there?" When Jake yelled, a flock of birds flew up from nearby trees, making him jump. A crow cawed in the distance, lending a horrific feel to the situation. No one responded, so he yelled again, "Anyone up there? Hello?"

"Captain Shepherd, is that you?"

Jake didn't recognize the voice at first but he stepped forward, squinting through the light to see who was sticking their head out of the cabin. "Yes, it's Captain Shepherd! Who is that?"

"It's me… Becky!"

Jake moved closer, finding a good spot where a grove of trees blocked the sun. He finally got a good look at her, his heart skipping a beat at her appearance. She looked worse than Colin, the whole side of her face covered in blood so bad that she was almost unrecognizable. She was laying on her side, barely lifting her head enough to look down at him on the ground.

"How does it look up there, Becky?" It felt like a stupid question - how in the hell did he expect it to look? And was Becky well enough to even look?"

"It's bad… Jake." It took her a while to get all of the words out, her words shallow pants. "I don't think… I don't think anyone's alive."

"Colin is up in the cockpit."

"How… how is he, Jake?" It looked like just talking was painful for Becky.

"He's alive but his leg is pinned. I can't get him out."

"I can try and get up and see if there are any survivors."

Becky went to sit up, lifting her head off of the metal but Jake held his hands up and yelled, "No! No, don't do that Becky! Just stay still! You don't need to do that. I can come up there."

"You don't look much better than me, Jake. And you're down on the ground. How are you going to…" Becky paused and closed here eyes, cringing. After a few seconds, she continued. "How are you going to get up here again?"

"At the front." Jake pointed toward the cockpit area. "The nose of the plane is buried and I can shimmy on up. The cabin is barricaded from a tree but I can climb."

"Your head is bleeding. Why did you get down, anyway?"

Jake touched his index finger to his head and when he pulled away, he saw the small droplets of blood on his hand. "I wanted to see how the plane looked. I needed to get an idea of how many people are alive."

"Not many," Becky said again, closing her eyes. "And with the way I feel... you might be adding one more to your count of fatalities."

"Don't say that. I'm coming back up there. I'm going to check on Colin and then I'll find a way to get into the cabin. I'll be right back!"

Jake moved as fast as he could, going to the front of the plane. It'd be the only way to get back inside, as the farther back the aircraft went, the higher off the ground it was from the nose being pointed downward. The metal was slippery and Jake had a hard time finding a way to keep from sliding. The screws and bolts that stuck out were helpful but he had to move fast. His legs burned, his head ached, and all his body wanted to do was lay down and sleep. But he couldn't do that. He had to do what he could until help arrived, whenever that may be. The fact that it had taken that long made him wonder what really was going on.

Jagged pieces of damaged plane and trees helped him pull himself back up into the cockpit. His arms were about to give out on him but Colin reached out, pulling Jake up the rest of the way. With his leg pinned, he had good leverage to get him inside, though more blood squirted from his injury. Colin even looked paler, his usual tanned skin appearing as white as a sheet.

"I'm back," Jake said, smirking. This was a serious situation so his attempt at lightening the mood fell flat. If he was pinned against the instrument panel of an airplane he wouldn't have much of a sense of humor either. "Thanks for pulling me up."

"Glad to be of use for something. I gotta get unpinned, Jake."

"Yeah but what if that is keeping enough pressure on your wound so you won't bleed as bad?"

"I need to help you. How bad is it?"

Jake bit his lip and glanced back at the tree that was hindering him from getting to the cabin. "Bad. Becky is alive but I don't know if she will be within the next hour. No one else responded. I can't really give an estimate of casualties. But one really shocking thing is how much the plane stayed intact. The wings are gone, the roof is crumpled up like a piece of tinfoil, but the fuselage faired a lot better than I would've guessed."

"You did a belly landing and that helped," Colin said, opening his eyes for a second before closing them again.

"You helped, Colin. Don't sell yourself short."

Colin scoffed and waved his hand. "I had no idea what the hell to do. I would've probably panicked enough that I wouldn't have even glided it in. And now I'm pinned, still unable to help you."

"None of that is your fault, Colin. Keep your leg still. I'm going to climb over this tree and get into the cabin. I don't know what to expect on the other side but we need to see how your leg is pinned so we can free your leg."

Colin grabbed Jake's arm and squeezed. He looked into Jake's eyes and forced a smile. "Be careful, Captain. You're not in good health either."

Jake patted Colin's hand. "I'll be right back, Colin. And then we'll get you out of this plane. We'll get some help."

Jake had a feeling the climb over the tree trunk wouldn't be an easy task. Running on pure adrenaline was the only thing keeping him going.

CHAPTER SEVEN

Going to the basement of the student union building wasn't the best idea Sophie had ever come up with. It was shielding them from the chaos happening outside but it was pitch black and she couldn't even see past the tip of her nose. She clutched onto Danny's hand, squeezing so tight that it hurt. Unwilling to let him go, she fought another wave of panic that coursed through her body.

"We need to get out of here!" she yelled, though it didn't feel like her voice was very loud. "Danny! Let's go back up!"

Crashing into Danny, Sophie caught herself before plummeting to the ground. He must have stopped in mid-step at her request to leave the basement. He grabbed her side and helped her keep her balance, a small laugh causing her cheeks to heat up. It was a good thing he couldn't see her face.

"Why do you want to go back up there?"

"It's dark. I can't see anything. And what if…" She scooted closer, feeling his body against hers. Knowing he was close was reassuring but she couldn't get her heart to calm down. "What if this all collapses on us? No one will ever find us. We'll just be dead inside all of the rubble."

"Sophie, we don't even know what is going on! What if it's a storm… a tornado or something?"

She couldn't recollect if there were storms in the forecast - she was an avid weather watcher due to her father's job. But that didn't matter - just because the weather said it'd be a clear and beautiful day was no guarantee that it would actually turn out that way. But they were also in Boston. It wasn't tornado alley, not by a long shot. There hadn't been a tornado in Massachusetts for years.

"I'm scared, Danny! What's… what is all of this?" The room around them shook, mimicking an earthquake and this time, neither of the were able to keep their balance. Falling to the floor, Sophie landed on top of Danny and though they were in the midst of something incomprehensible, they both laughed like it was all a dream they'd soon wake up from and it relieved some tension.

"I think you're right. We should probably get out of here so we can at least see what's going on."

They both ran up the stairs, and though it was day time, it was almost as dark as it was in the basement. A dusty haze covered the sky and Sophie's eyes burned from the smoke and dirt that lingered at eye level. The explosions had stopped and the crowd had thinned out. The building was destroyed in some areas, the walls caved in on themselves, the glass windows busted out, and parts of the ceiling falling in. The stability of the structure was compromised so her assumption of the basement not being safe was a good one.

"Where did everyone go?" Sophie asked, not really designated a particular person to answer her question. It was rhetorical - no one would really know.

Her mouth dropped open when they walked toward the courtyard on the north side of the building. Two smaller airplanes had crashed between the student union building and the gym. A fire was roaring out of control near the cockpit of one of them and when she stepped forward to see if she could help, Danny held her back, refusing to allow her to go.

"No, Sophie! We need to get away. It's spreading toward the gas tanks!"

"What if there are people inside?"

"By the looks of the airplane, I doubt anyone survived the crash. We need to get back."

The small crowd heard Danny and followed them as they ran through the building again, exiting on the south side, as far away from the two planes as possible. Sophie felt guilty, leaving the victims behind. What if that had been her father's plane? She'd want bystanders to help if they could.

"We should keep moving. Where did you park today?" Danny asked, his once calm demeanor seeming more panicked, his eyes wide, his grip tight on her as he continued to guide her away from the student union building.

"Over by the arena. About half a mile from here. I took a bus into class!"

Danny stopped near a crosswalk, looking down the street. It was as if they were in an end of the world movie. Buses weren't running, cars weren't driving by, and the once heavy population of students on campus was minimized drastically. An eerie feeling enveloped them - was the plane crash the cause of the damage? There were several crashed cars, some in trees and other buildings, as well as a bus that had driven up into the entrance of the alumni center.

Sophie didn't wait for Danny this time - she ran to the bus, climbing on board to see if there was anyone who needed help. Two girls in the very back were awake, bloody, and in shock. The driver's face was slammed into the steering wheel, his eyes glossy and vacant as he stared at Sophie. Scooting to the back, Sophie dug in her bag for some tissue, handing each girl a piece.

"Here. This is all I have. What happened?"

"We were driving along when the bus just swerved off the road. I thought the driver was trying to miss a pedestrian, but then I saw all the other cars and trucks around us do the same thing. It was like…" The girl snapped her fingers as she tried to think up a good comparison. "It was like they all had an on and off switch that someone had turned off. It was that fast."

Sophie glanced over at Danny who had followed her on the bus. "Kinda like the two planes that crashed near the SUB. Just right out of the sky. Right into the courtyard by the gym."

"I tried to call for an ambulance but my phone is dead. I was just listening to my music with a full charge before this happened!" The other girl held her phone up, pulling one of here ear buds out of her ear. "This isn't right! It's like the end of the world!"

That had crossed Sophie's mind too but she chalked it up to reading too many post-apocalyptic novels. Her imagination was healthy when it came to thinking up what if's and maybes.

Nudging Danny, Sophie tried to keep here voice from shaking. "You mentioned EMP's earlier. What if that's what this is?"

"EMP?" The girl with the phone cocked her head to the side.

"Electromagnetic pulse," Danny replied, staring down at the floor. "We just talked about them in class. But I don't know… We're jumping to conclusions and we shouldn't do that."

"We need to get some help. There are a lot of injured people who need to go to the hospital." Sophie stood up and started toward the front of the bus. It wasn't the safest place to be at the moment.

"Where are you going?"

"Campus police. It's not far from here and they might have some answers."

***

Alice couldn't process what was happening. The emergency room became flooded with people, many covered in blood, others walking around like they were lost. The paramedics had mentioned that they had to bring the patient the rest of the way on foot but what exactly did that mean? She stood frozen for a few seconds, watching the rush happen around her. Life was happening in slow motion, like a time lapse video, and she couldn't kick herself into gear and move in real time. Rose hurried past but turned on her heel, glaring at Alice in disbelief.

"What's the matter, Alice? We need to triage these people. There's a waiting room full of people waiting."

"What…" Alice licked her lips, feeling nausea in the pit of her stomach. The fear of her husband's plane crashing was still front and center despite the chaotic scene playing out in front of her. "What happened, Rose? What is going on?"

"We don't know. We're still running off of generators and there is a massive influx of people coming in with serious injuries. I heard someone mentioned a huge pile up on the freeway but it was in passing and I haven't had a chance to find out. Come on, Alice. We need to triage and get these people some help."

Alice stared for a few more seconds, and like a light switch, her training kicked into gear and she followed Rose into the main waiting room of the hospital. An influx of people was an understatement. Every chair was taken, people were leaning against the walls, and some people were lying on the floor. Taking a deep breath, Alice ran her fingers over the stethoscope that dangled around her neck and went to the farthest corner of the room - she'd work her way back and hopefully meet the other medical staff in the middle.

The first family had some minimal injuries so she tagged them as non-emergency, even though the father didn't agree with her decision. Alice ignored his ranting when she spotted a woman holding a child about Dylan's age in her lap. He was unresponsive, his eyes closed, and his white shirt was soaked dark red. Kneeling beside them, Alice checked his pulse, which was weak. His breathing was shallow and if they didn't get him some attention soon, he'd be dead.

Looking around the room, Alice searched for a stretcher or gurney, or even someone who could help her get him into an exam room. Standing, she glanced down at the woman who had a cold and vacant stare, like she had given up. In the disarray transpiring, it was easy for most to feel helpless, including her own situation with the uncertainty that plagued her worried mind about her family.

Patting the woman's arm, Alice forced a smile and said, "I'm getting him help. I promise, I'll be right back."

The stranger nodded but the blank expression on her face didn't change. She stroked her fingers through the boy's hair but didn't say a word, either patience winning the battle with her worry or she truly had given up and accepted that the child was a goner.

Weaving through people, Alice couldn't find anyone available. Everyone was working on other patients, all as bad off as the boy or even worse. A lump formed in her throat and she stopped to wipe the hair from her face. Sweat gathered on her skin, dripping into her eyes. To hell with it. She'd do what she had to do. Protocol or not, from the looks of the disaster playing out, none of it would matter.

She went back to where the woman and boy were and lifted him out of her lap. He was heavier than Alice had anticipated, his dead weight was a challenge. She had lifted many backboards with large people and now with her adrenaline pumping, she was able to get him up. The woman helped and Alice motioned her head through the doors and behind a curtain where a bed waited.

The boy was still unconscious, his pulse weak and thready, his breathing seeming to get worse. Alice took his vitals - blood pressure was way too low, respirations not good either, and his o2 stats were at a dangerous level. Lifting his shirt, she got her first good glance at his wounds. Something had punctured his chest and the bleeding wasn't stopping.

"Do you want a doctor?" A young nurse stopped near the open curtain.

"I don't think there's one available," Alice answered as she applied some gauze and pressure to the wound.

"You can't..." The nurse trailed off. "You can't do anything without a doctor, right?"

Alice swabbed the back of the boy's hand and inserted the port for the IV. Looking up, she blew some strands of her hair out of her face. "Watch me."

"I'll help."

The nurse went to the other side of the bed and applied an oxygen mask. To hell with protocols and rules. To hell with the doctors making final decisions on patient treatments. When it all came to fruition, it'd likely mean Alice's certification would be stripped and she'd no longer be able to work in the medical field but right now, the boy needed her. His young life was more important than waiting for a doctor to tell Alice what she already knew how to do. She didn't have MD behind her name but she had many years of experience and she was going to do what she could to help.

She applied pressure to try to get the wound to stop bleeding but didn't want to put too much on it - the extent of internal injuries was unknown and she didn't want to make it worse.

"What's his name?" Alice asked the woman as she inserted saline into the port of the IV.

"James. His name is James." The woman approached the foot of the bed, wiping her nose with a tissue. She had a few bumps and bruises which meant she was one of the few lucky ones. "It was so strange…"

"What was strange?" the other nurse asked.

"All of the cars… they just sort of… stopped." The woman's voice shook and she gripped the railing of the bed. "They just stopped and people just ran into each other. There was nothing we could do. There was nowhere to go. I've never seen anything like it."

Alice looked up, making eye contact with the woman. "We are going to take care of James for you, ma'am. You're both safe now." She hoped she wasn't lying. What was going on outside the walls of the hospital? Was her own family okay? A chill went down Alice's spine. Something told her it was going to get a lot worse before it got better, and she hoped her instincts were wrong this time.

CHAPTER EIGHT

Jake tried to push the pain aside. From constant vertigo and the mention of blood on his face and forehead, it didn't take a medical professional to diagnose him with a concussion. Getting over the tree trunk that had split the fuselage in two was a challenge but he needed to climb it to see who had survived and to attempt to get an estimation of casualties. He continued to remind himself that it was nothing short of a miracle that anyone had survived, and the fact that it was three crew members so far made it that much more strange.

Clutching onto the trunk, it was almost too fat in circumference for him to be able to grasp it. The bark worked in his favor, serving as good traction for his boots, giving him enough leverage to climb. His head pounded so hard that the edges of his vision grew black. Pausing, he allowed his body to adjust to the physicality of climbing the tree. Taking a deep breath, he continued again when things calmed down. The trunk was about five feet above the wreckage of the airliner and when he crossed the other side toward the cabin, he made the mistake of looking down. Five feet wasn't high but he wasn't level and his boots failed to grab the traction that he managed to do on the cockpit side.

He slid faster than he had planned and scraped his hands and arms up in the process. His shirt ripped, the fibers in the fabric tight on his skin until he got to the bottom of the trunk. Becky pulled him away, hugging him tightly.

"I'm glad to see you're okay," she said, finally letting him go. "What happened? And how is Colin?"

"Colin is okay but he's pinned. The instrumental panel is against him and the outer wall of the cockpit. I'm not sure how we're going to get him out. Have you walked through the cabin yet?"

Jake got his first good glimpse of the damage from that vantage point. It was breathtaking - various tree branches shooting in and out of the windows, many stripping the metal of the plane like it was tin foil. He had a feeling that the survival number would be a lot less than the casualties, and an instant wave of guilt hit him hard - he was the captain of the flight. The crash was his responsibility. People were dead because the flight he was in command over had been unsuccessful.

"Anyone alive?" It felt ignorant to ask but he hoped to get some response. The wind howled, rustling the trees overhead. A hand rose up several rows back and Jake and Becky hurried toward it.

"Back here," the man said, craning his neck toward a woman that was pushed up against the cracked window. "She's not... she's not breathing."

Jake knelt down and tried to assess the situation. The man didn't look good himself, the blood on his face and clothing so thick that he was unrecognizable. Most of the blood was from the woman sitting beside him. Reaching for the woman's wrist, Jake closed his eyes when he couldn't find her pulse. He tried her neck and her wrist again, neither proving to give any indication that she was still alive.

"Is she... is she gone?" the man asked, nudging her. "Oh my God... my wife..."

"I'm so sorry for your loss, sir." Jake stood up, the urge to vomit. The couple directly behind them had been impaled by a branch. A family toward the tail looked burned up. Jake couldn't recall if there were any fires on board, but with his systems completely crashing, nothing was reliable in alerting him about anything.

"Is anyone alive?" Jake asked again, his eyes scanning for movement. It was disheartening that no one was responding to his calls. That didn't mean no one was alive. It could also mean there were survivors - they might be too weak to alert him.

"Help me check everyone," Jake said to Becky. "I'll start in the back and work my way up. You can start in the front." How would they help those with serious injuries? The plane had a defibrillator and first aid kits but nothing past that. Hopefully, help was on the way and he wouldn't have to worry about those who were seriously incapacitated. He could do general first aid and though it wasn't going to take care of the overall picture, at least he was doing something to try and make up for whatever pilot error he had made.

Most people he came across were dead. Families probably going on vacation, businessmen traveling for work. He tried to numb himself to each person's story but it was impossible and what hurt the most was seeing children, in their seats, the look of shock on their face from the horror of the crash. Jake tried to glide the plane but it wouldn't prevent the objects on the ground from tearing up the plane and killing those inside. So far, the only people found alive was the man with the blood covering his face, Becky, Colin, and himself. He hadn't taken a second to ask Becky how she was faring toward the front of the cabin.

"Help me."

Jake stopped walking to try and here where it was coming from. "Where are you?"

"Help me." It was a small voice, a young child and he wasted no time digging through the rubble. Suitcases, bags, smashed electronics, and even other people hindered him until he found the little girl. Lifting her, he looked her over, her dress dirty, her blond hair messy, her face soiled with black around here nose and mouth.

"Are you hurt anywhere?" Jake asked.

She shook her head. "Where's my mommy?" She was tiny but she talked well, which made it difficult for Jake to guess her age.

"I'm not sure, sweetheart. We are looking." She appeared completely unscathed aside from being dirty. She was able to stand on her own, she seemed fully aware of her surroundings, and she was concerned about her mother. "What is your name, sweetheart?"

"Heather. My name is Heather. I want my mommy." Her lower lip quivered and she began to cry, her tears streaming through the soot on her face, leaving trails against her pale skin.

"Don't cry, Heather. I'm going to help you, okay? I'm going to help you find her." Heather made Jake think of his daughter Sophie. Had his family heard of the crash? He wanted them to know he was okay. It was unfortunate that so many families wouldn't be given good news today. Too many casualties. Too much destruction. Jake wasn't sure if he'd ever be able to live with himself after something like this.

He met Becky toward the front of the cabin again, holding Heather close. "Find anyone?"

"Two or three. There are a couple that need help or they're not gonna make it, Jake. I can't believe this is happening."

"Me either. This is Heather. Heather, this is my friend Becky."

"You gave me cookies!" Heather's eyes lit up and Becky took her from Jake.

"I did give you cookies. How are you feeling, Heather? Do you hurt anywhere?"

Jake allowed Becky to work with the young girl. She was better at it and his concern was on the survivors who might add to the death toll if help didn't come soon. Where was help? It had been at least an hour since the crash. Were they over a rural area that was making the rescue effort take longer? Scooting toward where the flight attendants had their supplies, he searched for a first aid kit. Everything was scattered around and he feared he might not be able to find one. If he sat idle for too long his head would play tricks with him and he'd comb through every second right before the crash. He'd soon face the FAA to go over every mistake he and Colin had made. They'd have to answer to it all and it's what he deserved for it. A small price to pay in comparison to so many people who had lost their lives.

Even if this crash was deemed mechanical failure, his pilot days were over. Cleared to fly again or not, seeing the victims faces made Jake certain that he would never get over this.

***

Sophie felt like she was in a post-apocalyptic video game and at any second, she expected zombies to pop out of all the wreckage and start chasing her. Danny kept pace with her as they fled toward the direction of where the campus police station was. Some buildings remained standing, a few were on fire, and though she wasn't certain, it looked like several planes had fallen out of they sky. Cars were left vacant on streets, many crashed into each other. Her gut instinct was to stop and help - there were victims still inside, some awake and responsive, some obviously dead from the amount of blood that was visible.

Stopping at a small truck, the girl inside had a bloody abdominal wound but her eyes were open, pleading for someone to help her get out. Sophie hated herself for debating on whether or not to provide assistance. It was likely impossible to move the woman without the Jaws of Life or help from others. Visible blood was dangerous - so many diseases were passed through bodily fluids and with no one knowing exactly what was going on, she didn't want to take any chances.

Her mother would be so disappointed in her - she was always ready to help, stepping in, which was why she was a damn good ER nurse but even in this situation, she wouldn't have been able to do it all herself. Sophie was nothing like her mother. She was an architect major, which meant minimal human contact, no bodily fluids, and no risk of contracting something. But this situation was different - this was a damn catastrophe that would force her into getting over the fear of illness.

Her conscience took over - what if she was the one stuck inside? She'd want someone to help her. From the amount of blood, she knew the woman wouldn't last much longer. Glancing at Danny, Sophie swallowed the lump in her throat, looking from him to the poor woman, knowing there were many other people out there like her who needed someone's help.

"I'm headed to the police station. We are going to get someone here to get you out." Sophie looked the truck over - nothing was leaking out onto the ground, no gas, oil, or anything flammable. "I promise you we will come back." A voice inside her head echoed - *Don't make promises you can't keep.*

"Please don't leave me," the woman whispered, squinting as she shifted her weight. "I don't want to die."

"You're not going to die, okay? The police station isn't far from here. They can dispatch an ambulance and get you to the hospital!"

Sophie heard a dull roar and the ground shake. Looking over her shoulder, she tried to decipher what was happening but took a hard fall to the ground, her head slamming into the dirt. The edges of her vision went black for a moment and faded. When she was able to grasp her bearings, she realized Danny was on top of her, his body shielding her from a large wall of flames that shot straight above them. The heat off of it made her sweat and the moisture dripped into her eyes, stinging them.

"What the…"

Danny's weight made her gasp and smoke replaced where the fire had just been, making it even harder to breath. Her lungs burned and Danny finally eased off of her, allowing her to sit up. The blanket of smoke was thinning but still present at eye-level, posing even more questions that Sophie needed answers to.

"What happened?" The truck was still there, the girl inside, her eyes wide.

"There was an explosion." Danny pointed toward the student union building. "I don't…"

"We need to get out of here. We need to get some help." Sophie's instincts were screaming at her to run and not look back. With the number of fires happening, another explosion would be imminent. "How far away is the chemistry building from here?" It was hard to tell exactly where they were but it didn't matter - if a fire was going on at that building, an explosion close to all of the chemicals stored there would wipe the entire campus off of the map.

Danny stuck his head inside the truck, and though Sophie couldn't hear what he was saying, she hoped he was reassuring the victim that they were getting help. She felt guilty for leaving her here but if they stopped for every person in a wrecked car, they'd never get help or make it out themselves.

"Come on, Danny. Let's get to the police station. Let's find out what the hell is happening." They ran past other wrecked cars and buses and Sophie shivered at the probability that they were all filled with casualties and people desperate for help. And here they were, able to run on their own two feet to hopefully find some form of safety.

Legs burning, lungs aching, they continued to move. One question bothered Sophie the most - why weren't the police already responding?

CHAPTER NINE

Jake glanced down at his watch, forgetting that it had been broken in the crash. He was a creature of habit, always checking to see what time it was. Looking up at the sky, he tried to estimate what the time would be by the location of the sun in the sky. The large blanket of trees over them hindered it, making it appear darker than it actually was. The only good vantage point he had to see the sky was where the plane had ripped through the greenery during its fiery descent into the forest beneath them.

After combing through the cabin with help from Becky, only a handful of passengers had survived the crash. Some were more incapacitated than others, some probably adding to the death toll if help didn't hurry and get to them. He felt vertigo and braced himself on a seat, preventing a quick tumble down from his body's betrayal from the apparent head wound he was suffering from.

"How long would you say it's been since we crashed?" Jake asked Becky, looking up at the sky again.

"An hour? Maybe an hour and a half? That sound about right to you?"

Jake squinted and looked back down - lifting his head only made the dizziness worse. "Hard to say. My watch is busted and I can't get my cell phone to turn on."

"Mine won't work either." Becky held it up and frowned. "I went right for it to call someone but it won't even turn on. I figured the crash had something to do with it. Odd that neither of ours works."

"Neither does Colin's. Speaking of him, I should probably go check on him. Keep an eye on the survivors. We should probably move them all together so when the rescue crews get here, things will move faster."

Jake dreaded the climb over the tree trunk, his body already sending out multiple warnings for him to sit still. The combination of vertigo and weakness wasn't making the tasks at hand easier but those who were left alive needed help, and though the plane was nothing but a shredded up piece of metal now, Jake was still the captain of the flight and he still held a level of responsibility for those who survived.

Scooting down the trunk, the second time climbing it felt a bit easier now that he knew what to expect. Colin was resting his head on the headrest, his eyes closed, but Jake saw the rise and fall of his chest, the first indication that his co-pilot was still awake.

"Colin, how are you feeling?"

The younger man's eyes opened for a second before closing again. "I want out of this chair."

"I know you do. I don't think we should move you until medical professionals get here. What if we cause more damage?"

Jake hunkered down to get a closer look at Colin's pinned leg. A large blood stain soaked his khaki pants. He had been married to Alice enough to learn a few things off of her, and if they moved his leg, the bleeding could possibly get worse. They didn't have the resources to ensure that if Colin moved from his current position, they could stop bleeding and prevent much more blood loss. All they had were the standard first aid kits - a band-aid wouldn't get the job done.

"The side of the plane is helping keep pressure on the wound. I can't tell how bad it is but I'm scared that if we move you, you'll bleed out. Isn't there a major artery in the leg?" Jake sat up and closed his eyes to stop the world from spinning.

"Yeah, I think so," Colin replied, the frustration evident in his tone of voice. "What if the plane is making me bleed more? The pressure is pushing the blood out?"

"I wish I knew, Colin. I'm not a doctor. I'd hate to make the wrong decision."

Colin swallowed and ran his hand down his thigh. "How's it look back there?"

Jake gripped what was left of the airplane yoke, so tight that his knuckles ached. "Not good. Five, maybe six survived. Becky is okay. The rest of the flight crew isn't." He'd never be able to wipe the death and destruction from his memory. "Trees ripped up the cabin and the wings on the plane are gone. I'm not sure how we managed to miss it up here in the front since most of the damage happened behind the cockpit. If I hadn't seen it with my own eyes, I'd never believe it."

"Was it a full flight?"

Jake nodded. "It was."

"Son of a…" Colin trailed off. "Surely they know we went off radar. They can pinpoint where we were located when it happened."

"Yeah, they can."

"So, where the hell are they?" Colin yelled out, mainly from frustration and pain. It was something Jake was wondering too.

"Becky estimates it's been a little over an hour and a half since we went down."

Colin clenched his jaw and closed his eyes again. "I know our flight path had us going over the rural mountainous states, but come on. This is America. It's not like we crashed into the damn ocean or something."

Jake shared Colin's frustrations. Reaching for the radio, he tried to send another mayday call out but he had the same luck as before. All ways of communicating outside of the crash site weren't working. Their radios were likely damaged in the crash, but why were their watches not working? Jake couldn't figure that part out.

"What do we do now, Jake?" Colin asked, opening his eyes again.

"I'm going to get the survivors out of the cabin and on the ground. I think I will start going through luggage - maybe someone packed something useful to assist with our injuries. With the wide range of people on the flight, it's possible, right?" Jake forced a smile and nudged Colin, though the other man didn't have the same reaction to his plan.

"Do what you need to do. I'll be sitting right here. I'm not going anywhere." Finally, a small smile parted Colin's lips until both men were laughing. It was an odd sentiment but a good release - Jake needed it before he went back and faced all of the death in the cabin.

"We'll get you out. I'll be back with a solution." Jake patted Colin's arm and nodded. "I won't be gone long."

It was a good distance from where the passengers were at in the cabin down to the ground. A healthy person might have been able to jump down but those that were still alive were in poor health. Moving them was iffy as it was - making them jump down from over six feet, jolting their already tired bodies could prove to be even more detrimental to what they were already dealing with.

Jake considered the evacuation slides that usually deployed in times of emergency. Just like with everything else on the aircraft, they didn't deploy. He inspected the front cabin door closest to the cockpit. It had been torn up in the crash and what was left of the slide had been ripped up with no chance that it would even hold air. Every window exit and the back cabin door were the same story.

"We gotta get the survivors down to the ground and off this plane," Jake said to Becky, keeping his voice low. "I don't know if jet fuel is leaking or what else could happen, but there's no reason to stay on here. The safety is compromised."

Becky nodded. "It's a long way down to the ground."

"I know. Any suggestions on how to get down would be appreciated."

Jake walked halfway down the aisle, stepping over bodies of people who weren't lucky to make it through. Emotions caught in his throat and he blinked back the warmth that gathered in the corners of his eyes. The wing was no longer connected to the right side of the airplane but it had somehow managed to get propped up on the side, wedged between a tree and the fuselage. There was a small gap between the side of the plane and the wing but it wasn't wider than two feet at most. They could use the wing as a makeshift slide to get down. The left side of the plane was not an option - it had scraped along a row of trees and there were no means of exit against the shrubbery.

"Listen up, everyone!" Jake spoke loud over the wind that continued to rustle through the trees. "We're going to need to exit the plane on the right side. Step off the edge and shimmy down the wing. It isn't connected to the plane anymore but luck is finally on our side - it's wedged just enough to use as our evacuation slide. We'll need to move quickly. I'm not sure how long that wing will hold with our weight on it."

He combed through the cabin again, helping a young child get off of the floor. He and Becky also assisted with the few that remained that had life-threatening injuries. The wing wobbled as they scooted down to the ground. It scraped against the side of the plane, the metal on metal contact rubbing together, the sound unpleasant like nails on a chalkboard, only twenty times louder.

Going back up the wing was the biggest challenge - an upward climb on a slippery slope with nothing to grab onto for bearings. It took Jake several times and he finally took a running start, his boots gripping the metal surface just enough to grab onto the jagged edge of the damaged plane so he could pull back into the cabin. His head throbbed from the abrupt movements but he had to make sure there was no one left behind that was still alive. He wasn't a doctor and he feared leaving people behind. What if someone was alive but unconscious? It'd take time but he needed to check pulses. He had done a quick job before but this time, he needed to be more thorough.

Becky wasn't able to help him. She went down the wing and just like him, struggled to make her way back up. He was glad he got back inside - if there was no way to climb back up, Colin would be left alone in the cockpit with his leg pinned. Jake had promised he would be back.

Stopping at each body, Jake checked for a pulse. If he couldn't find one in their neck, he checked their wrist. If the person was obviously dead, he'd move on without wasting time - those were the hardest bodies to come across. One man clutched onto his young son, both their eyes wide open and glossy, staring in different directions. A college aged girl still had her phone gripped tightly in her hand as if she was planning to call someone in the midst of the crash.

Jake began to second guess himself. What if he missed a pulse? What if someones was weak enough that he couldn't detect it? He tried to remind himself to take his time and double check. It was disheartening that everyone he came across didn't have one. There had to be more survivors. Moving toward the back of the plane, he held his breath as he continued, hoping he'd find at least one more person who had made it through.

It was horrible to think it but if someone's pulse was that hard to detect, if help didn't come soon, there would be nothing they could do for them. He had to hope they weren't feeling any pain and would die peacefully in their unconscious state. Reaching the very back, he checked the last person and had the same luck - he didn't find another survivor. The death around him was overwhelming and frustration coursed through him. Where in the hell were the rescue teams? The wind was a little high but nothing that would hinder a rescue effort to fly in. Maybe not as much time had passed as they had estimated and he was being impatient but seeing all of the dead bodies was like pouring salt on an open wound.

Swallowing the bile in the back of his throat, he went back to the spot they were using as an exit, checking to make sure Becky was handling everything okay on the ground. She was tending to a small girl, the same one who had asked him where her mother was.

"You good down there?" Jake yelled down.

Becky nodded and gave him a thumbs up. "We're fine."

"I'm gonna go check on Colin." He didn't want to have to make the climb back up the wing before getting Colin down.

Climbing over the large trunk again, his mind raced as it desperately tried to think up a way to get Colin's leg free. Patting the co-pilot on the arm, Colin opened his eyes and squinted from the rays of sun that shot through the greenery above them.

"I told you I'd come back."

Colin shook his head and forced a low, raspy laugh. He was probably thirsty and for the first time since the crash, Jake realized he was dehydrated as well. Scanning over the scene in front of him, he made note of the location of Colin's leg and what two factors had him pinned.

"Any ideas on how we're gonna get your ass outta here?"

Colin tried to move his leg again and cringed. "I thought you were worried about blood loss."

"I am. Hell, I don't know what to expect, Colin." Jake drove the heel of his hand in his eye, rubbing it. "I don't know when help is coming and I'd feel better if we got everyone off this plane. You're the last survivor left and I can't just leave you up here."

"Okay. Do what you gotta do, Jake."

Jake took off his belt and made a tourniquet around Colin's leg before releasing the pressure against it. He had learned it from basic first aid training in the military, as well as listening to Alice's stories from work. Having to actually apply it was challenging.

Jake looked at the massive tree trunk he had to scale multiple times going from the cockpit to the cabin. There were large branches and he could use one to wedge and lift the control panel off of Colin's leg. There were several large branches that were knocked loose from impact and he pulled at one, snapping it to have its size to give them more leverage.

"I'm going to wedge this near your leg. When I push up on it, try to slide your leg out."

Jake inserted the branch, making sure not to get it too close to Colin's leg. He put all of his weight on it, pushing it downward. It snapped almost instantly, causing Jake to crash to the floor. It wasn't the biggest branch to choose from and rather than ruminate on the failed attempt, he searched for a bigger one that would still fit under the control panel.

"Here we go again. This one seems a bit sturdier."

Colin nodded and Jake repeated the task. The branch held strong and he pushed as hard as he could, grunting out as the panel lifted. It was only a few inches and the damaged plane squeaked from the movement of the wreckage. Colin was able to slide his leg out and it was good he was quick - Jake wasn't sure how long he'd be able to hold the metal up, especially in his condition. His body ached, his head pounded, and more vertigo made him feel like he was on a tilt-o-whirl.

Letting go of the branch, the wreckage fell back to its original spot, only this time, Colin was free of it, his pant leg blood-soaked, his eyes closed as he clenched his jaw.

"Are you okay?" Jake asked, moving in to inspect the injury.

"I'm fine. It justs hurts like hell."

"Let's get you down on the ground. We can check it better down there."

Thankfully, Colin wouldn't have to climb the trunk to get to their homemade evacuation slide. The crash had caused the plane to impact the ground with the nose down and the tail high in the air, so they only had a few feet to go before they were safely on the ground. Jake aided in getting Colin down and just by the preliminary look of it, Jake would bet that the leg was broken. They could deal with that as long as the arteries hadn't been injured and the bleeding wasn't out of control.

Colin leaned on Jake as he led him to where everyone had gathered. Finding a soft spot on the ground, Jake sat beside him, finally able to catch his breath and allow the dizziness to stop. It looked like they were on an episode of *Lost* - he hoped that this was all a bad dream and he'd wake up next to Alice in their warm bed. The pain radiating in his skull was a sharp reminder that this wasn't a dream. It was a nightmare playing out in real time.

What would they do now? They had to stay close to the plane - it'd be the first place the rescue teams would look when they finally arrived. Becky tossed him a first aid kit and Jake chalked it up to good luck. He'd take it where he could get it.

Scooting toward Colin, he said, "Let's take a look at your leg. Getting you out of the cockpit was the hard part. Smooth sailing from here on out."

CHAPTER TEN

Alice couldn't believe how many people were flocking into the emergency room. She had been an ER nurse for years and there had been extremely busy times but this was a new one for her, a new definition when it came to the meaning of the word 'busy.' Every victim that came through the doors claimed they were in a wreck, that their vehicle had just stopped and had become uncontrollable.

The overhead lights flickered which meant that the generators were needing gasoline. The last thing they needed was for those to fail. Reaching for the phone, she selected the 'page' option to try and get into contact with maintenance. The option was unresponsive and it took her a second to remember that nothing was working - no cell phones, no computers, and even their medical equipment wasn't getting the job done. They were having to revert back to old school methods of treating everyone, which many of her staff panicked when it came to getting back to basic first aid and medical treatment.

"Has anyone seen Manny?" Alice asked out loud, not directing her question at anyone in particular. With the chaotic scene playing out in front of her, the best way to get someone's attention was by raising her voice.

"No, haven't seen him. Why?"

Alice smoothed her hands over her hair, pulling back wisps of hair that had fallen into her face. Her skin was sweaty, her body exhausted. The adrenaline was starting to fade despite all of the people needing care.

"I need someone from maintenance. We need to get the generators checked. How long have we been without power? An hour, maybe two?"

She had lost track of time. She relied heavily on her cell phone to know what time it was throughout the day and now that it was fried, she didn't know. The clock on the wall near the nurse's station had stopped along with everything else, which was enough evidence for Alice to put together that something beyond a normal power outage was happening.

"I haven't seen anyone," the ward clerk responded again with a shrug of her shoulders. If it wasn't for the fact that she was jumping in and helping, Alice would've felt annoyed with the young girl.

"I'm going down to the basement to see if they're down in their offices. I'll be right back."

Alice didn't wait for a response and wondered if anyone even heard her. Time wasn't on their side - one less nurse in the ER meant that the patients would have to wait even longer for someone to help them. She broke out into a jog, hurrying to the first set of stairs that would take her down. Elevators were completely out of the question and it made the hair on the back of her neck stand up at the thought of getting stuck on one. It hadn't occurred to her that there could be people on them. The generators were giving them electricity but the elevators were probably compromised like everything else.

Reaching for the stairway door, she glanced over her shoulder at the elevator across the hall. Hesitating at first, she backpedaled toward it and pushed the up arrow. She had no intention of hopping on but wanted to see if it would respond to the command. The light behind the button didn't even illuminate. The motor didn't hum like it usually did. There was no ding indicating that it was arriving on her floor.

Leaning in, she tried to listen to see if there was any movement on it. No one was yelling for help, there was no banging to get someone's attention. The shaft was completely silent. Blinking back the sweat that dripped into her eyes, Alice stepped backward, looking up at the floor indicator light. Of course, it wasn't working either. It didn't appear that anyone was on this particular elevator but it also wasn't the only one in the building. And it could've been on a higher floor and she just wasn't able to hear anyone inside.

Turning back to the staircase, she hurried down to the basement. Maintenance had ways of getting into the elevator shafts for issues and they'd have to be who fronted the rescue efforts if there were people trapped between floors. The most important thing at the moment was getting gasoline to replenish the generators. The lights flickered again, hinting that they'd be in the dark soon if someone didn't check on the only power source they had.

Once she got into the hallway of the basement, Alice broke out in a sprint. She passed the morgue, the training labs, and reached the maintenance offices in record time. Her once fading adrenaline kicked in full gear, her heart racing so fast that she feared it'd pound right out of her chest. Pushing the office door open, she let out a deep breath when she saw she was alone. Both desks sat vacant, sending a chilly vibe down her spine.

"Anyone in here? Manny?"

Nothing. No footsteps, no response… nothing. Alice pushed behind the counter, scanning the white board with notes on what jobs around the hospital needed to be done for the day. There were plans to work on an elevator on the south side of the building. It had a star beside it, which Alice assumed meant it was a high priority job. The elevator in reference was on the clinic side and she'd be willing to bet that was where Manny and his staff probably were when everything hit the fan.

Running down the dim hallway again, she took the stairs two at a time, bypassing the ER on her way to the clinics. The generators were a concern but it was now shadowed by the well-being of the maintenance staff. Rounding the corner, her legs ached, her lungs burned, but she pushed on. This had to be a dream. How could something go bad so fast, and at this caliber? Everyone she had talked to claimed their vehicles had died. Cell phones were fried. Computers were dead. They were dealing with hell on earth and she had no idea where to even begin on getting things on track to getting back to normal, whatever normal meant.

Reaching the clinic area, she knew of two elevator banks nearby. Reaching them, her heart skipped a beat when she spotted the doors to one of them wide open. Peeking inside, she looked down and saw someone on the top of the elevator, which was hanging between the first floor and the basement levels.

"Manny?" Her voice echoed in the shaft. The smell of oil and metal was strong.

"Alice! We're stuck! What happened?"

"I don't know, Manny. But we need to get you out of there. Who is with you?"

He looked down inside the elevator and back up, closing his eyes. "Bart. But…" he trailed off, bracing himself. "I don't think he made it, Alice. I think Bart is dead."

The lights flickered again, reminding Alice of the generator situation. It was happening too close together now. "We need gas for the generators, Manny. I think they're running on fumes. I'm going to get you some help! I'm going to make sure Bart is okay."

"Get the gas first, Alice. Running the generators on empty will fry them up."

Alice didn't want to leave the men behind but if she stayed there, she'd waste more time. Making eye contact with Manny, she nodded her head and forced a smile. "I'll come back, Manny. I won't leave you behind."

"I know, Alice. Go get the gas!"

She ran to the closest exit, trying to get a vantage point of what stores and resources would be available on that side of the hospital. There were two convenience stores right across the street and though nothing was working, she had to hold out hope that she could get her hands on enough gas to refill the generators.

Both stores were crowded with people, some running out with food, others demanding items from the clerk who stood behind the counter, wide-eyed and unable to control the crowd. A panicked atmosphere hovered around Alice, much like the looting and pillaging she had seen on the news after riots and massive storms that had come through. How was that possible? The power outage had only happened a few hours ago. Why were people already resorting to this type of behavior?

"Are the gas pumps working?" Alice approached the counter, knowing it was a stupid question, but one she had to ask anyway.

The clerk shook his head. "No. Nothing is."

"Damn it!" Alice wiped her brow with the back of her hand and looked around. "I work over at the hospital. We need gasoline for the generators so we can help everyone."

"Look, lady, he said they aren't working!" A woman near the coolers of drinks yelled at her, waving her finger in front of her face.

The large tanks under the ground were probably still full of the needed resource. But how in the hell would she go about getting down there to get some? With the chaos that ensued, there would be no way to go about it, at least, not right now. Running to the store next door, it was almost the same scenario, only the clerk seemed more in control.

"What are the chances that we can get some gas?" Alice asked, glancing toward the hospital. It was still daytime and hard to tell if the generators had completely died.

"Slim to none."

Vacant cars sat everywhere and an idea hit Alice blindside. Walking down each aisle of the store, she grabbed a red gas can and a short garden hose. Even though others were taking things and running, her conscience wouldn't let her take the items without paying. Reaching into her pocket, she pulled out a twenty dollar bill and slapped it on the counter.

"Ma'am, what are you planning to do with that?" The man pointed at her items.

"I'm going to siphon gas out of these cars. I don't think anyone is going to be using them anytime soon."

Walking outside, she ran across to the hospital again - there were plenty of cars in the parking lot to choose from. It was going to taste terrible but gasoline meant the generators would run and they would be able to continue to treat victims.

Unscrewing the gas cap of a pickup, she stuck the hose inside. It was too long to work with so she pulled the pair of clothing scissors from her pants and cut the hose down to half its length. Sucking on the other end, gas flowed up into her mouth, burning her lips and tongue. The flavor made her want to puke and she gagged, but the suction helped the gas flow and she quickly put her end inside the gas can. The trickling sound was music to her ears and the two gallon can filled quickly.

Alice wasn't sure how much gasoline a generator would hold, so multiple trips out into the parking lot was probably not out of the question. Once it was full, she pulled the hose out of the tank to get the gas to stop flowing. Whoever owned the pickup at recently filled the tank and she didn't want the rest of it to be wasted on the ground.

Putting the lid on the gas can, she ran toward the ER. It was the first generator that should be filled before anything else since most of the victims were in that area. It would also give her a chance to notify someone about Manny and his worker being caught in the elevator shaft. They had waited too long for help to arrive and she felt guilty for leaving them behind. The people at the hospital needed their help. It was a miracle no one had noticed they were missing sooner.

**

Sophie felt like with each step she took, the police station was moving away from them. She was never much of an athlete and running was something she used to always joke about and say if she was doing it, something was probably chasing her. Never in her wildest dreams would she have imagined a situation like this - car wrecks, plane crashes, and unexplained turmoil, would really be happening. She had read too many books and watched too many movies where the plot was almost carbon copy of the real life playing out before her very eyes.

Danny seemed to have better endurance than her and was now several steps ahead of her, continuously checking over his shoulder to make sure she was still behind him. They reached the police station and Sophie had to stop to catch her breath, bending at the waist to stave off the stomach cramps and nausea.

Going through the entrance, a sense of dread settled in the pit of Sophie's stomach. She had never visited the campus police station but there was a front desk reception area where she assumed someone usually sat to greet people who came in. No one was there and she was shocked when Danny went back to the large area where several offices were.

"Where is everyone?" Danny asked, opening each door, revealing an empty room each time.

"Maybe they're all out trying to help." Sophie tried to remain positive. Didn't one cop usually stay behind to protect the station?

"I don't know," Danny shrugged, slamming his fist into the wall when they reached the very last room at the end of the hallway. "What the hell is going on, Sophie? What is happening?" He raised his voice and it shook. She had never seen her friend upset and his extreme reaction made panic take over her worry.

"What do we do, Danny?" She lifted a phone off of the cradle. Maybe it was only cell phones that had been knocked out. There was no dial tone and she hung up, attempting it again. The phone didn't respond. "Land lines are out too."

The building shook, mimicking what Sophie imagined an earthquake would feel like. It was disorienting and she fell to the floor, the vertigo strong enough that she couldn't keep balance to get back up. Danny crawled to her, pulling her in for a hug. His embrace was comforting and for a second, she imagined that they were on a date and not stuck in the middle of some disastrous situation.

The building finally stopped shaking and when she opened her eyes, she hoped she'd be in her bed back at her dorm instead of on the floor at the police station. But she was there and whatever was happening wasn't going away. Standing, she took a deep breath and tried to calm down. Panicking would only cause them to make bad decisions, and one bad decision right now could possibly mean their lives.

"We need to get out of here, Sophie."

"Where are we gonna go?"

Danny's eyes widened and it took him a second to answer. "Off campus. We need to get the hell out of Boston."

Fleeing might be a good idea. Sophie wasn't sure how widespread this was happening. Was Boston under attack? Getting out of there was fine by her but how they were going to do it was beyond her. She wanted to get back to Dallas. She wanted to make sure her family was okay. Staying right where they were wasn't getting anything accomplished. Cars were not working, planes had crashed out of the sky, and from what she could tell, anything electronic had failed to remain functioning. Maybe outside of campus, things were okay. They wouldn't know unless they tried. It'd make her feel better if she could get to a working phone and make contact with her parents. If she could hear their voices and know they were okay, her panic would subside a bit.

"Okay, Danny. Let's go. I'm not sure how we're gonna do it, but let's get the hell outta here."

CHAPTER ELEVEN

Jake cut back Colin's pants with a pair of scissors he was able to find in some luggage. Becky found a first aid kit that had basic supplies in it - ace bandages, gauze, medical tape, and band-aids and Jake was thankful for that. His medical ability didn't go past patching up wounds and he could thank his kids for knowing how to do that much. Alice was the one who always handled the more gory things and sitting there now, among the plane crash victims, he wished he would've paid more attention to what she had tried to teach him over the years.

Colin's wound was still bleeding but Jake felt confident that pulling him from the plane wasn't going to put him in the grave. He applied a layer of gauze to it and wove the tape around Colin's leg, tight enough to put pressure on the wound to help stop the bleeding. His co-pilot cringed when Jake would move the leg around, which was all the convincing they needed to assume the leg was definitely broken.

"How you feeling?" Jake asked, patting Colin on the arm.

"Thirsty. Tired. Hungry. I'm in pain, Jake."

Jake laughed. "Anything negative, we'll just say all of the above." He wished he could do something for Colin's pain. Apparently, the ibuprofen and

Tylenol they had in the first aid kit wasn't even making a difference.

Colin nodded and closed his eyes. "Thanks for getting me out of there, Jake. I really thought…" He trailed off and opened his eyes, squinting from the sun beams that poured through the openings in the trees overhead. "I really thought I was going to die up there."

"I wouldn't have let that happen," Jake replied, standing up. "I'm gonna go find some water and maybe something to eat."

Becky followed him toward the rear of the plane. The storage area for the snacks and drinks was toward the back of the cabin and Jake hoped to find something useful in that general area. As he walked past, he took note of the survivors they had pulled from the plane, all of them spread out on the ground next to the wreckage. He was thankful for those who remained but it had been a full flight and only a handful would be left alive to tell about it. The statistics were against them - a 737 jet airliner held a maximum capacity of around one hundred and forty passengers and Jake counted ten survivors. Ten out of one hundred and forty - he felt ill over the numbers.

"There aren't any more survivors up in the cabin?" Jake pointed upward, looking at the tail end that was high in the air.

Becky shook her head. "If there are, they were unable to respond. Probably not in the best shape to move."

Jake began combing through the bushes and greenery on the ground, hoping snacks had fallen out onto the ground. "I can't believe that only ten of us made it out alive. How's that... How come we made it? I can't accept that." He tried to hide his emotion but his shaking voice revealed them.

"We're the lucky ones, I guess."

"I don't know if lucky is the correct word," Jake said, turning his attention to the cargo door. "Keep searching out here. I'm gonna start going through suitcases. Over one hundred passengers - we're bound to find something useful in all this luggage."

Some suitcases had already been tossed from the plane. Jake started with those, feeling like he was violating the person who it belonged to. Clothes were obviously not hard to come by and would come in handy if the rescue crews continued to take their time in getting to them. He could use a shirt as a tourniquet if Colin's wound wouldn't stop bleeding but they weren't quite to that level of first aid yet.

The first suitcase came up short - if they needed clothing or souvenirs they'd be set but there was no food or something to drink within it. Moving to the next, he pulled open a hot pink carry-on and almost yelled out for joy when the first thing he grabbed was a half gallon bottle of water. Hurrying to the children first, he allowed the three of them to drink as much as they wanted, each one slurping down several gulps before they were satisfied. Half of the bottle was gone by the time he got to Colin, extending it toward him.

"Did you drink any?" Colin asked, refusing it at first.

"Not yet. You first."

"You need it worse than me. You're running around here, trying to scrounge up things to help and I'm just sitting on my ass. Take a swing or two."

"I don't have a gaping wound that won't stop bleeding," Jake replied, both men's stubborn stance amusing and frustrating at the same time.

"You should find a mirror, Jake. You're not in tip top shape yourself."

Jake knew that - he could feel his body's warnings to stop and take a break. But he couldn't allow that. His plane had crashed and over one hundred people were dead because of it. The least he could do now was help the people who had somehow managed to survive it.

"Until the rescue crews get here, I'm going to keep going. Drink the damn water. I'll try to find more." Before Colin could refuse it, Jake hurried back to Becky. "Any luck?"

She held up three bags of peanuts. They were small but they were something and a small glimmer of hope in the midst of the wreckage and death that circled around them. The important thing was water and fluids - a body could go much longer without food than it could go without water. Jake focused on the suitcases again and Becky continued to search for the in-flight snacks that the airline had offered.

Eventually, Jake planned to organize and sort the items out of the luggage by type. Clothing in one pile, food, and water in another. But right now, the biggest priority was water. Every one of them was likely dehydrated from sitting in limbo on the crashed plane. In their poor health, dehydration could prove fatal for some of them.

Jake scanned over the survivors again. They sat in groups, none of them saying much. One child laid on an adult's lap, eyes closed, tears streaming down their cheeks, leaving trails in the dirt on their face. His heart ached at the sight in front of him. Most of all, his frustrations were heightening - why in the hell was this taking so long? It wasn't like they had crashed in the ocean or on some deserted island. They were in America. There was sophisticated flight data that broadcasted their exact location every second of the flight.

Being stranded for this long was unacceptable, and Jake wondered if something else could possibly be happening. He didn't have time to think about conspiracies or possibilities. The plane had crashed. And now they would wait. In the meantime, he had to find water and food. He'd sort out the what ifs and could be's later.

***

Alice sprinted across the parking lot, hoisting the gas can in one hand, weaving through people who were lined up outside the hospital. The crowd seemed to have dissipated some, which made her wonder what was going on. Maybe they had given up hope that they would receive help due to the long wait and left. It'd be a relief to the medical staff if that were true but she hoped they weren't in desperate need of care and left without any help.

She had to stop and think about where the generators were kept. They were likely down in the basement near the control room. She was thankful she had worked at the hospital for as long as she had and knew where everything was - she had walked past the control room when it was open but she didn't have any experience with gas or generators and feared she might mess something up.

When she got into the building, her heart skipped a beat. The lights were out and everyone was sitting in dark rooms. Her staff stopped what they were doing and watched her but she didn't have time to stop and talk. Hopefully, with the gas can in hand, they'd get the hint that she was working to restore the backup power and get things rolling again. Even though none of their machines or equipment were running and they were having to do basic first aid, it was still imperative to get the generators going again in case their systems kicked back on.

Going down the same stairs as before, she felt the gas slosh inside the canister and slowed her pace - gas was now like precious gold and she couldn't afford to spill any of it. There were tons of vehicles out there to siphon from but there was no set time frame on how long the power outage would last and she didn't want to be wasteful with the important resource.

The control room was almost too dark to see in. Patting her leg, she let out a groan when she didn't feel her flashlight in one of her pockets. She wondered if it would even work - it was like anything with batteries had been zapped along with all other electronic devices.

Leaving the door open, she felt her way around. Her habit had her reach for the light switch and she couldn't help but laugh at herself. Everyone was so predisposed to turn lights on in a dark room that even now, in the middle of the worst outage Alice had ever seen, she still tried to turn the lights on.

Being in the basement meant that there wasn't any natural light coming in from windows. There were small ones up high right underneath ground level that lent just enough that she could spot the generator in the far corner. It was large, almost half of the room, and her stomach was in knots as she approached it. The natural light from the small, rectangular windows on the side of the wall was very helpful, and she found where she needed to pour the gas. It was only a few gallons and this was a massive system, which posed the most important question of all - would this be enough? She had to try, and if it wasn't, she'd run back out to the parking lot and get more.

The liquid streamed down into the tank, the splashes echoing in the quiet room. Emptying the gas can, she put the lid back on and stood back, contemplating her next move to get the damn thing running. There was a button next to the tank that read 'automatic transfer switch.' Pushing it, she stepped back again as a low hum began. The lights flickered overhead until they were completely on and she yelled out in joy at the accomplishment of getting the power on.

Alice's victory was short lived when they blinked, mimicking how they were just before the generator had sucked up every last bit of gasoline and died on them. Hurrying back up the stairs, she went straight to the parking lot to siphon more gasoline. Her head was light from the fumes and the physicality of keeping the generator running. She didn't want to ask for help - her staff was needed inside to help victims, but this was going to take up all of her time if someone else wasn't able to lend assistance.

"Alice, need some help?"

Looking up, Alice spotted Rose running toward her. "How are the victims? What's going on inside?"

"We've done what we can do. General first aid, patching them up, but without our equipment, our hands are tied. Are you getting gas out of that truck?"

Alice put the hose back up to her mouth to create suction and inserted the end back into the gas can, nodding her head. "Yeah. It tastes horrible but I have to hurry. That generator is going to suck it all up before I can get back."

"Are gas pumps not working either?" Rose asked, looking across the street at the convenience store that Alice had taken the supplies from.

"Nothing is working, Rose. It's a massive outage."

"Let me help you so you're not chasing your tail. Where'd you get that stuff at?"

Alice watched the gas fill up and pointed across the street. "Over there, if there's anything left."

Rose ran across the road and Alice pulled the hose out of the tank again, fastening the cap securely so they wouldn't lose a drop. Following her previous steps, she ran back to the control room, relieved that the generator hadn't stopped running yet. It was close, and likely running on fumes from the gas she just recently put inside.

"Here, I've got some to put in too." Rose slipped in beside her, lifting her gas can to fill it up as well. "Four more gallons of gas added. How much does one of these things hold?"

"I'm not sure," Alice replied, skimming her hand down the hard metal. "I don't even know how long a few gallons will run this thing. We need to get Manny. He knows more and can maintain this."

"Where is he?"

"The elevator shaft over by the clinics. I wanted to get the generator filled back up so we could go get him. I think this is fine for now. If we do anymore we might mess it up enough that it won't run at all." Rose followed her out of the control room and to the maintenance offices again. "Look for rope or anything we can use to help them climb out of the shaft. They're in between floors and need to come up about twenty feet. I think he's already tried to climb up the elevator cables but wasn't successful."

Alice dug through their storage, shocked at how organized it was. Manny didn't seem like the type but she found several yards of strong rope that would have to be good enough. Pulling the rope tight, she patted Rose on the back and they headed back to the ER. What they needed now were a couple of strong men who could serve as anchors to pull Manny up.

Two men who seemed to be in decent health volunteered and when they got to the elevator shaft where Manny was, Alice stuck her head through the open doors again. "Manny! We got you some help!" Her voice echoed almost so loudly that it was hard to tell what she said.

"Oh, thank God!"

"We're gonna toss the rope down to you. These two men are going to hold it so you can climb up." She looked around for something to tie the rope to but there was nothing stable enough. Thankfully, she had their help. She and Rose wouldn't be strong enough to hold his weight. "Is Bart okay? Do you need to get him out of the elevator?"

Manny shook his head, his eyes downcast. "No. He didn't make it, Alice."

"Okay. Let's get you out and when the firefighters get here, we can have them get inside." It was cruel to just leave Bart there but they didn't have much time. Too many people were suffering due to lack of help and resources and it felt like only the strong were surviving. Things couldn't be that bad. It was only a power outage, right? Alice struggled with that idea, knowing this went well beyond the electricity being out.

One of the men threw the rope down and Manny caught it. It was a struggle at first but he used the sides of the elevator shaft as leverage to pull up. Groaning, he fought his weight and the swing of the rope, along with the grease used to lubricate the cables for the elevator to be able to slide up and down. The two men serving as anchors planted their feet on the side of the wall to help with the support and Alice and Rose stood by, watching helplessly.

Manny gritted his teeth, his hands gripping the rope tight. He was just a few feet away and grabbed onto the open door, using his arm strength to pull himself up the rest of the way. The two men helped pull him completely out of the shaft and out onto the floor. Manny lay still a few seconds, closing his eyes as he tried to gain his composure, his breath heavy and labored.

"Oh thank God, you came to get me!"

"I would've never left you in there," Alice replied. "I'm sorry it took so long, but we've got problems with the generator. I was hoping you could help out. We put gas in but I don't think it's enough."

Manny sat up and leaned against the wall, closing his eyes again as he caught his breath. "I'm on it, Alice. It's the least I can do."

Alice looked down the shaft again at the top of the elevator that was dangling in limbo. Bart was still inside, probably dead. Another casualty to add to the ever-growing list that was changing by the second. Her heart ached for the maintenance worker. She didn't know him well but he always came to work and he always got the job done in a timely fashion.

Hell on earth - and now that she had a second to stop and think about her own personal situation. Was Jake's flight the one that had crashed? Was Dylan's school experiencing the outage too? She hoped the administration had an emergency plan in place and he was safe where he was at. And Sophie was all alone in Boston - Alice hoped this wasn't that widespread. She wouldn't relax until her family was all accounted for, and by the looks of the chaos in the ER, she wouldn't be able to leave anytime soon to figure it all out.

CHAPTER TWELVE

Sophie was hoping that the farther they got away from the campus, things would die down a bit. She continuously checked her cell phone to see if it'd even turn on but it wouldn't respond. Either the battery was zapped or it just wasn't working - but the battery had been fully charged just before she had headed to class that morning. She hadn't been on it enough to have it go completely dead, so that theory wasn't a good one.

What made the situation even eerier was all of the cars left stranded on the roads. There weren't enough people to match up with how many vehicles were sitting vacant. Where were all the people? Did they all know something that Sophie and Danny didn't know? The hair on the back of her neck raised up and she glanced to the side, trying to read Danny's body language. Neither of them had said much since they had decided to get away from campus. Danny was usually a chatterbox, so his lack of input on what they were witnessing made Sophie worry even more. What was happening? Would they ever really find out?

"What are you thinking, Danny?" Sophie reached out and grabbed his hand, squeezing it. The human contact was calming and she was thankful she wasn't going at this alone.

"I don't know. I really don't know." He shrugged and looked up at the sky. Sophie followed his gaze, noting multiple jet chemtrails against the gray clouds overhead. It made her think of her father - had his plane crashed or was this isolated over the east coast and Massachusetts?

"I'm scared, Danny. Where is everyone?"

There were a few others, walking in the general direction that they were going, everyone surmising that the best idea was to get away from Boston. It was a sad world they lived in to immediately go to a terrorist attack when things like this happened, but unfortunately, it was the world they lived in. Getting away from heavily populated areas was the best idea, as that's where the majority of casualties would take place.

"Let's just keep walking this way. It's south and eventually, we'll get away from the city. Maybe we can find a TV with some news on it and can find out exactly what the hell is going on."

Sophie wouldn't bet on it. Her body ached and she was thirsty. They passed several stores and she couldn't believe that looting was already taking place. Was this really that bad that people felt that desperate to start taking things? Then again, if all electronic devices were shot, the cash registers weren't working anyway.

"We should go into that store and get something to eat, Danny. I'm hungry and the water we had earlier is gone. There might not be anything left the farther we get out of the city."

Danny nodded in agreement and they took a detour through the parking lot up to a grocery store. The front windows were broken out and people were coming and going, their arms filled with as much stuff as they could carry. Sophie couldn't believe what she was seeing - this was happening in real life.

Going inside, it was an even bigger disaster. Many shelves were already picked clean, there were no staff members in sight, and people were running around grabbing things, some pulling bread and milk out of the hands of others. It was a free for all, every man for themselves, and all Sophie wanted was a bottle of water and something salty to help with her appetite. She didn't realize they'd have to fight for such simple items, but she also didn't realize when she woke up this morning that it'd be like an end of the world novel.

The front coolers where the sodas and water were usually kept were wiped clean. She feared they wouldn't find even one bottle to share between the two of them. Hurrying down aisles, she grabbed a box of crackers, a bag of beef jerky, and when she reached the back of the store, she ran toward a large bottle of water in the back case. It was the last one, and three other people had the same thing in mind, all of them reaching for it at the same time.

Sophie's hand grasped it first and she pulled it away. The three other people, two men and a woman, stared her down as if they were in the animal kingdom and she had just picked off the carcass of a freshly killed antelope. They circled her, the woman lunging at her to try to pry it out of her arms. Sophie backed away, bumping into a nearby shelf. Danny was a few feet away, gathering his own food. Sprinting, her legs burned and she yelled out when one of the men pulled on her hair.

"Danny, catch!" She threw the bottle of water like a football and Danny intercepted it, hesitating to leave her there. "Go, I'll be fine! We need the water!"

The three looters lost interest in Sophie when they saw Danny now had the water. He was a faster runner and much stronger than Sophie, so she stayed back, attempting to catch her breath. Hopefully, Danny could handle his own. Once she gained her composure, she ran out into the parking lot, the three strangers were too far back to catch Danny. After a few more seconds of chasing him, they gave up and went back to the store. That was Sophie's cue to head in the direction Danny went.

Meeting back up with him near the freeway, he took a long pull off of the water and handed it to her. It tasted amazing and though it was no longer cold, it still quenched the harsh thirst she had felt.

"Did that really just happen back there?" Sophie asked, pointing over her shoulder at the store.

"It did. What were you able to grab?"

Holding up the items, Sophie smiled. "Crackers and beef jerky. We need the protein."

"Good! I got some bread and cheese. It's room temperature but if we eat it now, it shouldn't hurt us."

Sliding the groceries into her bag, Sophie grabbed Danny's arm and continued to walk south, following along the freeway where all the wrecked cars remained. "We probably shouldn't broadcast what we have. If people are already resorting to fighting like what we just saw, we'll be targets. Over bread and crackers. Not really worth dying over."

"How is this even possible? How could..." Danny trailed off, scrubbing his hand down the side of his face. "This is the twenty-first century. How could people be acting like that back there?"

"I wish I knew, Danny. We just gotta keep moving. There's nothing left here."

"Where do you wanna go?"

"Like we planned. Away from Boston. We need to get somewhere where we can find out what's going on. Where our cell phones will actually turn on. Where there's more people!" She waved her hand around. "Let me rephrase that. Where there's people who don't want to kill us over a box of crackers."

Danny pulled his cell phone out and mimicked like he was going to throw it, but stopped himself. "Son of a bitch! Son of a bitch!"

Sophie took his hand again and kissed the back of it. "I need you calm, Danny. Please... let's work together. We can figure it out together!"

He clenched his jaw and looked out over the freeway. "You're right, Sophie. We'll continue walking south. There's really nowhere else to go."

Hand in hand, they walked in silence. Sophie's stomach growled, she was thirsty, but after what had happened at the supermarket, the importance of rationing their food was front and center. As long as they refilled their water often and rationed their food until they found more, they would be okay.

She worried for her parents and for her little brother. Were they seeing what was happening on the news? Knowing her father, he'd be headed up that direction to get her out of harm's way. Sophie wished she could get on a phone and tell him not to come - it'd only make things worse. But what if he was already on his way, headed toward her dorm, only to find she had fled? She was always taught in disasters to stay where she was unless an evacuation was ordered. It was the safest way for loved ones to find you but her dorm and the campus was no longer safe.

They'd find a phone soon. She'd call her mom and dad and make contact with them. Things would seem a lot better once she could talk to them. Until then, the worry would be unbearable. At least they had a plan - it wasn't the safest or the most stable but it was better than sitting around. The future was unknown - it made Sophie's appetite fade quickly.

***

The sun was beginning to set overhead and Jake glanced down at his watch - it was a habit that was hard to break and he looked up at the sky, trying to guess what time it actually was. They had scoured several suitcases in the past hour, coming up with some food and water, as well as some toiletry items that would come in handy. He was feeling light-headed so he and Becky were taking a break, each of them snacking on bags of peanuts, compliments of the airline.

They had shared the snacks with the other survivors and the kids ate them up quickly. Jake sat back against a tree and heaved a deep sigh. Colin's leg had stopped bleeding, which was a step in the right direction. He felt ill, unable to even finish the small bag of peanuts. The water tasted great but he paced himself - there were people worse off than him that would need it more, and since help still hadn't come, it was important to ration what they had.

"What time do you think it is?" Jake asked, directing his question at anyone who wanted to answer. There was a smoky haze that hindered them from seeing the moon and stars, masking what time it really was.

Colin cringed and closed his eyes. The man was in pain but wouldn't admit it. "Evening. Probably a little after six."

"That was my guess, too," Jake replied. "You get enough to eat and drink, Colin?"

"I'm good. Give the rest of my peanuts to the kids over there."

Jake rested his head on the tree trunk and closed his eyes. What was Alice doing? Enough time had passed that she likely had seen the news about the plane crash. She was working a twelve-hour shift and if it really was around six, she was probably getting off work about that time. How was Dylan taking it? He had a game tomorrow and now all of the focus would be put on Jake and his crashed flight. And poor Sophie - she had made plans to visit home in a few weeks. What was she doing right now? Jake would be willing to bet she was hopping on the first plane into Dallas.

Alice had a number she could call for family members to get information on pilots. Jake hoped she was doing that, demanding a search party and help get sent this way. He could imagine it now, her voice raised, clenching the phone so tight that she could break it. And she had every right to - taking this long to get to a plane crash was unheard of, and here they sat, wondering what to do next.

"Becky, how are you feeling?" Jake felt guilty for focusing on Colin. He hadn't even taken a moment to consider her health.

"I'm fine. Bumps and bruises, but a lot better off than you two."

Jake opened his eyes again and smirked. That was one thing about Becky - if you wanted an honest answer, you'd get it from her. "We gotta come up with a plan."

"The safety plan is to stick as close to the crash site as possible," Colin chimed in, letting out a groan as he shifted his weight.

"But for how long?" Jake asked, looking around at the circle of survivors. The children were beginning to fall asleep, the others looking on, still depending on what was left of the flight crew to make the big decisions.

"I'm not sure. We should stay here tonight. If you can't tell, I'm not going anywhere anytime soon." Colin motioned toward his leg, his mouth set in a hard line. "If we have to move, how do you propose going about getting me mobile?"

"We'll figure something out. I agree, let's stay here tonight. We could all use the rest. Maybe by the time morning comes around again, the rescue crews will be here."

Becky pointed toward Jake and shook her head. "I don't think sleeping is a good idea for you. With that head wound, it wouldn't be far-fetched to assume you have a concussion."

"What happens if I were to sleep and did have one?" He wished he could just dial Alice's number and ask.

"Don't know but that's what I've always heard - no sleep if there is a concussion," Becky replied with a shrug of her shoulders. Standing, she moved closer to Jake and took a look at his wound. "We've got enough gauze and ointment to clean it up. At least keep it from getting infected."

"Sure, that sounds good." Jake hadn't suggested it before because he wanted to make sure they had enough supplies to help the others out first. Crashing the plane was enough - he didn't want to be the cause of no first aid items for those who were harmless victims in this mess.

Pouring some alcohol on a small piece or gauze, Becky gently applied it to the wound. It stung and Jake gritted his teeth to control the pain. Becky's brow furrowed and she grabbed a piece of clean gauze and the surgical tape.

"It's pretty deep. If I clean it up too much the scabbing will break and you'll bleed more. You don't remember hitting your head on anything?"

"No." Jake shook his head, which he regretted immediately. The damn vertigo was back and he had to look up to control the spinning world around him.

"Even more evidence that it's likely a concussion." Becky taped it up and scooted away from him. "Your eyes look pretty heavy. Keeping you awake is gonna be tough."

"I guess I can rummage through more bags."

"No. You need to rest. All of this will be here in the morning. Resting is good for you. Just don't sleep!"

Jake had seen this many times before - Becky always took charge of things. Some would say she was bossy, some would say it was just years of experience working as a flight attendant. Jake wasn't going to argue with her but she was definitely right about one thing - keeping him awake was going to be tough. His body had relaxed into the forest shrubbery and each time he closed his eyes, it was hard to get them to open again.

Colin had already given in and was resting soundly, which Jake liked to see but was also envious of. Even in his impaired condition, he made sleep look good. It was what his co-pilot needed - hands down, he was in very bad shape compared to most of them who had survived the crash.

"We've got a long night ahead of us," Becky said as she dug through a bag. "I'll stay up with you."

Jake shook his head and laughed, though he wasn't amused. It was more of an annoyance. "Great... just great."

CHAPTER THIRTEEN

With Manny rescued from the elevator shaft and controlling the generators, Alice was able to divert her focus back on the victims in the ER. When she got back to the chaotic scene, it was better organized when she had left but still like a madhouse. There was no hospital hierarchy anymore - staff didn't have time to consult with doctors to get the go ahead to perform certain procedures on patients. If they were capable, they did it. With most of their equipment not working, the chances of someone doing an extensive measure was unlikely. They had exhausted all of their resources and were left with basic first aid, which wasn't enough for the majority of victims who remained, begging for some help.

Alice felt helpless - standing at the entrance to the exam areas, she looked around at everyone. People were lying on the floor with minimal standing room left. Her staff backed off and Rose joined her, her scrubs bloody, her hair tousled from the long day they had just endured. The woman was defeated and Alice understood - she felt the same way.

"What do we do now?" Rose asked, her voice shaking as her gaze followed Alice's.

"Has anyone reached out to the authorities? Do we know what's causing this?" Alice asked, taking a step forward.

"Yes, with no luck. Phones aren't working and with the madhouse outside, it's becoming too dangerous to even go out there."

Alice understood that all too well. Looters were running rampant and people were already reverting to their base instincts to survive. It had only been a few hours and already, things were so out of control that anarchy was occurring before their very eyes. She couldn't accept that no one had any information. Pushing through a small crowd of people, Alice lifted the phone off of its cradle.

Slamming her hand down, she felt like she had swallowed a brick. "No dial tone."

"It's been like that all day."

"You know what this is, don't you?" A man near the nurse's station approached them. He had dried blood down the side of his face but he was able to walk - He probably had a head wound but his ability to move was a plus in comparison to so many around them.

"What? Please, if you have information, we need to know."

"It's the government. They control us with all of this shit. Cell phones, TV's, tablets… And now, they've shut it all down. And it's completely crippled us!" The man spread his arms and turned in a circle, his smile eerie, his laugh evil. Wagging his finger at Alice, he stepped closer - too close for comfort. "The look on your face tells me you're skeptical."

Alice backed away, getting some distance away from him. "After today, I'm up to believing anything."

"I've done extensive research. Call me a conspiracy theorist but just look at this place!"

"Why Dallas? Why are they focusing on us?" Alice glanced at Rose. Her eyes were wide and tears gathered in the corners of her eyes. It was a haunting sight. Rose was usually strong and collected. Nothing ever got to her.

"That's where you're also mistaken," the stranger replied. "It's not just Dallas, hon. This could affect the entire nation. The entire world!" He raised his voice and Alice motioned for him to keep his voice down. The last thing they needed was to invoke panic.

"How can we know for sure?" Alice asked, swallowing the bile in the back of her throat.

"Get your cell phone out and try to turn it on." The man motioned toward her pocket.

Doing as he requested, she pulled it from her pocket and tried to turn it on. It was the same story as before - it was completely dead.

"I bet it was fully charged right before the shit hit the fan, yeah?"

"It was." Alice nodded.

"And all of your fancy little machines in here. They're not working either, even though you've got the electricity running by way of a gas powered generator, yeah?"

"Yeah," Alice whispered.

"That's how we know for sure. If it was just a random power outage, electronic devices would work. Have you been outside?" He pointed toward an exit, his voice getting louder with each point he was trying to make. Alice gave up on trying to keep him quiet. Instilling panic would be impossible, especially since she was starting to feel her anxiety raise. Her heart pounded in her chest and all she could think about was the safety of her family.

"I've been outside, yeah."

"Cars are dead. Airplanes have fallen out of the sky. How much evidence do you need?"

The mention of airplanes crashing completely sent Alice into a tailspin. While this was something that people just read about on conspiracy websites and in fiction novels, there was no denying that the strange man was making good points. Her denial was clouding her judgment of what was really happening. Her first duty when the chaos ensued was helping every victim that came through the emergency room doors. But things had changed. They had taken a violent shift toward the 'every man for himself' mentality. Her family came before her job. Now was a fine time to think about the future - she had to make sure they were all okay.

Walking to her locker, she gathered her belongings. She couldn't make eye contact with those who remained in the ER. To her surprise, the crowd was beginning to disperse. Maybe the man's antics were enough to convince others that sitting here waiting for help was a lost cause. Everyone needed to channel their energy elsewhere, and though there were several patients who were completely incapacitated, Alice had to turn a blind eye. They had exhausted all of their available resources - for many of them, they were literally putting band-aids on bullet holes and they were wasting everyone's time, the victims included.

"Alice, what are you gonna do?" Rose grabbed her arm, stopping her.

"This goes against everything I believe in but I think it's time to cut our losses here. Think about your family, Rose. Go home."

"How are we gonna get there? Cars aren't working. It's dangerous out there!"

"All the more reason to get to your family, Rose. It's hard to believe, but that man is right. This isn't normal. You don't live far from here. Just get there. Run if you have to."

Rose pulled Alice in for a hug, her tight embrace comforting. They had worked together for years and it felt like a permanent goodbye. "Be safe, Alice."

"You too, Rose. Get to that boy of yours."

Alice wiped a tear from her cheek, slung her bag over her shoulder, and hurried toward the exit. Many other able bodied people were following suit, which made her decision a little easier. She tried not to look at those they were leaving behind. Those who were unable to move, who would likely be dead soon. She hoped they'd have a quick and painless death but that wasn't likely - without normal medical care, it was going to be horrible for them.

Her inspiration was her family. Fighting the urge to look back, Alice kept her focus on moving forward - the goal was now survival, taking an abrupt shift away from her medical oath to assist others in need. This didn't seem real - she was stuck in a continuous nightmare that cycled, sucking her into a world that only existed in high budget movies and TV shows.

Her house was miles away from the hospital. The trek to get there was going to be tough, but she couldn't give up now. Dylan was just a child and in the closest in proximity to her. One goal at a time - she had to get to her youngest child and then figure out what their next course of action would be.

***

Jake was having a hard time staying awake. The concern over the crash and whether or not anyone was coming was enough to plague him with insomnia, but his body was physically exhausted, urging him to get some shut-eye. Wasn't Becky getting tired? She had been awake and through just as much trauma as he had been through but she appeared energetic, picking through suitcases and gathering supplies that might prove useful if they had to sit through another day of waiting for help to arrive.

Looking up at the sky, it was completely dark. Due to the haze, he couldn't even spot the moon or the stars, which made it even harder to tell what time it was. The darkness made it hard to see Becky until she was close to him. She would walk back and forth, checking to make sure he hadn't fallen asleep. Her constant hovering was getting annoying and each time he felt frustrated, his pulse would thump, heightening his horrible headache.

"Would you please sit down?" Jake asked. "Your constant moving around is driving me crazy."

"I'm doing it to stay awake."

"I get that but how can you possibly see to go through those bags anyway?"

Becky took a deep breath and sat a few feet away from him, leaning on a tree. "I think everyone is sleeping. I hope they are, anyway. We might not like what the sun will reveal in the morning."

"What do you mean?" Jake asked, hoping his assumption of what she was implying was wrong.

"We'll be lucky if everyone makes it through the night."

"You haven't found the stash of drinks and snacks that y'all hand out?"

"Some but not all. Everything is spread out. I ran out of daylight."

Jake nodded and closed his eyes. "You've done enough for today. Get some rest."

"I'm not letting you off that easy, Jake. If I go to sleep, so will you."

He could barely see her through the darkness but spotted her wagging her finger at him. She was a mother hen and always had been since he knew her but it was probably what he needed. It's what everyone needed to ensure their survival.

"What's the harm in me sleeping? Enough time has passed, hasn't it? The crash was hours ago."

"I think you have to wait twenty-four hours," Becky replied.

"You're shitting me, right? You just pulled that outta your ass!"

"No, for some reason that's what I'm remembering about concussions."

Jake rested his head against the tree again, his eyes so heavy that he was getting to the point of ignoring her and giving in to the exhaustion. Grabbing a handful of dirt, he let the cool ground sift through his fingers, flowing back to the earth below. Like a lover waiting on an important text message, he checked his phone for the millionth time, hoping he'd get a different result.

"Your cell phone still not working?" he asked Becky, unwilling to give up on the chance to call for some help.

"It's dead. Was the radio in the cockpit dead too?"

"Yeah. I tried to call out several times and nothing happened."

Both of them fell silent again for the longest span since nightfall. Becky's breathing grew steady and Jake tried to see if she had finally fallen asleep. Sitting forward, he squinted but her face was turned away. Her breathing would indicate that she had lost the battle with her body. Finally, he could get a few hours himself. Shifting his weight, he closed his eyes and tried to relax - it was impossible to get his thoughts to stop but he tried to think about anything else, like making it home to Alice and the kids.

"You better not be sleeping!" Becky's voice echoed against the trees, pulling Jake from his daydream of Alice.

"Damn it, I was right at the point where I was about to be there. You know, when it feels perfect."

"I dozed too, but we gotta stay awake, Jake."

Grabbing another handful of dirt, he gripped it in his palm. "I'm thinking someone needs to go try and find help tomorrow."

"We might have to," Becky agreed. "But it's not wise to leave the crash site."

"I know. We'll have to split up. Two of us can go looking while the rest stay here in case someone actually comes. But you know, I don't think anyone is coming."

"No? Why do you think that?"

Jake was trying hard not to get discouraged but in their current situation, it was impossible to keep a positive attitude. "Don't you think they'd have been here by now? It's not like we crashed in the ocean. I'd be a bit more understanding with the delayed rescue time if that had happened."

"Patience, Jake. You were in the military - you should have the patience of a saint."

"Should being the operative word. We'll decide in the morning who will go get help."

He thought it'd be best to omit that he had every intention of being one of them who went. Sitting around by the wreckage was driving him insane. Without getting any sleep, setting off on a hike was probably not the best for his health, but neither was sitting around waiting for help that wasn't coming. He wasn't going to allow anyone else to die on his watch. Finding help was the least he could do for those who remained.

CHAPTER FOURTEEN

Morning came after what felt like an eternity of sitting in the darkness, fighting his body to stay awake. He couldn't be sure, but Jake guessed that both he and Becky had nodded off a few times throughout the night. There was still a thick haze in the air that allowed a few beams of light through, confirming that it was daybreak. Jake had a hard time pushing himself off of the tree - he had made it a point to move around so he wouldn't get stiff from staying in the same position but his body ached, his shoulders were tense, and the damn throbbing headache was still there.

It took him longer than usual to get to a standing position, the thought of his grandfather instantly coming to mind - as a kid, Jake never understood the complaints the old man had made about physical activity but now, he understood it all too well. Becky had gathered up some items and started a small fire in the middle of the circle where everyone was, throwing small twigs and dried up pine needles as a way to get it going well.

Kneeling beside Colin, Jake patted him on the shoulder. His eyes slowly opened, his irises red as he woke up.

"Morning, Colin."

"Morning, Jake. How'd you sleep?"

"Warden Becky wouldn't let me. How about you?"

"I feel pretty good today." Colin tried to sit up, wincing from pain as he scooted up against a nearby tree.

"At some point today we should probably take the bandage off of your leg and let it get some air." Jake pointed to the bandaged wound and looked toward the fire where the remaining survivors had gathered. "Don't say anything but I think I'm gonna go get us some help."

Colin's eyes widened and he shook his head. "I don't think you're in the best shape for that. How's your head? You probably need to rest more than I do after last night. When's the last time you got any shut-eye? The night before last?"

Jake rubbed his palm across his forehead, his fingers outlining the edge of the surgical tape holding the gauze in place. "I'll be fine. My adrenaline is keeping me going."

"You didn't answer my question, Jake. How's your head today?"

"It's fine. Don't worry about me."

"You telling me not to worry about you is like me telling you the same thing. How would you take it if this were reversed and I wanted to go gallivanting through the woods?"

Jake got off his knees and studied the group. Everyone was awake and moving around, and the kids seemed to be in better spirits than the day before. There were still some injuries that needed medical attention but they were not severe.

Looking down at Colin, Jake rested his hands on his hips. He didn't want to argue with Colin - his attitude hadn't improved from yesterday and he needed him on his side. "Listen, Colin... the situation isn't reversed. Looking at everyone, I'm the best for the job. Y'all will stay here in case someone shows up but honestly, man, do you really think someone is coming?" Jake spread his hands out, glancing over his shoulder toward the wreckage.

"Why wouldn't they?"

"That seems to be the million dollar question. We're going on almost twenty-four hours since the crash with nothing happening. I don't think I can sit and wait for another twenty-four. I don't think some of these people will last that long."

"What if something happens to you out there? I'm not even sure how far we are from the closest town."

"I'll take someone with me. What other option do we have?" Jake took a deep breath and rubbed his temples. "I need you on my side, man. Just like when we fly, we make these decisions together."

Colin looked up at him, holding eye contact for a few seconds. He didn't want Jake to go - it didn't take a genius to figure that out. They were stuck between a rock and a hard place. Every decision they made from here on out could mean life and death for people.

"No matter what decision we make, it's not going to feel right," Jake continued. "It's the least I can do, Colin. I was the captain of the flight."

"I know. You do what you need to do. We'll hold the fort down here. Where the hell else am I gonna go anyway?" Colin laughed and it was nice to see the scowl dissipate from his face.

"I'll come back. I won't leave y'all stranded."

Jake approached the group of survivors, nodding toward Becky who was still manning the fire. She knew his plans and her mouth set in a hard line. Jake guessed she figured he wouldn't go through with what he had talked about.

"I'm gonna go see if I can't get us some help."

Everyone stared back at him as if he had just spoken a foreign language. The fire crackled nearby, the smoke lingering against the humidity in the air.

"Why hasn't anyone come?" a woman asked, holding her young child on her lap. "Why have we been stranded so long?"

"I wish I could tell you, ma'am. That's why I'm gonna go see what I can find out. We need help and sitting here is just…" Delaying the inevitable, but Jake didn't say that out loud. They didn't need to hear that. "It's wasting our time. Now here's where I need your help." He spoke to the group, his leadership role changing, from making sure they had a safe flight that landed, to the one making the crucial decisions about their survival. It reminded him of the military all over again, only this was different - they were all civilians now. It was a bitter pill to swallow, looking at the helpless faces staring back at him. "I need one volunteer who is willing to come with me. It's not wise to go out there alone.

Someone who isn't injured too bad that will be able to walk for miles."

"But you're not even in that good of health," Becky chimed in, tossing another log on the fire. "I wish you could see yourself in a mirror, Jake."

Jake tried not to glare at her. The whole group didn't need to know he was far worse than he was letting on. That would instill panic. Ignoring her comment, he looked toward the group again, hoping someone would stand up and be willing to leave the crash site.

A man in the back raised his hand - he was a little older than Jake, stocky, but looked able-bodied enough to make the trek with him. Jake smiled and approached him - he didn't know the man but now was a good time to learn all about the man who would be accompanying him through the wilderness.

"What's your name, sir?"

"Larry. Larry Bailey."

"You got any family here with you?" Jake didn't want to separate someone from their children.

"No, sir. I was flying alone. Headed up to Seattle for business."

"You sure you wanna do this? There's no pressure if you'd rather stay here."

"I'll go. You're right, Captain. We can't just sit around and wait."

Jake held his hand up and squinted. "No need to call me captain. Just call me Jake. We're all even here. No ranks, no titles, okay?"

"You got it, Jake."

"I'm gonna see if there's any food and water we can gather up. I plan to leave here in about thirty minutes. You ready to go?"

Larry nodded and gave him a thumbs up. "I'll be ready when you are."

Jake went toward the cargo door and pulled out more suitcases. He gathered articles of clothing that looked like they'd fit him and Larry. Having extra would be beneficial in case they had to spend another night out there - it was cold and wet, and they needed to stay as warm as possible. The daytime temperatures were recovering nicely at a comfortable level which would make traveling a little easier. The blanket of trees overhead would block the sun and help slow down dehydration.

Becky scooted a small carry-on suitcase toward him and lifted the lid. Several bags of snacks were inside - Oreo's, peanuts, cheese crackers and cans of sodas and water. Jake's stomach growled and he reached inside, pulling a few packages from it.

"I hit the jackpot last night. Found a bunch of the airline snacks scattered behind the plane. There's definitely more than that but I just gotta find it."

"Have the kids been fed?"

"Yeah. And hydrated. Take more than that for you and Larry. You'll need it."

He picked out bottles of water and a few snacks but left the rest for the group. Becky tried to hand him more but he declined.

"Take more, Jake! You're gonna be burning a lot of calories. You need it for energy."

"Nah, we're good. I hope we won't be gone that long to need it. I have a feeling there's a town pretty close. I just need to get to the police station so they can dispatch out emergency services. Once we do that, we won't even need these snacks."

Becky ducked her head and closed the suitcase. A tear fell down her cheek and she quickly wiped it away.

"No, don't do that," Jake said. "Don't you do that."

"Do what?" She smiled through the tears.

"You're acting like this is goodbye. I'll be back. I'm not just gonna leave you here…" He patted his chest and she interrupted before he could finish his sentence.

"Oh, hush, Jake. I know you're gonna come back. I just… I think it's all catching up to me. All of this. The crash. The lack of rescue effort to get us out of this mess. It's just suddenly hitting me."

Jake glanced over his shoulder to make sure they were out of earshot from everyone else. "Just between you and me, I think something bigger is going on. I can't really put my finger on it but something doesn't feel right."

"All the more reason for you to take more snacks and water."

"We're good. Y'all keep it. And good job with getting that fire going." Jake pulled her in for a hug and her body shivered against his arms. Becky was cool under pressure - being a flight attendant for so long made a person develop a fight response in times of drastic measure. Seeing her so worried made Jake's stomach clench.

"You better get going. Daylight is burning." Pushing away from him, she wheeled the suitcase back to the group and stoked the fire with a stick.

Meeting back up with Larry, Jake took a quick inventory of everything they were taking. A pocket knife, extra clothing, a blanket, along with the snacks and water that Becky had found. It was the best preparation they could do with what they had. If things went in their favor, they wouldn't have to dip into any of it.

Jake's instincts were telling him there was a town just on the other side of the wooded area. It'd be a good hour hike due to the type of terrain they were in but it was doable. If there really was a town that close, it still posed the question of why no one had come to get them. They would've had to see the crash. Jake was ready to get his questions answered. He was ready to get in touch with his family and let them know he was okay. His heart ached when he thought about the anguish Alice was going through, presuming her husband had perished in the disaster.

Waving toward Colin, Jake patted his travel buddy on the shoulder. "Alright, Larry. Let's do this."

***

The scenery hadn't changed much between the campus and their walk to the outskirts of Boston.

Sophie took a second to stop and catch her breath, leaning on the railings of a bridge that led them over the river on the south side of town. Under normal conditions, it lent an excellent view of the city skyline. It was a popular place to take pictures and jog but today, it looked like the cover of an end of the world thriller.

The hazy sky had an orange hue, skyscrapers were burning, the trail of smoke rising high in the air, aiding in the gloomy appearance of the world surrounding them. There were other people on the bridge with them, all going with the same idea they had come up with - flee Boston and get as far away from urban areas as possible. Only now, Sophie wondered if it didn't matter where they went. Nothing was changing - stores were being looted, cars were left stranded, and the once heavily populated area seemed scarce and deserted.

Danny put his arm around her shoulders and pulled her in close. Neither of them spoke as they looked toward the city, their situation transitioning from a nightmare to the reality they were facing. Boston was in ruins. How were other major cities faring through this?

"I'm scared, Danny." Sophie rested her face on his chest, unable to pull her eyes from the disastrous view. It was like looking down when someone told you not to or staring at a horrible wreck. Human nature made people do weird things sometimes.

"I am too, but at least we didn't get split up. We're in this together."

Sophie shuddered to think how it would be without Danny. She was scared now - being alone would completely frighten her. "Should we keep going south?"

Danny nodded and ran his hand over her long hair. His touch was soothing and she closed her eyes, imagining that they were back at the dorm, lying together, watching a movie and not on some bridge with their lives being threatened by something they didn't know anything about.

"Yeah. There's nothing left in Boston for us."

"What about Dallas? Do you think it's the same there?"

Danny took her hand and kissed the back of it. "I do, Sophie. I think this is happening everywhere."

A chill shot through her body and she shivered. They continued to walk, both deciding that staying on a bridge would make them vulnerable. She allowed his words to sink in. Danny was a smart guy - when it came to science, he was amazing. For him to think this was widespread made her lose hope that she'd ever see her family again.

"So, what do you think is happening?"

"Don't ask questions you don't want to know the answer to," Danny replied, smiling.

"Yeah, you're right, I probably won't like what I'm about to hear but I still wanna know. Is this the EMP thing you mentioned earlier?"

"I can't say for certain but it sure does feel that way."

"That means we'll never make it back to Dallas, will we? No cars, no means of transportation. That's almost two thousand miles. There's no way we can make that on foot." Her voice quivered and she stopped walking again, this time, allowing the tears to fall. "I'm never going to see my parents again, am I?"

Danny took her hand again and rested his forehead on hers. "Don't give up on me now, Sophie. We'll get it figured out."

"I hope you're right, Danny. Everything seems impossible right now."

CHAPTER FIFTEEN

It took everything Alice had to step out of the ER doors and out into the parking lot. She wasn't the only one making the decision to do it - doctors, fellow nurses, and support staff were following suit, all of them coming to the conclusion that it was time to get to their families and figure out what they would do next. Before leaving, she had grabbed all of here belongings out of her locker, filled up a cup with coffee, and rummaged through the refrigerator in the break room for any food she had left in there.

There was a sandwich and some bottles of water and she handed a couple to some kids she saw in the waiting area. It was her last effort to try and help them, the least she could do for not being able to come through when the victims needed them the most. The coffee was cold - the coffee maker must have crashed with everything else, which was comical. Alice smiled at the thought - even something as simple as Keurig was dead, which made the man's words hang true - this went farther than a city-wide power outage. They were about to face some tough times that didn't appear to be improving anytime soon.

At least the coffee had caffeine in it. Cold or not, it'd give her a boost of energy that she'd desperately need on her trek home. It was normally a thirty-minute drive in traffic. She estimated it'd take at least two hours on foot, depending on what she'd run into on the way. Since it all had started, she hadn't gone past the convenience store across the street, not really getting a good perspective of what was really happening.

The sun was beginning to come up in the east but it was still too dark to see well. With no power, there were no street lights. She had lost complete track of time and hadn't even realized she was coming up on twenty-four hours spent at the hospital. Twenty-four hours of what felt like pointless work of filling up the generator with gas, only to fall short of getting medical equipment to work properly.

She checked her cell phone again and it felt ridiculous. Electronic devices they constantly had their faces buried in were gone. What she once used for games, texting, and emails was non-existent and the one time she actually needed it to make a real call out, it wasn't possible. She approached the last row cars in the large parking lot of the hospital. The parking garage was across the street sitting dark with cars occupying it. Cars that were now rendered helpless along with their cell phones - two items they used constantly and took for granted. Now that they weren't available, it made Alice realize how much the monotony of an everyday life pushed them into auto-pilot, going through the same routine day in and day out. It was a shame it took something like this to make here open her eyes to how good things were just a day before.

She stopped on the edge of the parking lot, like a caged animal that was being set free into the wild.

The hospital was her safety net away from home, a refuge that kept her close to her co-workers and people she trusted. Looking out at the city in front of her, it terrified her to think of what was out there. Random fires burned - cars, buildings, and even trees. The number of vacant cars around was surreal - many had crashed, just like the victims in the emergency room had claimed.

What made her pulse raise the quickest was the lack of people around. Dallas was a huge city - the sheer number of cars around proved it, but where had everyone gone? There were hundreds of people at the hospital, so that accounted for some of them. Were people hiding in buildings that weren't compromised from all of the crashes? Was she the only idiot outside, standing there like a sitting duck? Staying in one place out in the open wasn't her smartest decision. Seeing the violent looters just hours before meant that they were still around and would do anything to survive and take what they could.

Clutching her bag, she took a sip of water, making sure not to drink too much. She tried to push her fear aside by thinking of her family. It pained her to think it, but Jake was probably a casualty to add to the growing list of those who didn't survive the initial outage, or whatever the hell this all was. EMP, terror attack, power outage - labeling it really didn't matter.

The thought of her husband dying made a lump form in her throat and she took another drink to calm her squeamish stomach. She didn't have time to cry for him, which hurt even more. It'd hit her hard, blindsiding her when she least expected it but she also had to hope that maybe he was okay and deep down, she knew it. It was her positive attitude - until she heard otherwise, Jake was fine. They would reunite and things wouldn't seem quite so bad.

Sophie being in Boston was another stitch in Alice's side. If this was nationwide, how in the hell were they going to get her home?

"One thing at a time, Alice. One thing at a time," she whispered to herself. Dylan was actually *in* Dallas. Getting to him was feasible and didn't completely overwhelm her when she thought about it. She could trek all the way home - she used to run marathons, so walking wouldn't be too difficult.

Stepping out onto the street, she looked up at the sky. A dusty haze gave the surroundings a sepia tone. The sun was coming up over the tree tops, aiding in visibility, calming her racing heart. At least she could see for a few blocks now. Her problem was her imagination - thinking someone would hop out behind a wall or bush to get her. And though it seemed a little far-fetched, Alice couldn't let her guard down. She had to treat this like she was in South Dallas where muggings happened all the time.

She could feel eyes on her and this time, it wasn't her mind playing tricks on her. A group of men near the gas station was watching her, probably just as suspicious of her as she was of them. Attempting to not make eye contact, she walked along the edge of the freeway toward the overpass she took every day to get to work. Cars were stalled at the top of it - how in the hell did the occupants keep them from rolling down? Alice was to the point where she didn't understand anything, nor did she even want to try.

Glancing over her shoulder, the men weren't following her, likely unwilling to leave their post at the store. If she had tried to go get some items, she assumed they probably would've given her trouble. They had claimed the place as their own, a smart move since it had plenty of food and gasoline, should the need to use it ever arise. It was a precious commodity when it came to keeping the generators at the hospital going but now it was all a moot point. What was the point of the generators if the equipment inside wouldn't even work?

Sighing, Alice started up the overpass. It would allow her to get over the freeway and on the other side where the residential areas began away from the medical park. Her legs burned from the steep incline of the roadway, immediately reminding her that she hadn't gotten any sleep. She was used to it after pulling multiple double shifts but at least in those times, she was able to eat to maintain her energy levels. Right now it was a double edged sword. No sleep and no food combined made her want to curl up in a ball and pass out.

After she got to the other side, she'd pull the sandwich out and eat it. She had to ensure that there was no one watching who'd easily fight her for two pieces of bread, a slice of cheese and a slice of ham. It wasn't worth risking her life over.

The downhill side of the overpass allowed her to catch here breath and the wind in her face cooled her down. She got a good view of the turmoil happening, lending her a different point of view being so high in the air. The Dallas skyline was burning and Love Field airport looked like a war zone. Planes were crashed up and down each runway, not even able to take off. Maybe Jake's flight had gotten delayed and he never had a chance to even attempt a flight out.

Smiling to herself, Alice shook her head. They didn't have that kind of luck. If it wasn't for bad luck, they'd have no luck at all.

***

Jake hoisted the bag on his shoulder and took a deep breath. The hardest step was the first one and he shouldn't have looked over his shoulder at the people he was leaving behind. Becky was leaning against a tree, waving at him. Colin lifted a hand in acknowledgment and the remaining survivors watched. Larry gave him a quick nudge and smirked, his subtle attempt at helping Jake not talk himself out of this.

Turning around, he headed down the incline, his stomach clenching when he took one more glance at the wreckage of their plane, the emblem of their company scratched up but still recognizable. It'd be the last flight he ever took as a pilot with them. The way he was feeling, it was likely his last flight ever. When he closed his eyes, he could feel the shimmy of the plane, the fast decent toward the ground, and the loud whines from the engines as they sputtered into failure. He couldn't think about that now. His mission was to get help. Ruminating on the past and what he could no longer control was only going to set him back and prolong the rescue of those who remained.

"For some reason, my instincts are telling me to go that way." Jake pointed down the hill but the thick forest didn't provide a good visual of what might be on the other side. "What do you say, Larry? I need your input too."

Larry wiped the back of his neck and ran his palm down the front of his shirt. It wasn't really hot but the humidity was heavy, making his clothes stick to his skin. "I think you're right. Let's try out that direction and see what happens."

Jake didn't have enough time to gamble on a wait and see attitude but if both men had a hunch about that direction, that's what they'd do. Jake couldn't tell what direction it was - too many trees and hills, killing his internal compass. With all of the issues they were having with gear, would a compass even work? They had the type that wasn't electronic that would probably still be able to help them navigate, but the chances of finding them were slim.

Jake's head pounded and he closed his eyes to try and get control of the vertigo. Walking on uneven ground wasn't helping. Grabbing a bottle of water, he took a sip and screwed the lid back on. The uncertainty of their future and how long their hike would take kept him from downing too much of it. They only packed enough to get them through a few days, his guilt hindering him from taking more from the group he left behind at the airplane. If any more people died on his watch, he wasn't sure if he could take it.

"So, Larry, you say you were headed up to Seattle on business?" Jake tried to make small talk. It would get his mind off of everything and hopefully pass the time on their walk.

"Yeah. I'm a broker. There's a training up there that my boss wanted me to go to."

"Broker, huh? Hopefully, you don't deal with stock in our airline." Jake laughed. Surely it wasn't too soon to crack a joke like that.

"We invest in just about everything," Larry replied. "Been doing this job for about seven years now."

"Do you like it?"

Larry nodded and arched his eyebrow, the corners of his mouth turning up in a smile. "Yeah. I never imagined working in a job like it. As a kid, I always said I wanted to be a cop or a firefighter. No eight-year-old says they wanna be a broker."

Jake laughed again. "I hear you. Pilot can be iffy but I never imagined I'd fly commercially."

"No? What made you do it?"

"Well, as a kid I always wanted to be a fighter pilot in the military. Straight out of high school I joined the Army. Didn't exactly become a fighter pilot but I eventually changed my military occupational specialty and learned to fly. Mainly transport planes and supply planes. And once I got out, this job popped up and I took it. It was stable, which was important since I was about to marry Alice. She was ready to settle down with a family. And the rest is history."

"Alice, huh? You still married to her?"

Jake smiled at the mention of her name. He couldn't wait to hug her and let her know he was okay. The thought of her worried made him sick. "Yep. Still married."

"Kids?"

"Two. My daughter is going to school up in Boston. She's a sophomore. My son is an eighth grader. How about you? You tied down?"

Larry's mouth set in a hard line and he clenched his jaw. The question must have hit a nerve, as it took him a few seconds to answer. "I was. Ended in a big, dramatic divorce. No kids, so that was the positive in such a shitty situation."

"Sorry to hear that," Jake said, watching the ground as he took steps down an incline.

Rather than make an awkward situation worse, he stayed quiet, taking note to some of the greenery around them. The forest was beautiful and looked like a place he would've loved to take his family camping. After their jaunt in the wilderness, camping might be the last thing he ever wanted to do again. Larry was a few yards away from him and Jake looked up just in time, stopping dead in his tracks.

"Larry, don't take another step!"

The other man responded, his left leg lifted as his eyes widened. "What is it?"

"I think that might be poison ivy. A large patch of it." Jake pointed at the vine spread out right in front of Larry. Poison ivy had been his concern since exiting the plane - dealing with a horrible rash would make a horrible situation that much more uncomfortable.

Larry took a few steps back. "Are you sure?"

"I'm sure. I learned about it back during our long hikes. Three leaves, perfect shape. That's poison ivy and the last thing you need to do is step in it."

"I didn't even know. I'm just a city kid. I've heard about it but, you know, didn't really think it was a real thing."

Jake checked around them, noting it near trees and growing up the sides of their trunks. There were no trails to avoid it, so they would have to be extra careful not to step in some further down the mountain. Another concern was poison oak, insects, and even bears. Larry had mentioned he was a city person, so Jake would have to be in charge of Mother Nature and what she might have in store for them on the way.

"Just watch where you step. Snakes, bugs, animals… we're in their territory now."

Jake wished they had a gun with them, and then it occurred to him that he could've gotten the one off the air marshal. Not every flight had one but there was a chance. He'd have to dig but having the weapon would be added security. People were also allowed to check weapons in their luggage. They couldn't have ammunition with them, so the gun wouldn't be helpful. It didn't matter now, anyway - they were too far from the plane and they couldn't waste more time on something that wasn't definite. If they kept moving and watched what they were doing, they'd likely stay out of harm's way.

Reaching the bottom of the mountain, Jake was thankful to see flat ground. There was a winding road with several signs, indicating hiking trails and a campground up the road, as well as a fishing lake. Campgrounds and lakes meant people - maybe they had cell phones that would work and they could call someone in.

Wouldn't the campers have heard or seen the plane crash, being this close to the crash site? They were probably a little over a mile away, so it was likely someone had at least heard something. It all felt off and when Jake rounded the curve of the road, he spotted a truck crashed into the guardrail, the front tires hanging over the wooden barrier, stopped just in time before careening down the drop on the other side of the barrier.

Running to it, Jake's head throbbed but he ignored the pain shooting through his body. Swinging the passenger door open, he looked in the cab, his heart sinking when he revealed an empty cab.

"Hello?" Walking to the guardrail, he looked over the edge, but the thick vegetation hindered seeing anything. "Anyone out there? Are you okay?"

Larry joined him, both men calling out, their voices echoing against the mountainous terrain surrounding them.

"Something is going on," Jake said between breaths. "Something isn't right."

CHAPTER SIXTEEN

Jake continued to yell out for any possible survivors but there was no one around. Larry was a quarter mile up the road and Jake went toward him - the idea of splitting up made the hair on the back of his neck raise. This was more than just a plane crash with no rescue effort headed their way. It was eerie and silent. Everything was deserted – the absence of people was a good indication that something big was happening.

"See anyone?" Jake asked, approaching Larry.

"Nothing. I can see a few campgrounds from here but there's no one around. Isn't this usually a busy time for campers around here?"

Jake shrugged and took a deep breath. "I don't know. I'd assume so with it being springtime." Glancing over his shoulder, he tried to come up with a plan. The best thing to do was continue to the nearest town. The chances of running into someone there would be better, though he feared that they might not like who they came across, especially if one of his theories came true.

"Do you wanna go back to the crash site?" Larry asked as he wiped his brow.

"No." Jake shook his head and looked over the edge of the cliff, down to where there were several picnic tables. A few tents were set up and there was a camper nearby. "I'd say let's go down there and see what we come across but I think it's best to get to town. Stick to the original plan. Maybe when we get there, we'll have a better idea of what's going on."

"I agree. We need to find the police department. If there's some mass murderer going around, this is the last place we need to be right now," Larry said, taking a step away from the ledge.

Jake didn't say anything, though his hiking buddy was right. The uncertainty tied his stomach up in knots. There were too many questions and not enough answers. And now that there were people missing, Jake wished he had better protection in case they were attacked. A gun, knife, anything that would give them a fighting chance against whoever… or whatever might be out there.

They reached a sign that indicated that Jones Creek was three miles away. Jake had flown this route many times but being on the ground was a whole new perspective. According to the abandoned truck they had run across, they were in Colorado… that was if they truck wasn't from out of state. He had never heard of Jones Creek before so he couldn't guess what state and with the landscape around them it could very well be Colorado or Utah. He considered how long they had been in the air, which wasn't long. The flight time from Dallas to Seattle was almost four hours on average. Colorado was probably a safe bet.

"Do you think this is terrorism?" Larry broke the silence, glancing at Jake and back to the ground. It caught Jake off guard but it was something that he had thought about from the moment the plane had gone down.

"I honestly can't say, Larry. It's the world we live in now. Something goes wrong, we all assume terrorism. This could be as simple as a mechanical malfunction in the plane. The campground being vacant could mean several things - it's morning. Maybe they're all out fishing or hiking."

"But why hasn't anyone come to rescue us? You know people heard the crash. And the truck… why was the door hanging wide open? I get excited to fish like the next guy but I'd remember to lock up my truck."

Jake smirked and kicked a rock down the center stripe of the highway. Not a single car had passed by since they had been walking, which was also odd. It was a remote area but he expected to see a few here and there.

"I guess I'm just trying to be positive. I hate to jump to the worst case scenario right off." Jake knew it went deeper than what he was speculating. He didn't want to admit it out loud.

"What happened when the plane crashed?" Larry asked, stopping in mid-step as he turned to face Jake, making direct eye contact with him.

Jake pursed his lips as he recalled the worst thirty seconds of his life. He'd never forget what happened, though he wished he could wipe it clean from his memory like a magnet erasing a cell phone.

"Everything just shut down." He spread his hands wide, his muscles clenching at the thought of what they had all gone through. "Computers failed, communication dropped with air traffic control. We couldn't control what the plane was doing. It was like we were flying with a ton of bricks on us."

"And you still managed to glide us down into the forest," Larry replied, patting Jake on the shoulder.

"I wouldn't say glide. We dropped like a bag of rocks. I wish I could've set her down gently but all of our systems were just gone."

"Your quick action is what saved us. What saved those back at the plane."

Jake looked down at the ground, unable to hold eye contact with Larry any longer. He still felt guilty about the whole thing. So many people had died. "I can't take credit for any of it. Colin helped. And I wish we could've saved everyone. So many families are gonna have to deal with the loss of their children, parents, aunts, and uncles. We failed them - as a captain, copilot, and flight crew, we failed all of them." Jake kept his voice low, almost inaudible against the wind blowing through the trees.

"You said so yourself - the plane just shut down. And from what we've witnessed in the past few days, I think this all goes beyond you not being efficient as a pilot. We're dealing with something bigger than either of us could even imagine."

Jake clenched his fists so tight that his palms ached. He feared that Larry was right. In a time of great technology and discovery, they would've been rescued by now. People wouldn't have randomly disappeared, leaving their truck on the side of the highway. It was a scary thing for all of humankind. He wondered how widespread this was - was it just the west? The USA? Or the world?

He needed to get home to Alice and the kids. He needed Sophie home from Boston, Dylan home from school, and all of them at the house, prepping for whatever else would transpire. He reminded himself to take it one step at a time. The current course of action was getting to Jones Creek and see if they could find another living human being who might have some answers.

Larry and Jake continued to walk - three miles wasn't too far and they should reach their destination within the next forty-five minutes. Jake had to believe that what they needed would be there. Little town or not, *someone* had to be there to help.

***

Alice made it across the overpass to the other side of the freeway. A part of her was hoping she'd wake up safely in her bed next to Jake, ready to fill him in on the crazy dream her tired brain had conjured up. Things were all too real to believe this was all a dream. Her feet ached from hours on them, her clothes were sweat soaked and filthy, and she felt like she could sleep for hours. Her pumping adrenaline allowed her to press forward - her need to find Dylan and make sure he was okay. Her need to attempt to make contact with Sophie and Jake and know that they were accounted for.

Sipping on her water again, she paused in front of another convenience store that appeared to be vacant. There were no suspicious people looking out at her, no looters running in and out, and it didn't giver her a vibe to not go toward it. There probably wasn't anything left to take but she was going to try. Her bottle of water wouldn't last much longer and she still had quite a hike to do before getting back to her house.

The front windows were cracked and broken and a thin layer of smoke hovered at eye level. Alice must have been getting used to the polluted air - her eyes still burned but the coughing had stopped. Reaching for the door handle, she swung it open. It was dark and she had a hard time seeing anything and suddenly, her intuition told her to turn around and get out of there. Taking a step back, she felt something metal and cold press into her neck.

"Stop right there."

Doing as she was told, she instinctively raised her hands up, dropping the water bottle to the floor. The water sloshed around and thankfully, the plastic didn't bust. Water was like precious gold and seeing it spill out and wasted would be a tragedy.

"What are you doing in here?" The voice was a man's, deep and raspy with a wave of stale breath hitting Alice like a wall. She held her breath so she wouldn't gag.

"I just... I wanted to see if there was any food." Maybe the sympathy card would work. Maybe it'd just piss the man off more.

"There's not."

She looked to the shelf near them. There were typical gas station snacks and items available. Trusting her instincts, she kept her mouth shut. One wrong thing spoken would mean she was a dead woman.

"This is all for me. Not you. You're not gonna come in here and take what I've claimed." The metal jabbed harder into her skin, making her already tired muscles ache even more.

"Okay. I won't take anything." Alice's voice shook, revealing the terror coursing through her.

"You're in scrubs. Are you a doctor?"

"Nurse. I'm a nurse."

The metal moved away from her neck and she took a deep breath, though she knew she wasn't out of danger. She could see the man in her peripheral vision, moving around like a meth addict who had just hit his high.

"Come to the back of the store with me."

He motioned the gun in the direction he wanted her to move. Hesitating at first, Alice eyed the exit. Should she try to run that way and get out? If she went to the back of the store, she may never get away. Was he going to kill her once she got back there? So many things flashed in her mind - her family needed her and now she was in trouble, all because she took a wrong turn and had bad judgment about the convenience store. How could she have been so stupid about it? She should've just kept walking. The water would have held her over. Food would have been good but she could have lived without it.

The man continued to hold the gun on her, his index finger resting on the trigger. He was already antsy and clumsy and Alice couldn't risk him getting any more agitated than he already was. Doing as she was told, she turned on her heel, heading to the back where several signs noted that they were now in an employee-only area of the store. None of that mattered anymore. It had been a day since everything had crashed and already, people were acting chaotic. How could things escalate so quickly?

There was a curtain that led them into a back office. A computer, calculator, and cash drawer were sitting on the desk. Alice's heart skipped a beat when she saw the young girl lying on the floor against the wall, blood soaked into her white shirt, the majority coming from her abdomen. She eyes were slightly open, squinting up like a bright sunbeam was getting into her eyes.

"What… what happened?" Alice asked, taking a step toward the girl.

"Stop right there." The man raised the gun again, pointing it right at Alice's face. "That's my daughter. We were driving down the road and bam!" He slammed the gun against the wall, causing a loud thud that made Alice jump. Her first assumption was he had pulled the trigger. "We hit a pole and the next thing I know, Crystal is hurt. I can't get the bleeding to stop. She's gonna die!" Tears poured from the man's face and he wiped them away.

"I'm so sorry," Alice said, looking from him to the girl, still nervous about the gun in his hand.

"You said you're a nurse, right?"

"I am." Alice nodded to confirm, wondering where he was going with this.

"Help her. Get the bleeding to stop!"

Alice didn't have any equipment or even a first aid kit. If she declined, she was a dead woman. She didn't want to decline. She wanted to help the girl. "I need to kneel down and take a look at her. Can I do that?" Alice waited until she had permission and when the man motioned the gun toward the child, Alice moved in, lifting her shirt. The wound was deep. Without supplies, her prognosis was likely fatal. Alice wouldn't let that be known. She needed to gain trust with the man holding her hostage.

"You say her name is Crystal?" Alice asked, hoping her training would kick in.

With a gun pointed at her, her mind was going blank. Working in the emergency room had trained her to act on instinct and to work fast but she never had a gun held on her and she always had the needed supplies to get treatment rolling. Now they were on a dirty office floor in a gas station with everyone's lives on the line.

"Yes. Do something, damn it!" The man yelled, what little patience he had fading fast.

"What's your name?"

"Ed."

"I'm Alice. I'm gonna help both of you but I need you to do something for me, okay?" Alice paused to see if he'd answer but he just stared at her, the barrel still trained right on her. "Go out into the store and see if you can find a first aid kit. Anything that can be useful to clean this wound. Peroxide, bandages, alcohol. Anything you can come across, okay?"

Ed's hand shook and he hesitated. Desperation was getting the best of him, clouding his judgment. Glancing from Crystal and back to Alice, he clenched his jaw as more tears flowed down his sweaty cheeks.

"You better not leave out the back. Don't leave my little girl here."

"I won't," Alice promised. "I'm not going to leave. You need to hurry, Ed. The longer we wait, the worse off Crystal gets."

Backing toward the curtain, Ed continued to point the gun at Alice. "I'm gonna find the stuff you need. You better pray it works, Alice. If Crystal dies, so do you."

Alice's heart skipped a beat when she saw the hatred in Ed's eyes. Crystal was almost dead. Her chances of making it were slim. Alice needed a miracle, and unfortunately, a simple first aid kit and bandages weren't going to save the poor little girl. She was going to try her hardest but she also had to come up with a plan to get away from Ed once the inevitable happened to Crystal.

CHAPTER SEVENTEEN

Due to the mountainous terrain, Jake couldn't see that far ahead of them. Being unfamiliar with the area wasn't helpful but at least the highway sign had confirmed that there was a town coming up. The question was how big the town was. It could be a wide spot in the road where technology wasn't a big thing to begin with. With a large camping area and lake nearby, he had to hold onto hope that while not a big place, it was still a decent enough size due to tourism.

"You ever hear of Jones Creek?" Jake asked, hoping he could get some insight. Larry shook his head, shattering any chance that they'd know what they were walking into. "Must not be very big if we have never heard of it. I don't even know what state we're in."

"I'd guess Colorado. But I'm not sure either. The truck's plates back there said Colorado."

Jake nodded. "I noticed that too. There is still snow on the mountains but that can happen in Utah, too."

The road took a sharp dip downward. Road signs warned of the steep incline and for semi-trucks to use low gear and to slow down. Jake walked slower, allowing his shoes to gain traction on the asphalt. He was still in his pilot uniform and the dress shoes he wore with it weren't the best to hike in. He wished he would've thought to grab a better pair of shoes from someone's luggage but he didn't anticipate any of this. Hindsight was twenty-twenty and they only had a few more miles to go.

The steep downhill walk revealed Jones Creek just down the road, the highway sign confirming that it was now a mile away. Without a watch, Jake couldn't tell how long it was taking them but usually, a three-mile walk by two able-bodied people in decent shape was forty-five minutes to an hour at most. He glanced up at the sky, noting where the sun was. If his estimation was right, it was a little after ten AM. The mountain climate was cool, though exposure to the sun was making him sweat.

The sight of the town in front of them made both men pick up their pace. As they got closer, they ran across several more abandoned cars. Jake stopped at a small sedan when he saw the blood splatter right outside the driver's side door. No one was inside but a large amount of blood meant that whoever was involved likely wasn't alive anymore.

A cell phone, charger, and radar detector were left behind and Jake went ahead and checked to see if the phone was working. As expected, it was dead like all of the others he had tried. Throwing back in the seat, he got out of the car and looked around. Larry was standing away from him, his gaze down in a canyon. Joining him, Jake followed where the other man was looking.

"Holy shit…" Trailing off, Jake swallowed the bile in the back of his throat. "What in the hell?"

Three bodies were dead next to a different car, appearing as if they had all been ejected when the car went over the side of the road. There was no way they were alive and even though signs of death were obvious, Jake felt guilty that they weren't trying to get down there to help. What if there was a kid still inside the car?

Sitting down, he scooted toward the edge where the guardrail had been damaged, Larry's hand gripping his shoulder, hindering him from going any farther.

"What are you doing, Jake?"

"We need to see if there are any survivors."

"No! You can't climb in there. It's too steep. You'll die too!"

Jake came to his senses when he saw a rock tumble down, hitting the top of the car. Scooting away from the edge, he couldn't take his eyes off of the dead bodies. It was the first people they came across since leaving the crash site and he had high hopes that someone was there they could get another point of view on.

"Let's get to town. It's right down the road. Maybe we can send some help if anyone survived that crash," Jake replied, pulling himself to a standing position, continuing to look down at the damage. It was literally a bad wreck he couldn't pull his eyes from.

They quickened their pace, reaching the outskirts of town in record time. Jake's body continued to warn him of his own injuries - his head pounded, he was dizzy, and all he wanted was a nice long nap and some food. Drinking a sip of water, his worry of the size of town came true - there was a small grocery store, a bait shop and camping shop, and a post office. There were even more vacant cars, some crashed, some parked and untouched.

Pulling the door to the store open, Jake's heart sank when he saw the shelves completely picked apart. The back coolers were open, the glass doors shattered, the beverages and food all wiped clean. The cash register was also busted open with no money left in the drawer. Larry lifted a box of batteries, the only item left within the building.

"Double A's. We could use them," Jake said, wiping his index finger through some dust on a shelf. "I can't believe it. There's nothing." Opening the ice machine, all of the bags had melted, leaving a large puddle inside. With no electricity, anything perishable that hadn't been looted was already starting to ruin.

Dipping his water bottle inside, he hesitated before refilling it. What if it had been contaminated? The place wasn't clean and there was no telling who all had their hands inside. Until he knew exactly what was going on, he'd be careful about what he ate and drank. His water was still okay but he was rationing it carefully. With no signs of any other human life, he'd have to go back to the airplane and report the bad news to those who waited on their return.

After searching with no luck, Larry and Jake went back outside. Crossing the street, they checked the bait and camping shop. It was the same story - someone had already come through and taken anything of value. Jake slammed his fist against a nearby wall and closed his eyes. What was going on? Had this town been abandoned long before now? Nothing looked run down enough for it to be a ghost town.

"I think we're dealing with something bigger than a plane crash," Larry whispered, his eyes wide as he walked toward the exit.

"I think you're right. I don't guess they even have a police station here."

"What do we do now? This explains why no help has come. Where is everyone?"

Jake checked the cabinets to make sure nothing had been left behind. A camp store would have been perfect to pick through if they were going to have to continue to hike through the wilderness. Nothing had been left behind. Not even a damn fishing pole or can of earthworms for bait.

"I guess we go back to the crash site. We gather up everything we can use from the luggage and victims. And then we all go together and find a bigger city where we can get some answers. There's nothing left here for us. Besides, something doesn't feel right. I feel like we're being watched."

Larry smiled, though he wasn't amused. He was nervous, and Jake understood why. The man had admitted that he was a city guy. This probably felt like a foreign land to him.

"At least we're not leaving empty handed. We have a package of batteries." Jake forced a laugh but it fell flat. "On the way back we'll take a different route down by the lake. We can get a better look at the campsites. Maybe there are survivors down there. Until we talk to anyone else, the only point of view we have is that we were in a plane crash and we came across a ghost town. It'd be nice to hear from someone else. Maybe it'll help us piece things together."

"Or we'll come across people who will want to kill us. What if there's some murderer going around killing everyone?" Larry's voice shook, which was odd to see and hear. On the outside, he was a large man that Jake wouldn't want to take on in a bar fight. He couldn't fault him for being scared. Jake was terrified but he wouldn't allow it to cripple him. Freaking out would only hinder progress.

"You've seen too many movies, Larry. Looks like Jones Creek was pretty secluded even before this. People probably high-tailed it out of here once whatever the hell all of this is had happened. Not many resources left."

The lake was an excellent resource - fish, wildlife, and most importantly, they had a nice supply of water. Fear of contamination was the biggest hesitation Jake had about refilling their bottles. It was crucial that they talk to someone. They likely wouldn't know much more than the survivors of the plane crash, but actually coming across someone alive might settle everyone's nerves. Until then, Jake had to turn his imagination off. Zombie apocalypses, werewolves, and biological warfare all crossed his mind. Just as he told Larry, he had seen way too many movies.

Nothing like that would really happen, would it? This all had to be a coincidence. If they all stuck together and made it to a bigger city, things would start making sense along the way.

***

Alice's hands shook as she applied pressure to the child's wound. Ed still hadn't come back with a first aid kit but she could hear him in the front store area, throwing things around and yelling. His anger was enough to make him capable of killing her if she wasn't able to help Crystal and unfortunately, it wasn't looking like Alice would be able to pull off any kind of medical miracle with the situation they were in.

She needed a cloth or something absorbent to help soak up the blood. Crystal only had on one shirt and she needed to keep that on - she was in shock and shivering from the trauma on her body. Alice didn't have any clothing to spare either - just her scrubs and they weren't thick enough to do much.

Glancing around the room, she tried to find anything that would aid in putting pressure on the injury. Standing, she dug through the desk. There was a box of Kleenex, which she kept hold of. Pulling each drawer of the desk open, sorted through all of the paperwork, noting a roll of paper towels at the back. Bingo! Not the best thing to use but paper towels were absorbent and these felt like a decent brand. It wouldn't be the most sanitary but if Ed could get his hands on some peroxide or alcohol, Alice would be able to do some thorough cleaning and get a better vantage point on how deep and bad the wound actually was.

"What are you doing? Why aren't you helping Crystal?"

Alice turned on her heel, reminding herself to not make any sudden movements. Ed continued to train the handgun on her, his hand shaking, his knuckles white from gripping the weapon so tightly. Holding the paper towels up, she inched toward Crystal.

"I was looking for something to put pressure on Crystal's wound. Were you able to find anything?"

He tossed a red plastic box down near Alice. It was a cheap first aid kit, just like she imagined this type of store would carry. There were gauze pads, cotton balls, and cotton swabs inside. There were also antibacterial ointment, tweezers, band-aids, and small alcohol pads. It wasn't much but it was better than nothing.

Looking up at Ed, Alice tried to ignore the gun. "Did you find any peroxide?"

Ed slipped two bottles out of his pants pocket and rolled them toward Alice. "You better pray she lives, nurse."

"I'm doing the best I can, Ed."

"Your best better be saving my daughter or you're dead too."

Alice's hands shook and she tried to control the nervousness. Trying to convince herself that this was no different than a busy afternoon in the ER was a challenge. While people were unruly and demanding, having a gun held on her wasn't common practice. Soaking a gauze pad with alcohol, Alice applied it to the girl and the lack of response was disheartening. Usually, a person would wince or open their eyes but Crystal made no indication that she could even feel it.

Getting the blood cleared off gave Alice a good view of what she was dealing with. The wound was deep enough to see tissue and the bleeding continued. Putting pressure on it, she dug through the first aid kit with her free hand, glaring at Ed who paced above her. She'd ask for his help but he was already on edge.

"What are you looking for?" Ed asked, stopping in mid-step.

"Thread and a needle." Of course, the kit he brought her wouldn't have anything like that. It was the basics. Glancing over her shoulder, Alice wiped the sweat from her brow. "You think you might be able to check the store and see if there is a cheap sewing kit? You know, the kind they sell for repairing buttons and things?"

"Why the hell do you need that? How is that gonna help Crystal? You're just making excuses to get me out of here so you can escape."

"The bleeding isn't going to stop unless I can stitch her wound. Unless you have a better idea of how to do stitches, I really need you to go find a sewing kit." Alice's tone was sharp but she was over trying not to offend him. He was desperate to help Crystal and until she was deceased, he wouldn't pull the trigger.

Backing away, Ed's eyes widened and he adjusted his hand on the gun handle. "Don't you fucking leave!"

"I'm not. I'm not leaving Crystal here like this."

Turning back to the girl, Alice removed the soiled paper towels and applied a fresh package of gauze. Nothing was working and everything she used got saturated with blood almost immediately. Stitching her up with thread would give her a fighting chance but it wouldn't prevent infection and whatever internal injuries that Crystal might have sustained in the wreck.

It was hard to tell how Crystal got hurt. Did something puncture her? Anything could happen in a car crash and with all of the turmoil happening, the possibilities were endless. Not to mention the lack of first responder care - Ed probably moved her before he should have, which wasn't his fault. No help came and Alice couldn't fault him for attempting to get her out of harm's way quickly. She could fault him for panicking and threatening her life.

Maybe he'd come to his senses and drop the gun. Ed calming down was the only way Alice would get out of this alive.

"Come on, Crystal. I'm doing what I can for you," Alice whispered, waiting patiently for Ed to bring back what she had requested. If the store didn't have a kit, Alice would need to start thinking up a way to escape. Allowing Ed to swoop in and keep her from her family wasn't an option. Allowing Crystal to die hopefully wasn't an option either.

CHAPTER EIGHTEEN

Sophie felt more tense the farther they walked from Boston. The outskirts of the city was a heavily concentrated area with buildings, houses, and places of business. What lent to the eerie feel was the lack of people. There were a few other sparse groups, walking in the same direction they were down the sidewalks, but they were in a heavily populated area. Where was everyone? Held up inside their houses, afraid to come out? She could feel the eyes on her, watching her every move from atop the high lofts in the apartment buildings close by.

Clutching her bag on her shoulder, she glanced at Danny, neither of them saying much for the past half hour. Danny had always been a conspiracy theorist and she always took it with a grain of salt but as the disaster played out in front of them, Sophie felt it was important to listen to him. Electromagnetic pulse - just the mention of an EMP strike made the hair on the back of her neck raise. How in the hell was she going to get home to her family?

"We'll get back to Texas, Sophie."

"How in the hell did you know what I was thinking about?"

"I can tell. You've made it clear you want to make it back to your family. You haven't said much and you're usually a talker."

Glancing at a family across the street, her heart ached at the sight of the two young children following their parents, their clothing tattered, their faces soiled with dirt. It was like they were looking at photographs out of a National Geographic of chaos overseas. If Sophie didn't know any better, it looked like the scenes from Syria. Here on American soil. Was this war? Or was this just some breakdown in technology that no one saw coming?

"How do you think we're gonna make it back to Texas? Cars aren't working. Nothing is." Sophie spread her hands, motioning toward all of the abandoned vehicles. "How long will it take us to walk almost two thousand miles?"

"Believe me, I've thought about it. That'd be like six hundred hours, which would mean it'd take about twenty-five days if we walked continuously with no breaks." Danny flashed a smile and Sophie slugged him in the arm. "What? I'm just saying… it's doable. Not in twenty-five days but we will make it back there. Maybe we'll run across some horses or something. That'd cut it down to half the travel time."

Shrugging, Sophie sipped on her water. "No telling what we'll come across on the way. We already had to fight once. I don't trust anyone."

"And we shouldn't trust anyone."

"Do you really think this is an EMP?" Sophie stopped walking for a second. Her feet ached and her legs were sore. She had always been in decent shape but walking this much would take its toll even on the most seasoned marathon runners.

"I do."

Biting her bottom lip, she looked down at the ground. "Do you think our families are alive?"

"I wish I knew, Sophie. At least we're both needing to go in the same direction. I'll just have to walk a little farther to Abilene."

"It's just…" Reaching out, she grabbed Danny's hand and continued walking. "Airplanes crashed out of the sky. It'll be nothing short of a miracle if my dad is okay."

"Maybe he wasn't on a plane at the time."

"Maybe."

Danny pulled his cell phone from his pocket and grimaced. "It's just funny how we're so used to pulling out our phones and having instant contact with people. Now it's like we're back in pioneer times when people traveled by foot, horse, and wagon. They never knew how their families were doing unless they got a letter that took forever to get to them. I'm trying to view this as an adventure. It really helps with the doom and gloom of the situation."

"I should try to be more like you but it's hard to believe this happened. We almost got beat up back there at that store for simple items. We can't let our guard down."

"And we won't. We're good for now. We'll walk until we get tired and find a place to rest. The farther we get, the sooner we will find out about our loved ones. At least we're not going at this alone."

"I probably would've already panicked to death." Sophie finally cracked a smile and nudged Danny.

He was right - at least they were in this together, especially since it felt like the rest of the world was disappearing around them.

***

Jake walked slowly down the steep incline. The lake was below the road by several hundred feet and the campground was on the other side of the water. If they did run across anyone, it'd be people who would know what to do in this situation. They were campers. They knew how to survive without electricity and the comforts of their homes back in the city. That might not have been completely true but he had to convince himself of it to not freak himself out. Larry wasn't ashamed to admit he was a city person. Jake had grown up in the country but never without the daily items they took for granted now that they weren't available.

Larry wasn't able to keep up the pace with Jake so he slowed down to make sure they wouldn't get separated. Larry was a bigger man than Jake, outweighing him by at least fifty pounds and unfortunately, it wasn't muscle. His breathing was labored and he stopped, leaning on the side of the cliff to try and catch his breath.

"You okay?" Jake asked, feeling the sweat sting his eyes. It wasn't really hot but the humidity was a factor.

"I'm good. The last time I ever walked this far I was about twenty years younger. You never realize how out of shape you get sitting behind a desk all day."

Jake offered him the bottle of water. It was almost empty but he had a few more in his bag. "Drink the rest of that."

"No. We need it."

"Exactly. You need it right now. The last thing I need is you passing out on me, Larry." It was cut and dry but it was honest and Jake didn't have time to sugarcoat anything. They were in a mess. They had to move fast in case anything else happened. "There are some motor homes and campers just down that way. And it looks like the tent camping is on the other side of the lake."

"And why are we doing this again? Why not just go back to the plane?"

Suddenly the once quiet, reserved hiking buddy was now becoming whiny. Jake had to consider their situation - it was bad enough to make anyone cranky and wishing they were somewhere else.

"I want to see if we can find anyone who might know what happened. And we might find some things we can use. Camp stoves, lanterns, those kinds of things."

"You want to steal?"

Jake glared at Larry as they continued to walk, finally reaching a point in the trail that was a bit more level, allowing their pace to quicken until they reached the ground below. "You see anyone around here who might be wanting this stuff?" Jake spread his hands, motioning toward the abandoned campers.

"I don't think we're in a position to really have a moral debate. Do you understand the seriousness of what's going on?"

"I really don't. What do you think happened?"

Jake hesitated before reaching for the door of a camper. A pickup truck was still there, parked by a fire pit that looked like it had been recently used. The charred wood in the hole looked like it still had some use and he'd love to be able to take some back to the plane to keep them warm overnight. If they needed to, he'd go back to the crash site and bring a few more people back to help gather things. But his overall plan was to get the hell away from the area and somehow find a way back to Dallas. If things went his way, he'd only spend a few more nights there and be gone.

"First thing my mind went to was terrorism. The plane was in fine shape. I assumed someone tampered with something. Someone who knew exactly what they were doing." He opened the door to the camper, being cautious to the possibility that someone could be on the other side, waiting with a shotgun. Just like everything else they had run across, it was vacant. Taking the steps inside, Larry followed.

"But now what do you think?" Larry asked, staying close to the door as Jake walked through, opening up the cabinets as he passed by.

Jake clicked his tongue between his teeth, pulling out food from the pantry. Cookies, beef jerky, a few bottles of water, and a bottle of scotch. Jake wasn't sure if he'd admit it out loud, but seeing the bottle of booze excited him more than the water. He needed an escape or something to at least take the edge of the reality they were facing.

"I don't know. I don't even know where to begin, which is why I wanna find someone to talk to. Getting another perspective of someone on the ground might give us a better idea." Jake put the waters, scotch, and cookies in his bag. It wouldn't be able to hold much more but at least they knew where to find more items if they wanted to come back later. It wasn't too far of a hike if they got desperate for something.

The very back of the camper exposed a bed and chemical toilet. Lifting the pillows, he felt something metal and cold under his fingertips. Clamping down on the item, he yelled out in joy when he realized it was a handgun - a nine millimeter just begging to be plucked. Stealing a gun was a felony but things had changed - this was for protection and survival, and Jake felt he could walk with more confidence knowing he had that with him.

Sliding the magazine out, the gun was loaded with fifteen bullets. It wasn't much but hopefully, he wouldn't come across a situation where he'd need to use any of the ammunition, much less all fifteen of them. He slid the gun in his waistband, the weight of it reminding him that he had just stolen a major item from someone - it wasn't just food. Taking the gun catapulted Jake into the complete reality they were now living - normal, everyday laws didn't apply anymore. The world had changed in a matter of seconds and it was becoming every man for himself.

It took Jake a second to relax. Hoping he was hiding his anxiety from Larry, he forced a smile and waited to see what Larry's opinion was on the theft of the handgun. The man didn't say a word, which was good and bad. Jake tried to ignore the worry. They were now protected, whether it was from some other person or even wildlife - they were deep in the woods and could easily run across an animal that would take their lives.

Exiting the camper, they moved onto the next, finding the same story with each one. Jake was beginning to feel discouraged when he saw something sprint into the trees about two hundred yards away from them. It was quick and a streak in the corner of his eye and he wondered if it was just a wild animal attempting to get away from them.

"Did you see that?" he asked Larry, patting the other man on the chest.

"What?"

"I think I saw someone go into those trees."

"They obviously don't wanna talk to us if they ran."

Jake ignored Larry and walked toward the thick grove, holding his hand against the butt of the handgun in case he needed to draw it quickly. Leaves rustled from footsteps and he blinked back the sweat, swiping his cheek with his shoulder.

"Hello?" Jake stood still, attempting to listen if whoever it was would respond.

The crackling of the leaves stopped and he peered through the thick vegetation. The body shape looked like a man and he held his hands up at shoulder level, his back turned toward Jake and Larry.

"We're not here to hurt you," Jake yelled. "We just wanna talk!"

The man turned around, his face shielded by the brim of a baseball cap. He kept his hands up but didn't move an inch. Jake got closer, moving slowly so he wouldn't spook the person even worse.

"Please don't shoot me!" The man finally spoke up but kept his face low. "Please…"

"I'm not gonna shoot you." Jake was finally close enough to get a good look at him. He was younger – Jake would estimate him to be in his early twenties. His clothes were tattered and his face was bruised and bloody.

"Please…" the man pleaded, his voice low, his body shaking.

"I'm not gonna hurt you. I just wanna talk. Do you know what's happened?"

The stranger shook his head and looked up completely. Tears streamed down his soiled face, he grit his teeth, and anger replaced the sorrow and pain he had revealed to Jake.

"They killed them. My family…"

"Who did?"

"Do you have a family, Mister?"

Jake nodded his head but was hesitant to reveal much more information. For all he knew, this kid was playing him. No one could be trusted. "I do."

"Are they still alive?"

"… I think so. Why?"

"You're lucky if they are. You should probably get home to them. They won't be alive long."

"What do you mean by that?" Jake asked, glancing over his shoulder at Larry, who had stayed back. Figures. Jake knew he didn't have backup with him.

"Nothing. Never mind." The boy wiped his face with his sleeve and took a few steps back. "They're gonna get us all. We're all dead." He turned around and ran, sprinting through the trees until Jake couldn't see him anymore.

"Come back! I'm here to help!" Jake's voice echoed but got no response from the mysterious person. "What in the hell was that about?"

It gave him the chills as he heard the warnings replay in his mind. Was the kid another doomsday conspiracy theorist? Probably. But it still didn't answer all of the lingering questions Jake had on his mind. If anything, it made his curiosity worse and his panic to get back to his family heighten.

"Let's get the hell out of here, Larry. We need to keep moving."

CHAPTER NINETEEN

Alice looked around the small office for anything that might help her with the child. It was taking Ed a while to get back but she could hear him looking around. Would a gas station have a needle and thread? They had lots of odds and ends and maybe they'd have a small repair kit. People who traveled lost buttons, didn't they? She dug through a desk drawer, searching for anything that might help her sew up the wound but was coming up short.

There was a pair of scissors in a pen holder and she grabbed those. But nothing for thread. Kneeling next to Crystal, Alice sterilized the scissors with some of the peroxide, making sure not to use too much. It would come in handy later on if she found a way out of the mess she was in.

Ed came back through and tossed a plastic package at Alice. It fell beside her and she grabbed it, shocked that he actually found what she had requested. What were the chances that the gas station would have something like that? She wasn't going to ponder her good luck and convenience of the situation because Crystal's injury was anything but convenient. Ed pacing around her with a loaded gun made this far from easy.

She sterilized the needle with more peroxide, trying her hardest not to infect Crystal even more. Threading it was tough and she tied a knot, securing the thread. Wiping the blood clean once again, Alice tried to ignore the fact that Crystal likely had lost so much blood that getting the injury stitched up was a moot point. Maybe she hadn't lost as much as Alice was predicting and this would help. Maybe she had lost so much that it was already too late.

Checking Crystal's pulse, Alice glanced up at Ed who wasn't looking her way. He paced back and forth, grumbling something she couldn't understand, mimicking the actions of a drug addict at the peak of his high. Leaning forward, she pushed the injured skin together, attempting to match the sides up like a puzzle piece. Forcing the needle through the skin, she punctured one side, expecting Crystal to yell out in pain but she didn't respond. That was good and bad. Good that she didn't have to handle a wailing child, bad that the kid wasn't feeling anything. Being in shock was the best case scenario. Being on death's doorstep was likely.

Weaving the thread down the wound, Alice formed a braid and pulled it tight, joining the skin together. More blood oozed out and she moved fast. Every second was crucial to Crystal's survival - and not to sound stupid, it was crucial to hers as well. She continued to keep Ed in her peripheral vision, making sure he didn't get trigger happy and shoot her.

Tying a not, she cut the thread loose and put it in the first aid kit. If she could get away, it would be a good item to carry with her. Though she lived somewhat close, there was no telling what else she might run across between here and there. It was a big if on whether or not she'd get away from Ed. Either the wreck they were involved in had hit him in the head and made him crazy, or he was fitting the mold of a drug addict. There was possibly more to the story than he was volunteering to her.

"I have it stitched up," Alice said, scared to even speak.

"Good. Is she gonna make it?" The gun shook in his hand and his shirt was covered in sweat.

"I don't know, Ed. It's hard to say."

"Fix her, nurse. Damn it!"

Alice checked Crystal's pulse - it was so weak she struggled to find it. Her breathing was slow but at least she was still alive. "I've done everything I can, Ed. This will help stop the bleeding. There are gauze pads to make sure the wound stays clean. Sleeping is good for her. It's allowing her body to heal." She would omit the details about Crystal possibly having internal injuries that Alice had no way of fixing.

"You're talking like you're leaving." Ed lifted the gun at her, his knuckles white from gripping the handle so tight.

"No. I just want you to know that I've done everything I can with the supplies we have."

"You're a nurse. Do you just give up on every patient that you see?"

"Of course not, Ed. I work in a hospital where we have equipment that helps us do our jobs. I have doctors that give me advice. I don't usually work on people in the middle of gas stations."

Ed cocked his head to the side and waved the gun around. His hair was plastered to his forehead from his sweat and he was unable to keep eye contact with her. "You don't have to be so damn rude, nurse. I told you I'd kill you if Crystal doesn't make it."

"I wasn't meaning to be rude." Alice lifted her arms, holding her hands at shoulder level. Keeping him calm was key but no matter what she said, he found a way to twist her words around, making the circumstances even more dangerous. "Crystal is still alive. She's breathing and I did feel a pulse."

"But you're acting like she's gonna die."

"She might." Alice cringed, certain a gunshot would ring out but Ed didn't pull the trigger. Instead, his eyes widened and he lowered his arm.

"I'm a man of my word. If she dies, I have to kill you too."

"Why? What good would that do?" Alice asked, hoping if she continued to talk through it, he'd eventually drop the gun completely.

"I just can't deal with this shit. I just can't do it." Ed began to cry, covering his eyes with his free hand. The gun was still in his possession and Alice couldn't take her eyes off of it.

"There's more to this, isn't there, Ed? What really happened with you and Crystal?"

"That's none of your business, bitch!" He lifted the gun again, the look on his face pure evil.

It was enough warning for Alice to dive toward the corner, shielding herself from a bookshelf. Gunshots rang out, echoing in the small office. They were flying close enough to her that she could feel the heat off of each one. Ducking on the floor, she crawled and kept the desk between her and Ed. She lost count of how many shots Ed had fired and wasn't even sure how many the gun could hold.

The shots subsided and her ears rang from being in close proximity of the gun. Hunkering in a fetal position, she listened to his footsteps, moving throughout the room, kicking items aside, paper sliding on the floor. Had Crystal been hit in the crossfire? It might've been a favor for the child - it would put her out of the misery and spare her a continuous, painful death.

"Oh, nurse? I know you're in here. I'm standing between you and the exit!"

Alice didn't say anything. She tried to hold her breath, fearing that it would give her position away. A dusty haze was at eye level, confirming that most of his shots hit the wall above her, spreading out the drywall underneath the horrible paint job.

"This gun is all out of ammo but who's to say I don't have more?" His tone was condescending, taunting her to try and evoke even more fear. It was working. Her heart raced so hard she could see it against her scrub top. "Guess I'll need to reload."

She heard the click of the magazine. She had about thirty seconds to make a move before he got reloaded. Standing, she ran toward him. The door was right there and if she could fight her way past him, she could make a run for it. He didn't notice her coming at him for about three steps and when he looked up, she lunged at him, swinging and grabbing for anything that would hurt him.

Her nails dug into his arm and she had underestimated his strength. Flinging her to the side, Alice hit the wall and the edges of her vision went black. Ed didn't try and reload. Instead, he pocketed the gun and swung at her but she ducked, anticipating his first moves toward her. Scooting on her knees, she dodged a kick, the distance between her and the exit just a few feet away.

Ed's arms wrapped around her midsection, lifting her off of the floor. He outweighed her by a good seventy-five pounds and held her up with almost no effort.

"I got you now, nurse. I should take advantage of you before I kill you."

Laying her across the desk, he reached for the elastic on her scrub pants, pulling at them. He got them as far down as her hips before she kneed him in the groin, sending him to the floor, doubling over in pain.

"You bitch!"

Sliding off the table, Alice grabbed the scissors from the first aid kit and jabbed them in his back, as close to the spine as she could get. Blood squirted out and he cried out in more pain, closing his eyes as he squirmed to try and get away from her. The scissors were still stuck in his back, covered in red.

She didn't have much time to get away. His anger would overcome the pain and he'd be even more pissed. Unwilling to chance her luck further, Alice grabbed the first aid kit and checked on Crystal for safe measure. She couldn't find a pulse and the child had stopped breathing. She immediately felt guilty for being relieved - no health care professional in their right mind would ever wish death on such an innocent person - but she couldn't leave the girl with Ed. Her passing away was probably for the best. There was no way Alice could take her with her and leaving her behind didn't sit well. She didn't know their story or if Ed really was her father. His behavior said otherwise - possibly a kidnapper, child molester, or even both. It was all assumption but Alice had been in nursing enough to be able to tell when something wasn't right. It didn't matter now - Crystal was gone and away from whatever Ed was doing to her.

Walking back to Ed, Alice looked him straight in the eye. He cringed and gritted his teeth, still rolling around from the scissors jabbed in his back.

"Rot in hell you bastard."

"You better hope I don't find you. I will rape you and make sure you die slow, you whore!" Ed pursed his lips and spit at her. A wad of blood fell on his lips.

"Judging by the way you look, you're not making it out of this gas station. I know you hurt Crystal. Car wreck my ass, you pervert!" Making sure to stay out of arm's reach from Ed, Alice circled behind him and jabbed the scissors even deeper, feeling the crunch of bone against the blade. Ed's body flailed from the trauma and he screamed.

It took almost a city block for Alice not to be able to hear his yells of agony.

***

Jake wanted to take his time going through the campsites but running across the suspicious person in the woods made his need to hurry that much more important. There were key items they could use and even some that were more novelty than necessity. The scotch sloshing around in his bag was a reminder that they had something they might possibly enjoy when they made it back to the crash site.

"What do you think that guy meant? Saying they're gonna come for us? Who is gonna come for us?" Larry asked as he lifted a sleeping bag up. Jake expected there might be a dead body or something each time they did that but so far they had come up short on finding anyone except the creeper.

"I wish I knew," Jake replied.

"So what do you think about all of this? It's like the end of the world or something."

"And we're the chosen ones?" Jake arched his eyebrow and shook his head, looking off toward the lake. "You must've read Revelations in the Bible at some point in your life."

"Yeah. You don't think that's what's happening?"

Jake kicked a dirt clod and it rolled to the edge of the water. So many things had crossed his mind about possibilities and reasons why the plane had fallen out of the air. He also pondered why cell phones and electronics had crashed. Electronic warfare was something he read about. Not once did he ever think it'd actually happen.

"I gotta be honest, Larry. I really don't know. My focus now is getting home to my family. At first, I figured we needed to find someone and get another viewpoint but just the little we've come across has told me enough. I want my family. If this does happen to be the end of the world, I wanna spend it with the ones I love."

"How do you plan on getting back to Dallas?"

"Any way possible," Jake said. "Let's get back to the crash site. We know this is here if we need any supplies but we need to check on everyone. They're probably wondering about us too."

Both men walked in silence on the way back. It was uphill and harder on the body, and Jake was trying to preserve oxygen. Being so high in the mountains made the air thin and he wasn't used to the altitude. When he was high in the sky, the cabin was pressurized to help with those issues. He meant what he said about getting home. He feared his family was dead but instead of speculating about their well-being, at least he could get there and know for sure. Alice was a fighter - he'd put money on her still being alive through this.

The air was cool but the humidity made Jake sweat. Wiping his brow, he took a swig of water, noting it was almost empty. The lake was nearby but contamination was possibly an issue. Maybe Becky was able to comb through more of the items from on board - the plane was fully stocked with snacks and drinks and as long as they hadn't been damaged, their food supply should have been in good shape.

"It feels like the walk back is longer." Larry struggled to talk, panting between each word.

"Uphill climb. We're almost there." Jake had noticed a grove in the forest near where they plane was located. He could see it a quarter mile down the road, indicating that was where they had to go off road and climb up the trail. "You okay to go farther or do we need to take a break?" Jake hoped he would agree to rest for a few minutes. Larry was a bigger man, slightly overweight, and Jake wanted to make sure he wouldn't fall out and need some kind of medical treatment. With Colin's leg, they were already in for a treacherous trip when they decided to head back toward Texas.

"Yeah, I could use a break," Larry confirmed as he leaned against a boulder on the edge of the road.

Jake handed him a handkerchief and he saturated it with sweat. "Drink the rest of this bottle." Tossing Larry the water, he pulled another from his bag and sipped on it. "This is my last one but I think we'll make it back before I run out."

Larry took a second to catch is breath and Jake took the time to catch his as well. His legs burned and his lungs were tight. He was also worried about the injured left behind. How would they get Colin to travel? Leaving him behind definitely wasn't an option but there was no way he could walk on the broken leg, especially with the distance they'd have to put in on foot. They could build a travois but that would mean taking turns pulling it. If they could run across a farm with horses on it, it'd be like winning the lottery.

Jake glanced up at the sky, attempting to get some idea of what time of day it was. The trees hindered seeing it but he guessed it was getting to be late afternoon.

"I guess we better start moving again. We need to get back to camp before it gets dark. I really don't feel like running across any wild animals out here." Having the gun he found at the camper helped but he wanted to preserve the ammunition for all of the possibilities they may run across when they finally began to travel.

"Let's do this," Larry said, though his body language spoke something different. The man was exhausted. His shoulders slumped and his clothes were soaked, appearing like he had just jumped in a pool of water.

"Once we get back, we can take a load off. I figure we can spend one more night at the crash site, gather up everything we can, and tomorrow morning we'll move on."

Getting the others in the group to agree might not be so simple but Jake's mind was on his family and survival. Staying there was no longer the best option. They had to go against everything they were taught.

Staying close to where they went off the radar wasn't feasible. A rescue team wasn't coming.

CHAPTER TWENTY

"You wanna move away from the crash site?" Becky placed her hands on her hips, her eyes wide as if Jake had just suggested something horrible. He couldn't blame her - it went against every bit of training that had been drilled in their heads. Always stay close to where you went off the radar. That's where the search team would look. This was a totally different circumstance.

"Yeah. Hear me out before you look at me like I ran over your dog." Jake glanced down at Colin. He was pale and though his leg wound looked okay, he was probably in a lot of pain. He needed to call Alice. She'd know what to do. Not having easy access to cell phones was proving to be a bigger challenge than he could ever imagine.

"I found a lot of stuff we could use. It'll hold over until someone comes." Becky motioned toward the pile of snacks and items dug out from suitcases and the galley of the plane.

"That's just it, Becky. No one is coming." Jake kept his voice low. Larry was chatting with a couple of other survivors, hopefully telling them their plans. Maybe they'd agree to it. Lying around hoping for something to happen was frustrating and getting old.

"How do you know that?"

"There was no one in town. We passed a campsite. Ran into some psychopath claiming that something is going around killing everyone."

"You're gonna let a psycho sway you to leave the plane?" Becky shook her head.

"No. But seeing how abandoned the area is makes me wonder." Jake knelt down beside Colin and looked over the wound. "How are you feeling?"

"I'm fine. But how do you suggest I travel with everyone?"

Jake looked up, the question already something he had considered during his hike back from town. "We can build you a cot out of tree branches. Sort of like a travois like the Native Americans used to use to haul supplies behind horses."

"We don't have horses. Who's gonna pull me?"

"We'll have to take turns. Hell, I don't know." Jake shrugged. "I didn't realize you two would be so against this. Don't you wanna get out of here and back to your families? Believe me when I say that no one is coming. It's like the end of the world out there. Abandoned cars, empty campers, and no one to be found. Since when has a rescue taken days? Think about it."

Becky sat beside them, looking over the supplies. "Of course I believe you, Jake. You're our captain. It's just… It's really hard to take it all in. We haven't seen the world outside of this area and you have. There's just a lot to think about. How far from Dallas are we? Can we actually get back there on foot? And what exactly is happening?"

"Sitting here worrying isn't getting us anywhere. The time is gonna pass no matter what we do." Jake patted Colin's good leg and forced a smile. Moving him was scary but leaving him behind was never an option. "We'll get you fixed right up. Between me, Larry, and a couple of the other guys, we can take turns and move you right along. Who knows? Maybe we'll run across a car that'll actually work."

Colin scoffed and laughed. "Wishful thinking. I guess I'm at your mercy. I'm not exactly in a situation to make decisions. I guess if I become too much dead weight you can leave my ass. Just make sure it's near water." He laughed again, this time it was genuine.

"You're my co-pilot. If you stay behind, so do I."

Standing, Jake started working on gathering branches that would be strong enough to pull Colin long distances. With as far as they were having to go, the chances of them having to replace the travois were likely. There were several downed trees from the impact of the plane and he piled up what could be used.

The canvas emergency slide would be perfect to stretch across for Colin to lay on. From the friction of the ground, it would also need to be fixed so keeping a good amount of the slide with them was a necessity. It was thick enough that it wouldn't hurt Colin and he'd be lifted far enough off the ground that just his feet would catch the brunt of the friction.

"You seem to know what you're doing," Colin said.

Jake cut thinner strips of canvas from the slide and braided the branches together, making a V shape large enough to hold Colin and supplies. It'd be a perfect way to carry what Becky had gathered without leaving much behind. Everything was a precious commodity. Being on foot meant days and days of travel and they'd need plenty of things to eat to stay nourished.

"I am appearing like I know what I'm doing but really, I have no idea. I guess taking my kids camping is helping but I've never made something like this before."

To make the canvas sturdier, Jake used smaller branches to go across the back of it. The more support he could make, the better and easier it'd be on Colin. Jostling him around would only hurt his health. Standing back, he looked over what he had created. Two branches crossing at the top in a V shape - whoever was dragging the cot would stand there. The canvas was spread between the branches where Colin would lay, appearing like a hammock. It wasn't pretty but it'd hopefully get the job done. There was no other way for Colin to travel.

Jake put his weight down on it. Colin was about the same size as him and it seemed sturdy. The only issue was Colin slipping out of it due to traveling at an incline.

"Now, how do we secure you?" Jake asked out loud, looking around at what they had available.

Looking toward the plane, it dawned on him like a light bulb coming on. Seat belts! He could try and sew them into the canvas. Surely someone had a sewing kit in their luggage. He'd have to climb back up into the plane but it wasn't as daunting as hiking up the side of the mountain like earlier. His energy was fading but a new burst came when he came up with the idea. The more they prepared, the sooner they could start their trek back toward Texas and the sooner he'd get to see Alice and the kids.

Striding to the plane, he went for the lowest part, which was right in the cockpit. That's exactly where he needed to be - at least in the cockpit, they had shoulder harnesses. Those would prove most useful in keeping Colin from falling out of the travois.

"Where are you going?" Becky yelled from the ground. Jake was already halfway up, his shoes sliding on the slick metal.

"Getting some seat belts. I'll be right down." He'd grab more than one. The travois was turning out to be something they could use, and Jake planned to make more than one - with the items Becky had pulled from suitcases and the children traveling along, having a couple more would be helpful in hauling the supplies and aiding in carrying exhausted children for miles. It'd mean more work on the adults but leaving things behind didn't sit well with Jake.

Glancing up at the sky, Jake noted the position of the sun. It'd be night time soon. He had to work fast. Their goal was to set out toward Dallas as soon as the sun came up in the morning. Having the travois ready would help them get a head start.

It took a while for Alice to calm down after her
encounter with Ed. Working in the ER provided her
with enough experience to know how much evil was
out in the world, but now that the area was pretty
much a catastrophic zone, she wanted to think that
the good would come out in people and they could
help each other. She thought about Crystal and how
she had died - what was the back story with her and
Ed? She was better off not knowing and she tried to
find comfort in the fact that the little girl was no
longer suffering. The pain she must have felt from
her injuries sent a chill down Alice's spine and she
cringed at the thought of Ed kidnapping her for
extremely malicious reasons.

She had to refocus on her initial plan - she needed
to get back to the house and find Dylan. He was the
closest to her and once she knew he was okay, she
could focus on Sophie and Jake. She had enough
water to make it home if she rationed it and didn't
stop. It was still a good trek but doable. The biggest
issue was it was getting dark - if she ran into danger
in the daytime, she shuddered to think what she
might come across after the sun went down.

Her body ached and begged for her to stop.
Blisters were forming on her heels due to being on
her feet for so long. She lost track of time, not even
realizing how long it had been since she got any
good amount of sleep. Her adrenaline was serving

much like caffeine normally did for her but even it was wavering. Sipping on the water, Alice swished it around in her mouth. The dusty haze that had been present since the chaos had hit hindered her from being able to see much of the sky. She wanted to see the location of the moon to get an idea of what time it was but even that wasn't coming through the blanket of destruction that lingered over what was left of the area.

Out of habit, she pulled her cell phone from her pocket and tried to turn it on. Nothing happened, and a sinking feeling of pessimism fell hard in her stomach like she had swallowed a pound of bricks. The good thing was, there weren't that many people around. That also could be construed as a bad thing. Alice felt like she was being watched - shadows around the corner, though she wasn't sure what could be casting them. The streets were dark and there was nothing from the moon. Maybe it was just her imagination driving her crazy - she had seen one too many crime movies, not to mention end of the world movies where there was one sole survivor, left on their own to try to make it.

She reminisced about those movie nights wit her family - they always asked each other the hard question of what they would do if they were stuck in that very situation. Alice always claimed if she was the last person on earth, she'd just want to die. What would be the point of trying to make it when there was no possible way to replenish the population and there were limited resources for food and water? It was a painful and slow way to die, knowing each day the person was running out of things to keep them alive. It was a hard question to answer - a person would have to be put in that situation to truly know how they'd act and what they would want to do.

Alice laughed to herself. She wasn't the last person on earth - there were others, including evil people like Ed who she hoped had finally bled out and died on that gas station floor. She couldn't put her finger on how many had died and who still remained. Without knowing exactly what had happened to put the area in this position, it would be hard to know about casualties. The high number of cars that had crashed and the lack of people around was a bad sign. Those lucky enough to have made it through were left to either help each other or run around like criminals, looting businesses and houses just because of the lack of law enforcement.

Where exactly were the people who always had the answers for the public? The ease of turning on a television when something big was happening was gone - just a few days ago the local news would spout off what was going on around Dallas, and even some information that wasn't relative. And now, nothing. Poof. The world was changed in a matter of seconds.

Alice hugged her midsection, shivering from the chill of the wind. Dry air replaced the normal humid climate of Dallas and cold swept through, matching the mood. She reached another freeway that needed to be crossed - a freeway she sometimes took on her way to take Dylan to school. It was the same story as the freeway near the hospital - crashed cars, fires, and this time, more people than she had seen since she left the ER. Her first instinct was to head toward the family that was camped out by their crashed SUV but she stopped herself. Immediately trusting strangers is what got her in the mess with Ed. She tried not to make eye contact and told herself to stick to her task - it was about Dylan and her family. Everyone else would have to fend for themselves. No more helping strangers. The world was different now. Her duties as a charge nurse in a busy emergency room were gone.

Hurrying across the asphalt, she heard the woman's voice in the distance, muffled by a gust of wind. Alice fought hard not to look over her shoulder. If she looked, it would commit her to listen to what the woman was saying. If she continued to walk, pretending she didn't hear, a few things could happen. The family could follow Alice and pursue her or they could just chalk it up to Alice not wanting to help. Alice hoped it was the last option, but the yelling got louder, this time, the man's voice deeper over the windstorm.

"Hey, excuse me!"

Alice closed her eyes. Maybe if she kept them closed, the urge to turn and look would go away. Heavy footsteps came closer and Alice began to run, but she wasn't fast enough. Fingers dug into her bicep, stopping her, the grip strong enough to finally get her to turn around. When she saw who it was, her heart skipped a beat. Finally, someone she recognized.

"Tom?"

Her brother nodded, his face masked by a trail of blood that appeared to be coming from a wound on his forehead. "I…" he trailed off, his eyes darting to the ground. "What the fuck, Alice?" The tone in his voice made her jump and she took a step back. He was family - estranged family, but still, a relative that she cared about, even if he didn't believe it.

"Who's the woman?" Alice pointed in the direction of their wrecked car.

Looking up again, tears welled in his eyes and he shook his head. "She's my wife, Alice!"

"Your wife?" Alice rubbed her temples, her brain unwilling to take any more bombshells in. "I guess that's what we get for not talking for years. I didn't know you got married. I'm so…"

"Sorry? Yeah." Tom bit his bottom lip. "You were just gonna leave us here and keep walking? I guess I'm more of a black sheep to the family than I thought."

"No, that's not it, Tom. I didn't realize it was you. I promise. Your face is covered in blood and it's dusty. I'm sorry. Truth be told, I'm happy to finally run across someone I actually know." Know was a strong word. It had been at least five years since she had any interaction with her younger brother. She really didn't know him at all. What she should have said was it was nice to see someone she recognized.

"What the hell is going on, Alice?"

"Let me guess. You and your wife were driving and then suddenly your car just stopped working?"

"Yeah. Same story for everyone, as you can see." Tom spread his arms to motion toward the freeway and the massive pileup behind them. "I don't understand."

"Me either. I'm headed home to see if I can find Dylan. Y'all are welcome to come with me, though I don't have much in the way of food or water." Alice hoped she wouldn't regret the offer. Tom was a thief - the main reason they had fallen out of touch was his multiple stints in prison for robbery. She couldn't leave him behind, regardless of his mistakes. There was strength in numbers, even if she couldn't completely trust her own flesh and blood.

"Sure. Let me go get Randi and our things out of the car. We're right behind you."

CHAPTER TWENTY-ONE

Sophie's legs ached. She was in pretty decent shape having to walk everywhere at school but she had never conquered the distance she and Danny had covered without stopping. Her body longed for nutrients - a big glass of water without having to worry about how much she was drinking and a huge plate of spaghetti would be like heaven on earth. It was like when she carb-loaded before a race. Her body needed carbohydrates from the extensive physical demands she was putting on herself.

They had made it past the urban areas surrounding Boston to the outer county. Buildings were more spread apart now, houses on more acreage, and highways without that many crashed cars like they had witnessed on the freeways miles back. There were a few groups of people heading in the same direction they were going but no one said much to each other. The silence was good and bad, and Sophie wondered where everyone else was going. Did they know what was happening? She couldn't take any more conspiracy theories or speculation - dealing with that was almost as exhausting as the long hike they were enduring.

Stopping along a wooden fence, she pulled her water out and sipped on it. Her body longed for more than a few gulps but she reminded herself that rationing was important. Her stomach growled, another reminder that nourishment would probably make her feel better. The sun was going down, the darkness unsettling against the unknown future they were facing.

"You okay?" Danny asked, nudging her arm. He seemed energetic, like none of this was bothering him. Or maybe he was just really good at hiding it.

"Gonna have to be. What other option do I have?"

"We should probably find a place to stop for the night. We need to rest and you know…" Danny trailed off, looking past her into the distance.

"I know what?" Sophie knew exactly what he was referring to. It was exactly what she feared - people were up to no good after dark. EMP or not, that's when the bad guys came out to rob, rape, and plunder.

"We should probably just find a place to rest off the radar." Danny side-stepped her question and that was fine - he knew how freaked out she could get and it was avoiding drama.

"Where do you think we should go?" Sophie looked around. Some people continued to walk, some were following suit to camping out for the night.

"There are some houses back off of the road. The only question is, are there people there?"

Danny walked toward a driveway and Sophie followed, her feet hurting, her body longing for a chance to just collapse where she stood. The first house they came across was nice - two stories, a three-car garage, and a big garden in the side yard. Sophie jumped at the sight of it - most of the plants weren't in their mature producing stage yet but a tomato plant had small, unripe fruit that would still provide some nutrition. She was so hungry at that moment that she could eat the plant itself.

Both of them dug in, searching each plant for anything edible. A small bell-pepper, cherry tomatoes, and black-eyed peas that Sophie didn't even bother to shell. It didn't even occur to her that someone could be in the house - things were very competitive now. They could easily lose their lives over a couple bites of vegetables without the owner even thinking twice about killing them.

Stopping, she patted Danny's arm to get his attention. "Danny…"

He bit into a green tomato and winced, but finished it. "Yeah? What's wrong?"

"What if someone lives here? What if they're watching us from the window?"

Danny wiped his mouth with the back of his hand and looked toward the closest window on the side where the garden was. It was dark enough that they almost couldn't see the house now - with no electricity, there were no street lights to aid in seeing anything. The dusty haze overhead also hindered the light from the moon to help.

"I don't think anyone is here," Danny assumed, taking her hand in his.

"What makes you think that? I can't see anything." Sophie's voice shook. She usually wasn't such a baby about things but people were fighting over bottles of water now. Survival seemed to be bringing out the best or worst in people, both on the extreme side.

"They would've been out here by now. Come with me. If it's vacated, this will be the perfect place to get some sleep."

He tugged at her hand and led her through the garden, closer to the house. She could feel his pulse against her palm, which didn't help her calm down. His clammy skin was another indicator that he wasn't so sure that his assumption of the house being vacant was accurate. She followed him, mainly because she didn't want to be alone.

The patio was closed in and unlocked. Danny motioned to a far corner where several bicycles were. "Transportation! It won't get us there as fast as a car but it'll sure as hell beat walking on foot."

Sophie smiled at the find - a bike would also be better on them physically. None of it mattered if the owner of the place met them at the door with a gun to their face. The patio had a screen door that was shut, but the main door leading into the house was wide open. She wanted to yell out to stop but she followed Danny inside. Her gut instinct was to reach for the light switch. She felt like a moron - they had been without electricity for days now and still, she wanted to flip on a switch like it would magically come on.

Everything in the kitchen was in its proper place. Looters hadn't gotten to it yet. There was also no indication that anyone was home unless they were upstairs sleeping but who would do that in this situation? A place this nice would need to be guarded on the ground-level floor. Sophie's nerves began to relax as they went from room to room, discovering that it indeed was vacant, just like Danny had predicted.

"I guess this is our hotel for the night," Danny replied, locking each door. "I'm not sure if it'll keep anyone out to do this, but better safe than sorry."

He opened the refrigerator - all of the food inside was spoiled and a rotten smell permeated the kitchen. Sophie backed away, her ravenous appetite quickly gone from the rancid food that had sadly gone to waste. Backing away, she checked the pantry for non-perishable items that would still be okay. Crackers, bread, and peanut butter were the first things that caught her eye. She slipped them in her bag - finding the peanut butter was like hitting the lottery. It was nutritious and would help hunger pangs better than anything.

"Sophie, come upstairs!"

She glanced toward the landing above her. She hadn't even realized Danny had left her alone and went up to meet him. Motioning toward the large bedroom, he pointed to the closet. Padding toward it, Sophie's breath caught in her throat when she saw the open gun safe. Her father had guns in the house and she had shot handguns but they still made her nervous. Right now, it meant added protection.

"Oh my God."

"Looks like we chose the right house to stay at tonight. Bikes, food, and guns." Danny's smile made him look like a young kid on Christmas morning.

"Where are the people who live here?" Sophie asked. Finding the items they had was great but there was still an eerie feeling around them.

"I don't know, Sophie. Maybe they were at work and never made it home." Danny pulled out a shotgun and ran his hands up and down the handle. "Look at this. It's a beauty!"

Edging away from the closet, she shrugged off her backpack and sat on the edge of the bed. It was perfectly made with a floral bed set - someone had been there right before the EMP hit, preparing for the day ahead, not realizing they'd never make it back home. The same could be said for Sophie - she didn't know she'd never walk back into her dorm room again. She may never make it back to her home in Dallas. Having a pessimistic attitude wouldn't help them but it was a grave situation.

The bed dipped beside her, pulling her from her daydream. Glancing to her side, Danny sat beside her and put his arm around her. Neither of them spoke for a few minutes but it was a comfortable silence. Sophie took in the sounds throughout the house - the only noticeable thing was the wind blowing right outside the window by them. She was scared to even look in that direction. What if others were trying to get in too? What kind of fight would they endure if everyone got news of guns and food in the place, not to mention the garden outside?

"We should probably get some sleep," Danny said, breaking the silence.

"Yeah." Nodding, Sophie scooted backward, pulling the covers down. It was a chilly night and without electricity, it'd get colder, depending on how well insulated the house was.

Danny slid in beside her, hugging her from behind. She imagined they were back at her dorm, safely in her bed, and none of this had happened. For a split second, with the feel of his body up against her, it almost seemed real. It almost felt like she had dreamed up all of this and she couldn't wait to tell everyone what her imagination had come up with. The dark, unknown house was a stiff reminder that this was beyond what dreams were made of.

***

Jake woke up early the next morning, having never truly fallen asleep. The sun wasn't up yet but he spent time double checking the travois he had made. Four total - one large enough to carry Colin and the other three would be used for the children and supplies. They couldn't make more than that so people could trade off dragging them. It would take a lot of energy, especially as far as they had to go. He hoped along the way they would be able to find something that would aid in travel. Cars were pretty much out of the question - though he wasn't sure what the criteria was for something to stop working, if his assumption of an EMP was true, anything newer than around 1970's would be out of the question. Most people were driving much newer vehicles than that.

For those who weren't dragging a travois, they could pull a suitcase. They wouldn't be too heavy and would be another added benefit to hauling the supplies that they didn't want to leave behind. The more food and water, the better, and pulling a suitcase wouldn't be so bad with the new fancy, three-sixty wheels that a lot of luggage had. Going off road and on rugged terrain might prove to be challenging but the plan was to get on a main highway headed south toward Texas.

Jake would be naive to think that they would have a direct trip with no hiccups, and the heavy weight of the gun he had gathered reminded him that trouble would loom wherever they went, especially as people became more desperate and knew of all of the supplies they were carrying. For the most part, he had to believe that the good would be brought out in people but there would always be the few who would prey on the misfortunes of others and take complete advantage of a very bad situation. Ammunition was sparse so he had to be smart when it came to weapons.

Sitting next to Colin, he noticed his copilot was awake, his brow creased as he looked up at the sky. "You really think you can drag me all the way back to Dallas?"

Jake patted Colin's arm. It was going to be tough but leaving him behind was definitely not an option. "We can and we will."

Colin shook his head and closed his eyes, the tension palpable. "I'm not a little guy. I'll be dead weight."

"What do you propose we do, Colin? Leave you here? You'll be some wild animal's lunch in no time. Or you'll starve."

Colin shifted his weight and cringed. The bandage on his leg had soaked through the gauze. The stitching job was helping but his wound was still in bad shape.

"I just don't want to bring the group down, Jake. You gotta do what you gotta do. I'm injured. I'm a liability and am risking the survival of the rest of the group. You have that gun you found, right?"

Jake glanced down at Colin, knowing exactly where he was going with his question. Patting his pocket, he felt the cold metal against his skin. "Don't even think that, Colin."

"It'll prevent me starving or being some bear's meal, right?"

"No." The anger built up in Jake and he chewed on the inside of his cheek to keep his voice down.

"I'm a liability, damn it! Shoot me or let me do it myself."

"You're a bastard for even suggesting something like that," Jake replied, standing up. "The sun is coming up. We're about to start moving."

Walking away, Jake couldn't even look back at Colin. He got where the man was coming from. If the situation were reversed and he was the one with the broken leg, he'd suggest it too. It would be tough with Colin's lack of mobility but the thought of killing him made Jake sick to his stomach. He wasn't a dog that needed to be euthanized. He was a human being and a friend. A broken leg wasn't going to decide his fate.

"There's three travoises we can use for supplies and the children," Jake said, letting Rose know. "The bigger one is for Colin. I wanna get moving. I wanna get away from this damn plane."

"Slow down, Jake. What's the matter?"

"Nothing. It's time we go. It's time to get the hell outta here and back to our families. I'll pull Colin first. You make sure we have every bit of supplies we can carry loaded up."

Larry helped Jake load Colin on the travois. Thankfully, Colin made no more mention of putting him out of his misery. Jake wasn't sure how he'd handle it if he had. Positioning himself between the two branches, he gripped them tight and began walking. As expected, Colin was heavy and getting him down the mountain and to the road was going to be rough. Hurting his leg worse was a worry but still a better alternative than leaving him behind.

Glancing over his shoulder, Jake watched the others in the group follow him down the path they had come the day before after exploring the campsite. For the first time since the plane crash, he felt productive, like they were actually moving forward instead of sitting around and waiting on a rescue effort that never came.

Each step was moving them closer to getting home. Each treacherous, hard step meant one second closer to seeing Alice, Dylan, and hopefully Sophie again. He prayed to God they were all safe and sound. He prayed to God that this was the right decision. It was too late to second guess himself now.

CHAPTER TWENTY-TWO

"You know, usually when a person hasn't seen family in over five years, there's a lot to say. You haven't said more than five words to me since we started walking. Not even last night when we found that place to sleep." Tom spoke the truth that Alice wasn't willing to face - he was brutally honest but despite the shortfalls, the resentment and anger she had harbored toward him were still as strong as the first time she had felt them.

She let his words sink in before she spoke. Choosing her words wisely was a good idea. She had no idea what he was capable of.

"I guess when my brother decided to hop on the wrong side of the law and become a felon, it made me put up a ten-foot fence to keep the disappointment away." It wasn't the nicest thing she could have responded with, but just as Tom had spoken the truth, she felt she needed to as well.

"I guess I deserve that," Tom replied. "Believe it or not, I'm trying."

"How many times have we heard that line?" Alice glanced over at Randi who hadn't said a word, not even when Tom had introduced her. She was very skinny and her hair was a mess, but now definitely wasn't the time to judge appearances. Everyone was in need of a shower and clean clothes.

"Man, we're really going for the cold hard truth now, aren't we?" Tom clicked his tongue and kicked a rock down the road until it rolled into a ditch.

"It's just hard for me to believe you when you say you're trying. You said it the first time you made parole. Then the second. Then that third trip down you served every bit of your sentence. Apparently, the State of Texas has gotten like the rest of your family. We don't believe you when you say you're trying."

Tom cringed and shrugged his shoulders. "I deserve that too. Would you believe that this has been the longest amount of time that I haven't gone back in? I've got a wife now. I have... had a good job. Go figure. I actually start doing something with my life and the damn world ends."

His comment made Alice smile. Finding humor in a horrible situation broke up the tension, even if it came from her criminal kid brother who she couldn't trust. "Okay, we can blame you for all of this. I'm good for that." Alice nudged him. "You were the scapegoat before... might as well carry on the tradition now." Alice looked over at Randi again. The woman kept her eyes on the ground, walking two steps behind them. Whispering, Alice said, "She always this quiet?"

"Not really. I guess she's trying to figure you out."

"No. I'm just listening to your sister berate you when it's unnecessary." Randi glared at Alice, finally looking up from the road. "He's done his time. He's paid his price. I think it's best to put it all behind you since there's so many who have died around us."

Alice felt guilty. Randi was right. Times were different now and with her being separated from her immediate family with no idea of their well-being, sticking together was important. Tom was a criminal, there was no doubt about that. But now they lived in a world where the laws didn't matter. Thieves were everywhere and sadly, stealing was becoming a way of life to survive. Though it killed her to think it, his downfall might become their saving grace.

"You're right, Randi. I apologize for the bad attitude." Alice nudged Tom again. "How'd you two meet?"

"Prison," Tom smiled. "Before you say anything, hear me out. She used this pen pal thing they offer and we started off conversing in the mail. Then she started visiting. And here we are now."

"Wow. That's interesting." Alice forced a smile. She had heard about the pen pal system but didn't think it was real. "Well, Randi, welcome to the family. I hope married life has been treating both of you well."

Randi gave a half smile and looked back at the road. Alice had ruined her first impression and there was no getting it back. She had enough of other things to worry about and ignored it. Dylan was number one on the checklist. Jake and Sophie were a close second.

"You and Jake still married?"

"Yep. Still married."

"Of course you are. You two were Riverdale High School's sweetheart couple back in the day. It'd be an act of Congress if you two ended up getting divorced. When he left for the military I thought for sure that'd be the end of your relationship, and here you are, still married to him. He still flying?"

Alice nodded, her stomach sinking at the mention of Jake. Her memory instantly flashed to the news story of his flight number and the confirmed crash right before the electricity went out. She had to hold out hope that they got the information wrong. With everything between then and now happening, she hadn't taken a second to think about it until Tom mentioning him.

"Yeah. He's still a pilot." It came out in a whisper and Alice had to stop and sit on the curb. The world around her was spinning and she closed her eyes to try and gain her composure.

"Woah, are you okay, Alice?" Tom sat beside her and grabbed her hand, which surprisingly was helpful. It helped Alice brace herself and the vertigo finally subsided.

Opening her eyes, she grabbed a bottle of water from her bag and drank the whole thing. Rationing it was important but it tasted good and her body needed it.

"I'm fine. Just a little lightheaded." She omitted the worry of Jake's plane crash. Talking about it would make it worse. She had to keep focused. She had to get back to their house and find Dylan. One thing at a time - if she tried to cross bridges she hadn't gotten to yet, she'd lose her mind. "We should keep going. My neighborhood isn't far from here and Dylan might be at the house."

"Take a few more minutes to rest, Alice. Where are Jake and Sophie?"

"Sophie is at school in Boston. Jake was at work when this all happened."

"On a flight?" Tom's voice cracked and he leaned forward, offering Alice a package of crackers, which she gladly took from him. They'd help settle her nervous stomach.

"I'm not sure. I'm not sure if the flight got canceled or if he was already in the air when this all happened." The news report confirmed he was flying but Alice still held hope that they were wrong. They had to be wrong. Something inside her felt like Jake was still alive.

"I sure hope he wasn't flying yet. Every aircraft in the sky crashed. Every car crashed. All cell phones are dead. This was an EMP. I read about them a lot in the prison library. My cellmate was all about science and theories regarding all of this. I always thought he was a nut job but…"

Alice held her hand up to stop Tom. His constant chatter was making things worse. "I'd rather not talk about it. Let's get moving. I need to get home to Dylan. You two can come with me or you can go where you need to but nothing else is keeping me from getting home to my son."

Neither Tom or Randi spoke up and followed Alice as she composed herself and continued to walk. She was determined before but now there was a desperate need to get back to the house and find Dylan. The speculation of what happened didn't matter. The fear that Jake was dead had subsided. Her family was alive - there was no other option. Reuniting with them was priority over anything else and she'd get there come hell or high water. They were already going through hell. Bring on the rain. Alice was ready for anything.

***

Jake struggled to get Colin and the travois down the side of the mountain. There was a footpath that aided in it not being such a steep incline but it wasn't helpful for someone lugging a human-being behind them in a very unstable apparatus. He failed to consider his own injuries sustained from the plane crash, hoping that if he ignored them that they'd fade away. Lugging his co-pilot was a stiff reminder that he was hurt too, though he didn't want to admit it out loud to anyone. Anything to make Colin feel guilty about this wasn't an option and Jake pushed through the strong headache that was growing by the second.

He felt the back of the travois lift and the weight eased a bit. Glancing over his shoulder, Larry had picked up the other side, lifting Colin completely off of the ground. It was helpful and he nodded toward Larry, thanking him. The walk down was still steep and they had to take each step carefully. Jake could see the road from where they were but it still felt like miles away. As far as he could tell, the rest of the group was keeping up, even the kids, though most of them had hopped on a travois that was hauling supplies and suitcases.

Taking a deep breath, Jake pressed on. The edges of his vision grew black but he wasn't going to give up that easy. Succumbing to his body's injuries would mean he was giving up and they hadn't even gotten a mile away from the plane. He survived a damn plane crash - he was going to survive the hike back home too.

"Just a little farther," Larry grunted from behind. He was probably struggling too - from what Jake could tell about him, he wasn't in the best shape.

His legs burned, his lungs ached, and his head was pounding but Jake felt triumphant when they finally reached the road. It was almost like a mirage and hard to believe until he actually set foot on the asphalt. Setting the travois down, he moved his arms around. They felt like noodles and he took a deep breath, enjoying the spectacular view around them. Despite the situation, they couldn't argue that the mountain range was beautiful and the lake lent an even better nature-like feel.

"It's a shame we can't hang around and enjoy this," Colin said, sitting up to see. "Looks like a place I'd love to bring my kids."

Jake nodded and handed Colin a bottle of water. "Yeah. A nice, long weekend doing some camping and fishing. But not for a while. I think we're all camped out for the time being." He laughed and took the water from Colin, finishing it off. "I guess whatever empty bottles we have we can go fill up in the lake. Since we're not sure how clean the water is we can still use it for washing our hands or clothing. Could put it to use for something."

"We can do it," Becky said, stepping through the group, motioning to another lady. "You and Larry have worked so hard for us."

Jake hesitated, remembering the odd person he had ran into not far from where they were. "Are you sure? People aren't the same now. If you come across someone they're not gonna welcome you with open arms."

"I've dealt with grouchy customers for years. You know I can handle my own, Jake."

Jake looked down at Colin. "Oh, shit. Your bandage came open and you're bleeding." Kneeling beside him, Jake took out the first aid kit in the backpack next to Colin. Looking up, he saw that Becky and the other woman were already halfway to the lake before he could say anything. If they made it quick, they'd be fine.

"I guess that smooth ride did it," Colin replied, laughing. "I felt like I was in a luxury car."

Jake peeled the old bandage off. "Very funny, co-pilot. I'm about to put some alcohol on the wound so brace yourself." He dabbed a cotton ball in the cleaner and smoothed it over the gash. Colin didn't even wince and Jake hoped he was just used to it and not because he was losing feeling in his leg.

"I think you missed your calling, Jake. You should've been a nurse."

"I think you're right, seeing as I crashed an airplane and all."

Colin's smile faded and he went to say something, but before he could, a loud scream echoed against the mountains, making the hair on the back of Jake's neck raise. It sounded just like Becky, yelling for help, and in the vicinity of the lake. Dropping what he was doing, he made sure he had the gun in his pocket and ran in that direction.

The same man who had confronted Jake earlier at the campground had Becky and the woman cornered. From what he could tell, the stranger was holding a knife on them but there wasn't a gun, which gave Jake the upper hand. He slowed his pace as he got closer. The man didn't give any indication that he knew that Jake was coming, so he hid behind a large tree and peered around it, knowing if he moved too fast, the stranger would hurt Becky and the woman. If he took too long, it could be too late and the damage would be done.

Edging closer, Jake gripped the gun, his palm moist against the handle. Becky's hands were raised at shoulder level, fear on her face, though her body language showed confidence in handling whatever the stranger had planned.

"Give me what's in the bag!" The man pointed with the knife, just a few feet away from Becky.

She didn't move, her defiance her strong point but also what would get her killed. "Why?"

"Are you kidding me, bitch? Give me the bag! I'll kill you!"

He slashed the knife toward Becky, too close for comfort. Jake had seen enough, already knowing how unstable the man was from their previous encounter. Making himself visible, he came out from behind the trees and pointed the gun right at the stranger's head, his adrenaline pumping so hard that any pain he felt from carrying Colin down the mountain was momentarily gone.

"Drop the knife!"

All three of them looked Jake's way, though his focus was solely on the stranger who was inches away from stabbing Becky or the woman.

"Oh, we meet again! I thought I warned you to get out of here!"

"We're leaving. Believe me, we're leaving," Jake said, his voice low, though they all could hear him.

"Looks to me like you're still here at the lake. *My* lake. I told you that they're coming."

Jake ignored the stranger's comments. Any more speculation about what was happening was unimportant. The only thing important was getting out of there alive and getting home. The rest would be sorted out later.

"Drop the knife and we'll leave. We're not giving you the bag so don't even ask for it again."

The stranger cocked his head to the side and smiled. His sunburned skin was red and looked hot to the touch. If he only knew what they had up on the highway he'd already be trying to kill them to get to all of the supplies they were able to pull from the plane.

"You're not running this show. I am." The stranger pointed the knife toward his chest and then put it back on Becky, even closer than he was just a few seconds ago.

"Gun versus knife. I don't think you wanna know how this will end." Jake held the gun steady, his index finger resting on the trigger, ready for immediate action if the stranger moved any closer to Becky. Things were different now. Laws seemed to have gone out the window and it was survival of the fittest. There would be no immediate repercussions for killing someone, which was a scary thought.

"Shoot him, Jake!" Becky gritted her teeth, taking a step away from the stranger.

"He doesn't have the sack to shoot me. You'll be dead before he gets to me," the stranger replied, lunging toward Becky.

It happened in slow motion, but it also happened fast. Jake pulled the trigger, the hard metal reacting and the loud echo of the gunshot rang out against the mountains. The gun kick was hard in his palm and when he opened his eyes, the stranger was on the ground, his forehead bloody from where the bullet had hit him. Becky was standing, her mouth open, shocked at what had just happened.

No one said anything at first. All three of them stood in a circle around the stranger's body - his eyes were wide open and glossy, staring up at the sky overhead. The bullet hole was a perfect circle with a small trail of blood that dripped to the ground. It took a second for Jake to realize what he had done. He had killed a man. It didn't matter that the man was after Becky and going to kill her - he had still taken a life. A human life. It was a bitter pill to swallow, especially as he stared down at the body that was alive just a few seconds before.

"Y'all okay down there?" Larry yelled from the highway and Jake couldn't even bring himself to answer.

"We're okay!" Becky waved and patted Jake on the shoulder. "It had to be done, Jake. You saved our lives."

"Did I?" He glanced at Becky.

"Yes. No doubt about it."

Jake knelt beside the body and checked every pocket for anything they could gather, unwilling to leave anything behind that might be useful. The stranger was dead. Jake had pulled the trigger. And now they were picking apart the clothing for things they could take with them. A part of Jake hoped that the crucial situation they were in was nothing more than a plane crash and the rescue effort was just taking longer. The past ten minutes confirmed that their way of life before was over and now it was survival mode. Kill or be killed. There was nothing they could do to stop it.

"Let's get back up to the highway. I don't know if he was with anyone that might come looking for him."

Jake glanced over his shoulder one last time, getting one last glance at the first man he had ever killed. Something told him it wouldn't be the last life he'd have to take. They were in for more on their trek back home.

CHAPTER TWENTY-THREE

Sophie woke up periodically throughout the night. Without her cell phone working, she couldn't tell what time it was but the sun hadn't come up yet, allowing her to stay in the bed next to Danny. Her body ached, her mind raced, and fear settled in the pit of her stomach. They were in a stranger's house, rifled through their garden, and while the fresh vegetables were refreshing and satisfying, there was a nagging feeling that something was very wrong. Her guilt and worry were the main culprit of her insomnia - her fear of her family's well-being ranking right up at the top of her list of reasons why her mind wouldn't shut down.

Danny was sleeping like a log and she envied his talent of being able to shut the world out. It was comforting having him near. She couldn't imagine how this would go if she were by herself, especially after being attacked for simple items like water and convenience store snacks. She'd probably already be dead and the thought of that made her shiver. Warmth gathered in the corners of her eyes and she buried her face in the pillow. It was an unknown scent of the person who once inhabited the house. Where were they? Did they flee like everyone else? Or were they dead?

Sophie's body shook under the blanket and she rolled on her back, feeling the tears trickle down the sides of her face. She hadn't had a chance to stop and let things catch up with her. She hadn't had a chance to really sit and think about what had happened. Now all of her emotions were overflowing like a swollen river from torrential rain. It never occurred to her that the last time she had left Dallas after Christmas break might possibly be the last time she'd ever see her family.

Closing her eyes tightly, she hoped that when she opened them again she'd wake up in her dorm room and this would all be some crazy dream her mind conjured up from the stress of school and upcoming tests. But it didn't happen - she opened her eyes again, finding herself in the same unknown room, in a bed that wasn't hers - the only familiar thing was Danny lying next to her and she was extremely thankful for that. Without him, she'd be another casualty caused by whatever the hell all of this was.

"Sophie, are you okay?" Danny's warm breath tickled her neck and she found herself leaning into him.

"Yeah. Yeah, I'm fine." She sniffed, revealing the congestion from crying. Danny wasn't stupid. Even in the dark, it was evident she had been crying.

"You can talk to me, you know? What's going on?" He rolled on his side and propped himself up on his elbow. There was enough light cascading in from the moon that she could see him, his brow creased in genuine concern for her well-being.

"I just can't sleep. I keep thinking about… everything."

"Me too. My dreams… I keep dreaming that we're back on campus and everything is fine. We're in psych class and I'm stealing your notes off of you." He laughed and shook his head, clasping his hand in hers. "I never thought I'd say I want to go back to school."

Sophie squeezed his hand and brushed her lips over his. The kiss grew deeper and his hands slid down her sides, pulling her as close to him as possible. "I'm so glad you're here," Sophie said between kisses. "Promise me you won't leave me behind."

"Are you crazy? I'd never do that to you."

They kissed again but it ended quickly. The sound of glass breaking down the stairs pulled them from their embrace and Sophie's heart almost skipped right out of her chest. "Did you hear that? What was that?" She kept her voice low, her temples throbbing from the immediate pang of fear replacing any other emotion she was recently feeling.

Danny sat up and grabbed the shotgun they found. "I heard it."

"What if it's the people who live here?" Sophie's voice shook as she eyed the bedroom door.

"That would be the least of our worries. I think it's a looter. Someone just like us trying to find a place to rest for the night."

"What if they… what if they're violent like those people outside of Boston?" Sophie scooted out of bed and stayed close to Danny, unwilling to allow him to get even just a few inches away from her.

Grabbing his hand, she clutched onto it tight, so tight that her grip ached.

"We should get out of here. We could go out of the window and shimmy down the side of the house." Danny looked out the window and cringed. "There's really nothing to hold onto and I don't want to risk either of us getting hurt. That'll really slow us down." He paused for a second, arching his eyebrow as he thought. "Let's go down the stairs to the patio where the bikes are. We can't leave those bikes behind."

Sophie nodded and bit her bottom lip. She was two steps behind Danny as they edged out of the bedroom on the landing of the stairs. Another sound came from below - this time it was a chair scooting across the floor. They had to be in the kitchen, which meant getting to the patio was going to be a challenge. She felt her clammy palm against Danny's, the fear heightening with each step they took down the stairs. Danny glanced over his shoulder at her, his quick smile possibly a desperate attempt to get Sophie to calm down.

Reaching the last step, they walked slowly, hovering near the closest wall. Danny held the shotgun in one hand and though Sophie was raised around guns and knew how to use them, having it in their possession was worrisome but also a good thing.

"Who the hell are you?" A raspy voice broke the eerie silence behind them and they both turned to see who it was. Danny was quick to get in between

Sophie and the woman near the pantry in the kitchen. She looked tired and weathered like the rest of them - dirt caked on her face, her hair was disheveled, and her clothes draped off of her.

"Who are you?" Danny asked in return.

"I asked you first." The woman's eyes widened. "This your house?"

"No, ma'am. We were just getting some rest before we head out."

"Where you headed?"

Sophie looked at Danny and back to the woman. The less she knew, the better, and thankfully Danny was in agreement. Skirting the question, he said, "Away from here. We're not meaning any harm. We just wanted some sleep."

The woman nodded and Sophie didn't spot any noticeable weapons on her. The patio was behind them and all they had to do was stop talking to her and get to the bikes. Danny tugged at her hand and they both moved toward the back door. Danny stopped abruptly and when Sophie looked up, they had run into a much larger man standing right in the threshold of where they wanted to go. His stare was cold and vacant, his body language hinting that he had no intention of moving out of the way for them.

"Where do you think you're going?" The woman laughed and stepped closer, closing the gap between them.

"We just want to leave. We're not here to cause trouble," Danny said. The man towered over Danny and he was over six foot tall.

"You punk ass kids think you can come around and do whatever the hell you want." The man finally spoke up, getting right in Danny's face. "Without your precious cell phones and electronics, you don't know what to do with yourselves. And I'm not gonna just step aside."

"Please…" Sophie finally spoke up, not even realizing she had said anything until the words fell out of her mouth.

"Please what?" The man made eye contact with her.

"Let us leave. We don't have anything for you."

The man took a few steps back and for a second, Sophie thought they had reasoned well enough with him to let them through. Turning, he balled his fist and hit Danny in the face, sending him to the floor. The shotgun slid out of his hand and across the wood floor, right next to the woman who put her foot on it, hindering any chance that Sophie could get her hands on it. The man kicked Danny in the stomach, causing him to curl up in the fetal position, a groan escaping from deep in his throat.

"Oh my God, you're hurting him!" Sophie knelt beside Danny and rested her hand on his forehead. Blood dripped from his nose and lip and he closed his eyes as he cringed, gritting his teeth from the blunt force trauma.

The man stopped and laughed, motioning toward the woman for the shotgun. Placing the barrel right under Danny's chin, he lifted his head to look at him.

"You two aren't going anywhere. Might as well make yourself comfortable."

Sophie's fears were coming true. They were already in way over their heads. Now the hole they had fallen into was just getting deeper and deeper.

***

Jake was in a haze when they rejoined their group back on the highway. Things were moving in slow motion, like a dream sequence he wanted to wake up from. The scene played over and over in his head – the bullet hitting the man in the forehead… the man falling to the ground… Jake's action taking his life in seconds. Colin said something to him but it sounded like someone playing a tape on the slow setting. Becky and the other woman were in danger. Had he not pulled the trigger, they'd be the dead ones. Or was he too quick to act without allowing the man a chance? This must've been how cops felt with split-second decisions they had to make every day, only for it to be picked apart for hours by a group of judgmental people who had the time to dissect every second of the incident.

Regardless of the circumstances, taking the man's life was a punch to the gut. Hundreds of people had died on the plane he had crashed and now another was dead from him pulling the cold metal trigger of the gun. He was on a roll, and not a good one.

"Jake? Did you hear me?"

Colin's question pulled Jake from his trance. "No. What did you say?"

"Are you okay? You were looking right at me."

"I'm… I'm fine."

"Do you want someone else to pull the travois for a while? You don't look so good."

Jake glanced at Becky who put her hand on his forearm, her expression comforting with just a small shade of judgment in it. Or maybe that was all in Jake's head. "No. I'm fine. Let's get moving. I don't wanna come back here."

Jake didn't even wait for the rest of the group. Once they saw he was moving Colin, they'd follow suit and easily catch up. The wood of the travois dragged on the asphalt but at least he wasn't jostling Colin around as much as on the mountain trail. They were still having to deal with uneven land and steep inclines but for the majority of the highway, they were going downhill, which helped them move a lot faster than before.

There were a few abandoned cars on the side of the highway and other people in the group would go through them, pulling out anything useful. Jake also hoped they'd run across others, as long as they were civil, but it was like they were the only ones left of the human race. That posed another problem - they needed to keep an eye out for wildlife who might be looking for food and water.

"Jake, don't beat yourself up about what happened at the lake."

Looking up, he noticed Becky was walking right beside him, hoisting a large backpack full of supplies. Larry had picked up the other end of the travois again, helping with Colin's weight. He didn't respond to her. It wasn't just shooting the stranger that was bothering him. He needed to know why this happened. He wanted to know who was responsible.

"Are you listening to me? He was going to stab me. He was seconds away from doing it."

"I don't want to talk about it," Jake replied, his tone quick and to the point.

"You're blaming yourself for all of this and you need to stop."

"For all of what?"

"The plane crash. Us being stranded. Shooting that man at the lake. Stop it, Jake! I don't like you acting this way."

Jake licked his lips and tasted the salt on his skin. Sweat stung his eyes but he couldn't let go of the travois to wipe his brow. "The plane crash was my fault, Becky. I was the captain of the flight. I didn't fulfill my duty of getting the passengers to their destination. Even after a crash, it is the captain's responsibility to get the survivors rescued and I didn't even get that done."

"You're kidding me, right? This wasn't pilot error and you know it. This goes beyond your flying abilities, Jake. We're dealing with some serious shit here if you couldn't tell."

Jake looked over his shoulder at Colin who was hearing every bit of what Becky had to say. He felt embarrassed that the younger pilot was witnessing his guilt trip - He was Colin's mentor and wasn't being a good role model by wallowing in his own self-pity. Even if he felt he had come up short with the crash and the rescue team he could start from there and get everyone back to Texas. A sudden wave of desire to keep going was instantly replaced by his body's warnings to slow down, reminding him that he was an injured man who hadn't been treated for the damage he had sustained in the crash.

Jake sat his end of the travois down and wiped his brow with the back of his hand. "I need to take a break." Grabbing a bottle of water, he walked away from Colin and Becky, down the highway to be alone. The vertigo was stronger than he had felt before and his legs felt like noodles. Nausea got the best of him and he bent over the railing, heaving the little he had in his system, the acid burning up his throat and nose.

"Jake, are you okay?" Becky yelled down the road but it was like she was in a tunnel. "Jake, sit down!"

He tried to but the dizziness was stronger than his ability to control his body, and his legs gave out from underneath him. Crashing to the blacktop, he scraped his arm and hit his head on the wooden post of the railing. His vision blurred but he could tell that it was Becky and Larry standing over him.

"We're never…" It was a struggle to get the words out and Jake laid his head back, closing his eyes. "We're never…"

"Never what, Jake?"

Opening his mouth to answer, he didn't want to give in and pass out, but despite his resistance to giving in, the world went black around him.

CHAPTER TWENTY-FOUR

Alice's stomach did a back-flip when they reached her neighborhood. It almost looked normal with several cars in driveways, appearing like a street where most of the people were at work for the day. The main indicator that things were not normal was the dusty haze at eye level and the crashed cars of the unfortunate who happened to be driving when the incident had occurred.

She quickened her pace, not even worrying if Tom or Randi were able to keep up. Her house was another block down and her desire to find Dylan heightened even worse than before. Breaking out into a run, she heard Tom yell something but didn't stop to see what he had said. He knew where the house was even if it had been years since he had visited it.

Alice's legs ached and her lungs burned, and when she reached the front yard, she came to a screeching halt, staring at the home where things were recently perfect. Now it was eerie - the front bay window was cracked and the front door hung wide open - they were likely hit up by looters and now that she had taken a second to look around, the next door neighbor's house looked similar.

"Dylan!" Running up the sidewalk, she kicked the door completely in and stopped in the entryway. The house was dark and she opened the blinds to allow the sun to come in. "Dylan! Dylan, are you home?" Her voice echoed, making the hair on the back of her neck stand up. Seeing their home abandoned confirmed that this was a grave situation.

Walking through, she felt a debilitating level of sorrow course through her. Lamps were knocked over and broken. One of the couches had been ripped open - the insides all over the floor. The TV had fallen off of the wall and shattered. The kitchen was the worst. The walk-in pantry was empty, the refrigerator hung wide open with nothing left in it either. Even the liquor cabinet held no contents. Sliding against the wall, Alice sat on the floor and hugged her knees to her chest, allowing more tears to fall.

"I'm so sorry, Alice." Tom and Randi had caught up to her and he patted her on the shoulder.

"I can't even get a drink to calm my nerves." Alice motioned toward the liquor cabinet. "Those sons of bitches! Son of a bitch!" Her voice echoed again and her body shook as she cried. "He's not here. Dylan isn't here."

"Where could he have gone?" Tom asked, sitting next to her on the floor, the crack of broken glass under the soles of his shoes.

"I don't know." Alice shrugged and wiped her cheeks. "I have no idea."

"Does he have friends that live nearby? Where was he when this happened?"

"School. I'm pretty sure he was still at school. He has friends who live in the area."

"Good. He probably didn't want to be alone." Tom patted her again. "You're allowed to have a momentary freakout but remember that Dylan needs you. Have your meltdown and then try to think about where he might've gone."

Alice ducked her head and took a deep breath. Standing, she wiped her hands down her scrubs and continued through the house. She wasn't sure why she was doing it - seeing it in the shape it was in was heart-wrenching. The family pictures on the wall, Jake's belongings in the bedroom, Dylan's room, and Sophie… poor Sophie. She was all alone in Boston. How was Alice going to get to her? How was she going to bring her daughter home? She needed Jake there. She needed his rational thinking and the calming effect he held over her. His years in the military would be helpful in a time like this.

"God, I hope they're all still alive," Alice whispered to the empty room. Tom and Randi were downstairs waiting on her, giving her a moment alone, which she needed but also feared. "Please make it home. I hope we all make it home and can be together."

Tom's suggestion ran through her mind. She was allowed a moment like this. It was due and everything had all come to the surface, revealing the real amount of trouble they were all in. But she could only afford a few minutes of acting that way. She had to come back to reality. She had to be strong, especially for Dylan. He was somewhere close and come hell or high water, she was going to find her youngest child. They were already going through hell. Bring on the high water.

Walking down the stairs, Randi and Tom watched her from below. Alice forced a smile and smoothed her hands over her ponytail. "Let's try the school first. Maybe the administration held them all there and didn't let them leave. It's about ten blocks to the north if you're both up to walk some more. If you aren't, you're free to stay here and rest."

"We're here for you, Alice. We'll be right there with you." For the first time, Randi spoke up, her compassion genuine as she held Alice's hand. "We've been walking for miles. Ten more blocks will be a piece of cake."

Alice smiled and this time it wasn't forced. "Thank you. I appreciate that."

***

"Jake? Jake, can you hear me?"

He could hear the voice but it sounded like it was far away. Struggling to open his eyes, he squinted from the bright light above him, his head feeling like someone was driving a nail right through his forehead. Why in the hell was it so hard to open his eyes and where was he? Groaning out in pain, he tried to sit up but something heavy was on his chest, preventing him from moving very far.

"Jake, don't move. Just lay back."

"No. What is..." he trailed off, his head resting on something hard. Attempting to open his eyes again, that same damn light drove right through his skull and he felt the urge to vomit. "Where am I?"

"On the side of the highway. You fainted. Here, drink some water."

He finally recognized the voice. It was Becky and everything came back to him. They were stranded in the wilderness. Colin's leg was broken. And he had killed a man. The guilt hit him hard and he was finally able to open his eyes, though his vision wasn't clear. Blinking to clear the blurriness, he fought past the person whose hand was on his chest and sat up, drinking over half the bottle of water before he reminded himself that he needed to ration everything they had.

"Are you okay? How are you feeling?" Becky sat beside him and handed him a sleeve of crackers, which did not sound appetizing. "Eat a few. They'll settle your stomach."

Jake pulled one out and took a bite. "What happened?"

"What's the last thing you remember?"

Jake made note of what time it was, estimating the placement of the sun. With the mountains around them, it was hard to get a good idea of where the sun actually was, but it was dusk, and they'd lose daylight very soon.

"I shot that man at the lake. Then I started pulling Colin down the highway again. And here we are." He spread his hands and glanced to his left. Colin was staring at him and Jake felt his face heat up. He was supposed to be the leader and he had passed out.

It wasn't exactly a way to instill confidence in the group.

"That's pretty much how it all happened. I think you have a head injury by how you're acting."

Jake heaved a deep sigh and ran his hands through his hair. That was his assumption since his symptoms presented themselves but he was in denial. He didn't have time to deal with it. "How long was I out for?"

"At least an hour."

"More like two," Colin replied. "You hit your head on the way down. You sure you're okay?"

"I'm fine. Nothing we can do about it anyway."

"Well, there's no sense in keeping on tonight. The sun is about to go down and though you're going to disagree, you need to rest. There are more campsites nearby and we can make a fire in one of the pits."

Jake didn't even have the energy to refute Becky's suggestion. Attempting to pull Colin in the shape he was in was a recipe for disaster. Becky helped him stand up and it took him a second to get the world to stop spinning. Larry and another man in the group helped get the travois down to the campsite where they were already working on getting a fire started.

"How far would you say we went today?" Jake asked, knowing he wouldn't be happy with the distance.

Colin arched his eyebrow and contemplated the question. "I'd say about four miles."

"Shit. That's what I was afraid of. We keep at this pace and we'll get back to Texas in a couple of years." Traveling on foot wasn't an efficient way to get anywhere fast but without cars, they really didn't have many options.

After a dinner of airplane snacks and canned sodas, most of the group turned in for the night. Jake set up a pallet next to Colin's travois, close enough to the fire for warmth but far enough he wouldn't get too hot. The crackle of the flames was soothing and the flicker of the orange flames on the side of a nearby mountain made him pretend he was out camping with his family, much like they used to do before they all got busy with school and work. Long before Sophie ever left for Boston.

Insomnia plagued him again. What could they do to travel faster? At this rate, they'd never make it home and that wasn't an option. Sitting up, he rubbed his throbbing temples and looked around. They were in a rural area. There had to be ranches nearby, especially as they got closer to town. Grabbing the backpack Becky had been carrying, he rummaged through it. There was plenty of supplies to tide him over for the night, including the handgun he had used to save Becky and the other woman. One day he'd learn everyone's names but right now that wasn't an important detail.

Grabbing a piece of paper from a notepad, he jotted down a quick note, letting them know where he was in case someone woke up and noticed he was gone - also, just in case if something happened to him. He didn't have a set plan on what he was going to do but the goal was finding quicker transportation. Pulling the travois by hand was going to send them all to an early grave.

It probably wasn't the wisest decision to run off alone but he had to be useful. Lying on the ground and contemplating the what if's made him feel like he was spinning in thick mud. At least it was a full moon, helping him see. The gun was heavy in his pocket - it'd be important for more than one reason. Wild animals or people with bad intentions - he felt safer having it in his possession.

The small town they had visited before wasn't far, though it proved to be a waste of time. The mountain range spread out farther as he reached what used to be a somewhat heavier populated area where more houses were popping up on the side of the road and down into valleys. If he could find an old vehicle that was still running he'd probably scream out in excitement. It was a plausible plan since it was ranch country and a lot of old timers hung on to things like that.

Taking a detour down a long driveway, Jake quickened his pace to a slow jog. Head aching, world spinning, he pressed on. There was a fairly decent sized farmhouse about two hundred yards away, separated by a large vineyard that spanned to the front and sides of the house. Jake plucked a few grapes from the vine and ate them - they were sour and not ready yet but it was still something to help nourish his body.

Going up the steps of the porch, he tried the front door, which was locked. Peering through the window, he couldn't tell if anyone was inside. It was almost pitch black and so eerily silent that he could hear the faintest rustle of leaves on the nearby pecan tree. Pecans would be another good source of protein, so Jake gathered up as many as he could into the backpack.

He heard the loud neigh of a horse in the distance. Stopping his tracks, Jake looked around to try and figure out where it was coming from, hoping it wasn't something his imagination conjured up. It was like a mirage in the desert, only he was hearing something that would be extremely beneficial for his group.

"Come on, neigh again."

Everything fell silent and the wind rustled through the vineyard. Jogging to the back pasture, Jake felt like he had hit the lottery when he saw the horse barn and barbed wire fence a quarter mile up the dirt trail. Stopping at the gate, he hesitated. The ranch was kept up nicely. The horses belonged to someone. He couldn't just snag horses away from people.

Leaning on the fence, he counted four. Four would be enough as long as they shared. They could each pull a travois and the children could still ride on them like they had been. It was the perfect plan and it almost felt too good to be true - too easy, like disaster was waiting right out in the bushes.

Going in the fence, Jake looked at their food and water area. Their troughs were empty and the water was bone dry. Maybe the owners were no longer there. Maybe they had run off like the rest of the world seemed to have done. But why would they leave something as precious as horses behind, especially since automobiles no longer worked?

He padded over to the shed and opened the door, the metal squeaking from the friction. A nauseating stench stung Jake's nostrils and made him gag. What in the hell was it? He couldn't see but when he opened the door all the way, he got a good look inside and yelled when he saw the corpse of an older man staring back at him - his mouth was wide as if he died in mid-scream. His head had a bullet hole in it and his hand was clutching a black revolver. The first assumption was the man had killed himself.

"Son of a bitch!" Jake took a few steps away, falling backward against a shelf that held various tools and ropes. Were things already bad enough for people to feel the need to commit suicide? Standing, he approached the man again, looking to see if he had left a note. Jake was hesitant to touch him but patted down the front of his shirt, feeling the crackle of a piece of paper in his front pocket. As expected, he had written a note to whoever was left to find him.

"I was already so alone. And now this is happening. I won't let the evil take me. I'm going out on my own terms."

Jake folded the note up and slipped it back into his pocket. He wouldn't let the evil take him? What evil? Apparently, others knew more than Jake did. And now he had found four horses that he could use. Grabbing the ropes, he searched for saddles but only came across two. Carrying both of them, he went back out to the pasture and cornered the horses. He had experience riding but it had been several years since he had been on one.

They were tame and trained which was another stroke of luck on his side. He'd take it where he could, seeing as everything before now was a strike against him getting back to his family. Sliding the saddles on, he maneuvered the rope to group them all together, the length barely enough to get around them to constrain them. Hopping on the lead horse, Jake guided them up the driveway and back to the highway. Glancing back at the house, he thought about the old man in the horse barn who felt that times were desperate enough to take his own life. One man's misfortune was another man's flicker of hope. It also made Jake second-guess himself. Two people now had mentioned evil and someone coming. It posed a big question - was it worth even trying to survive through?

Shoving the doubt aside, he thought about Alice, Sophie, and Dylan. They were worth trying to survive for. That would be his continued inspiration despite all of the death and uncertainty lingering all around them. They now had horses. It'd cut down travel time tremendously. As he thought before - he had to take the good things as they came, even if it felt too easy. Even if it felt like he couldn't celebrate for too long with the possibility of danger around every corner.

With an effective way of travel, they'd have a target on their back. People would be gunning for them. Jake made a mental note that they would stop at the houses along the way tomorrow when they came back through. Farm houses and ranches meant they'd probably run across more guns and ammunition, which was now just as important as food and water.

CHAPTER TWENTY-FIVE

Sophie felt Danny's heavy breathing next to her but she couldn't see anything. It was pitch black around her and the air was cold and damp. The scent was musty and if she had to guess, she'd say they were in a basement or a cellar. Her memory was fuzzy but it came back to her fast when she heard Danny's groans of pain. They had been kidnapped by a man and a woman and Danny had gotten kicked several times.

Sitting up, she tried to squint into the darkness but she couldn't even see her hand in front of her face. The only comforting thing was knowing that Danny was right there beside her - his labored breathing was worrisome and she scooted up against him, skimming her hand through his hair, hoping to get some kind of reaction out of him. Another grunt vibrated in his chest and Sophie slid as close as possible to him, her pulse racing at the situation they had gotten themselves into.

"Danny, can you hear me?" Whispering, she looked off in the distance, fearing her captors were in the same room, off in the corner, listening to everything they were doing. The thought of them right there made her frantic and it was hard to keep a lid on panicking. "Danny? Are you awake?"

Silence ensued, confirming that Danny was out of it. That added on top of the fear she was already experiencing - how bad were his injuries? The man had beat him pretty hard and the last thing Sophie could remember was Danny's bloody face as they were pulled from the bedroom they had been sleeping in. At least he was breathing. It wasn't calm respirations but it was better than nothing.

Running her hand down his side, she blindly searched for his arm to attempt to find a pulse. His skin was cold and clammy and the sweat gathered on her palm. It took longer than usual to find his pulse, partly from the dark, partly because it was weak. Tears stung the corners of her eyes. This couldn't be happening. Danny had to be okay. They had to make it back to Texas and not allow their kidnappers to win.

An unnerving thought hit Sophie hard - what if they had thrown her and Danny in a cellar or basement and left them for dead? There was no way for her to know what their intentions were and her sense of time was off due to no windows or light getting in. She couldn't just lay around and let Danny suffer. Even if she couldn't see, she could at least try and find a set of stairs or a ladder if they really were in a basement.

Standing, she took a second to try and gain a vantage point. Now she understood what blind people went through every day and it made her knees wobble. Counting the steps from Danny until she found the wall, she made a mental note so it wouldn't be so hard to find Danny again. The walls were cold and hard, feeling like brick and mortar under her hands.

Walking the perimeter, the dust got thicker, the smell of mildew stronger, and her heart beat faster with each step she took, memorizing how many steps it was taking to go to different spots. It was a nightmare mimicking a dream she often had as a child - waking up in her room, unable to find the light switch or lamp to help her find her way. Her dad always came in to rescue her but now he wasn't there. Her father wouldn't come to the rescue and turn a light on, getting her far away from the danger that ensued.

She heard the strike of a match close by. The friction on the box hissed and the flicker of a small flame was right in front of her, illuminating a man's face. Jumping back, Sophie let out a squeal. It was the man who beat up Danny – middle-aged, wrinkled, his skin weathered from the sun. Even from the little preview of his face from the match, the hair on the back of Sophie's neck stood up. The man's intentions weren't good ones and there was no one there to help her.

"What in the hell do you think you're doing?" His voice matched his gruff appearance. He sounded just like a person who smoked two packs of cigarettes a day.

"I'm trying to help my friend. He's hurt really bad." Playing the sympathy card probably wouldn't help but it was the only line of defense Sophie felt that she had.

"I know. I'm the one who hurt him."

"What do you want from us?" Sophie's voice shook and she really didn't want to know the answer.

"You realize what's going on out there, don't you?" The man lit a lantern, brightening the room better. It was just what Sophie had guessed - a cellar of some sort with boxes on a far wall. Danny was lying in the middle of the floor on his stomach, his face bruising and most importantly, he was still breathing.

"No. What's going on out there?"

"The end of days. We are under attack."

"Under attack from who?" Sophie had to take every bit of speculation with a grain of salt but the EMP theory had been tossed around. She wanted to see what their kidnapper had to say about it all.

"From terrorists. They've always hated America. We have the best military so they know they can't defeat us that way. What better than to completely cripple us by wiping out everything we rely on? Computers, cell phones, electronics - send a pulse through here that sends us into a tailspin. Man, they were right, weren't they?" He arched his eyebrow and wagged his index finger, laughing.

"That still doesn't tell me what you want with me and my friend."

"People are dying out there. We are killing each other for food and water to survive. It's an all out war."

Sophie balled her fists and tried to keep from crying. The man was creepy and without Danny's help, she didn't think she would ever be able to get away. She didn't want to leave Danny behind. He needed to wake up. "That still doesn't answer my question, mister."

Looking up, his eyes were almost completely black against the flicker from the lantern. "I need you to help replenish the population. There will be some survivors. We will be left to get America back on its feet." Stepping close to her, the man ran his fingers down her jawline and rested his hand on her shoulder. "You're young. You're beautiful. Perfect genetic makeup to bring us back stronger than ever."

Sophie grit her teeth and backed away, dodging his hand as he reached for her again. "You're not gonna touch me."

"No. Not yet, anyway."

He walked to Danny and sat next to him, lifting his head off of the cement floor. Danny let out another groan and opened his eyes, making contact with Sophie, though she couldn't be clear if he knew what was going on.

"Please, don't hurt Danny. He can help in your mission." Sophie was going to tell him what he wanted to hear. If it meant keeping Danny safe, she'd play along. "He's got a good genetic makeup too."

The man grabbed a plastic box from the supplies in the corner and applied first aid to Danny's face. "You both will know your role in this soon. Until then, don't you worry. Neither of you are going anywhere."

***

Jake got back to their campsite around the time the sun was coming up. Becky and Colin were awake but the rest of the group was still sleeping. Becky stood over the fire, warming up something and Colin lifted his head as Jake got closer, a smile brightening up his face when he realized what Jake had accomplished.

"Holy shit! You come bearing gifts!"

Jake slid off of the lead horse and tied it to a tree. "A complete stroke of good luck!"

Becky petted the mane of the horse Jake rode and offered him a cup of coffee, which he gladly took. With no sleep along with his headache, it'd be a long day ahead, but hopefully a much more productive day. "When I saw your note I figured you'd ran off and we'd never see you again. Then you completely redeem yourself with these horses! Where in the heck did you find them?"

"Up the highway closer to town. It was a ranch that we should probably stop at again on our way through. I didn't have time to gather supplies but I bet there are some things we could definitely use."

"What if we run into the people who actually live there?" Colin asked.

Jake's heart sank when the image of the man in the barn flashed in his head. "I don't think that's gonna be a problem."

"What makes you sure?"

"I ran across a man in the barn. He killed himself and left a note. He feared the evil headed our way and wanted to go out on his own terms."

Becky sighed and shook her head. "Poor man. It really makes you wonder what is going on. We probably won't ever know."

"I have an idea," Jake replied as he sifted through their snacks. His stomach growled and he needed some nourishment to prepare for the rest of the day. Going only four miles was unacceptable. He wanted to cover lots of ground and get as far as possible before it was time to rest again.

"What's your theory on all of this?" Colin spread his hands and smirked. "We've heard from Larry and some woman. It'd be interesting to see if your story jives with what they're thinking."

"Let's not talk about it right now. We should eat and get moving. I wanna make up time from our disaster yesterday. We can tie up the travois to the back of the horses. If the ride gets too rough, Colin, holler at me so I can slow down or adjust for you." He got closer to Colin and Becky and lowered his voice. "Having these horses is good but it also means we'll have a target on us. People are already competitive over food and water. They see we have a good way of traveling and they will stop at nothing to get them from us."

"With one gun, we won't last long." Colin pointed to Jake's pocket. "We need other ways to protect ourselves.

"I know." Jake nodded. "That's why I wanna stop at the ranch house that I was at last night. I'm certain we'll find some guns there. Anything we can use, we need to grab. We're living under different rules now. Killing someone is no longer a crime - it's a way of survival so we can all get home to our families." He was saying it out loud to take his own advice - the guilt he felt over the man he had killed at the lake had to go away. It was about the group. More death was inevitable. Jake had to make damn sure it wasn't going to be anyone in his group.

"One foot in front of the other, Jake. We'll get there. We may be going as slow as molasses in wintertime, but we'll get there." Becky patted him on the shoulder and gathered up the supplies they had unloaded for the night. "Finding the horses is a giant leap forward. Thank you for doing that last night, even though it was dangerous and probably a little bit stupid."

Jake forced a smile. "I never claimed to be a smart man."

"Oh, hush. So far, you've saved my life and found us better transportation. That's all we can ask for. And if you expect me to stand here and continue to feed your ego, you're wrong. Now go load up the travois and get the horses ready."

Becky smiled and Jake left her last comment alone. He checked on Colin one more time to make sure the bandage on his wound was fresh and he was still feeling okay. Everything looked normal, including Colin's morale, which made Jake feel better. Being stuck, unable to walk or help would kill him. He could only imagine what it was doing to his friend.

"Here we go. Another day closer to home. Let's do this."

CHAPTER TWENTY-SIX

After Alice's mental breakdown, she pulled herself together and focused on where Dylan might be. The school was probably her best bet since that was where he was when everything had happened. Taking a deep breath, she stood with Tom and Randi in the living room. Neither of them spoke to her, the silence deafening as all of the possibilities of where her family was ran through her mind.

"What do you need us to do?" Randi was talking now more than before and it was comforting to know that Alice had support in two people she hardly knew.

"I don't know…" Alice trailed off and picked up a family photo off of the shelf, running her fingers over it. "I think… I think I need to get to the high school. Even if Dylan isn't there they might need help. There could be tons of children there who are stranded." Alice couldn't do it alone - the thought of hundreds of scared children who were probably hungry and injured made her kick into nurse mode again, pushing aside all of her personal problems and focusing on helping others survive.

She double-checked the kitchen one last time, hoping to add to their small stockpile of food she was carrying in her bag but whoever had looted the place left no trail of anything helpful behind. Hurrying out the door, she felt Tom and Randi behind her, matching her step for step as she hurried down the block to the main road that would lead to the school.

It was ten blocks. Ten blocks wouldn't take long. But ten blocks also felt like a lifetime when it involved her son and his well-being. Everything moved in slow motion as she broke out into a sprint. Her legs burned, muscles ached and she was running on pure adrenaline. Her body begged for rest but her heart and mind dismissed it – this was her child and she had to find him, pushing her past the breaking point to get there and help wherever she could. Alice didn't even look over her shoulder to see if Tom and Randi were behind her. None of that mattered.

Rounding the corner, she ran through the soccer field, the mist of a light rain shower invigorating on her dry skin. It helped settle the dust that was everywhere, and the rumbles of thunder made her think about how they would sit out on the patio and have a few drinks while storms rolled in. She'd give anything to have that happen again with Jake, Sophie, and Dylan. Having them all home would be heaven. It was something she had taken for granted.

Reaching the parking lot, Alice stopped abruptly, getting a good glance at the two-story building. Windows were completely shattered, one wing off to the left was scorched from fire, and just like everywhere else she had gone, there was no human presence except for a few people who wouldn't even look her way. The same unsettling feeling she experienced back at the house nestled in the pit of her stomach. Where in the hell was everyone?

Going to the front entrance, the main doors were gone, allowing easy access inside. It was abandoned, dark, and eerie. The main office looked like an old building that was left to rot. Out of habit, Alice lifted a phone off of the cradle, getting the same result as she had the many other times she attempted to use the phone. It was dead, the electricity was out, and Dylan wasn't there.

Padding down the hallway, she tried to think of where large groups might gather. In times of severe weather, she remembered Dylan saying something about going to the library since it was the center-most room in the school. Maybe that's where staff had gathered up the students and they were still there, waiting for help to come.

She ran again, sprinting down the long hallway, following the signs directing her to the library. She had only been in the school a few other times for open house and teacher meetings but her memory led her right where she needed to go. Stopping at the entrance, she pushed the door open and shattered glass fell in her hair. Wiping it free, she was surprised at how dark the place was. With it being the tornado shelter, there were no windows, so she couldn't tell if anyone was inside.

"Dylan? Is anyone here?"

There was a terrible stench that stung her nose. It didn't smell like a normal library would - not the smell of books, paper, and dust. This was more like something rotting and it made her stomach churn. Something was dripping in a puddle and if she had to sit and hear it all day, it would drive her insane.

"Hello?" Her voice echoed and with each second that passed where she didn't get a response, the more defeated she felt.

Alice's instincts screamed at her to leave. The rotting smell was similar to what a dead animal or body smelled like. What if she had just walked into a room where there were mass casualties? What if this is was where the teachers had led the students and something had happened to all of them? Without a light to see, she wouldn't know. Most importantly, what if Dylan was in with that group?

She had to fight back the what if's and fear. Assuming the worst was only going to cause her to make bad decisions. Leaving out of the same door she had gone in, she ran down another hallway - with windows, she could see better and headed toward the gym. Running past a locker room, she screamed when a hand reached out and grabbed her.

"Mrs. Shepherd?"

Alice recognized the boy - It was Ben, a friend of Dylan's. "Oh my God, Ben! You scared me!" The familiar face calmed her down. Maybe she would finally get some answers.

"What are you doing here?"

"I could ask you the same thing." Alice noticed the dirt caked on Ben's face. His clothes were tattered and he looked like he hadn't slept in days. "Are you the only one here? Where is everyone?"

"The library. A lot of the school went to the library when it all happened. We were at soccer practice. The gym was as far as we could go."

"Who is we? Is Dylan here?"

"We all just started running, Mrs. Shepherd. Cars started crashing. An airplane hit the south wing. I heard that everyone in the library died. The explosion from the crash got them all."

Alice's stomach sank. Seeing the tears well up in Ben's eyes tore at her, especially since he hadn't answered her question about Dylan. Wouldn't he have come out by now if he had heard her voice?

"Where's your family, Ben?"

"I don't know. My phone isn't working. I've been too scared to move."

"You've been here this whole time? You must be starving and thirsty."

Ben pointed to an orange Gatorade cooler behind him. "It's full of water. I've been living off of that. The rest of the team left. They were gonna chance it and leave. I knew this is where my parents would come and look once everything was clear. But they still haven't come. I've been waiting and then I heard you."

"Was Dylan one of the ones who left?" Alice already knew the answer to the question but had to ask it anyway.

"I'm not sure, Mrs. Shepherd. We all took off running here. I never saw Dylan. I don't know if he even made it to the gym."

"Oh my God…" Alice whispered, wiping the tear that fell down her cheek. "Here, you probably need something to eat." She handed him a package of crackers she had grabbed from the gas station near the hospital. "Come with me. I'm trying to find Dylan."

"What if my family…"

"I'm not leaving you here, Ben. It's just me, my brother and his wife. There's strength in numbers and you can't stay here alone."

"What about the cooler?" Ben pointed over his shoulder again. "It still has a lot of water in it."

"It'll be too heavy to carry but I'd hate to leave it behind."

"We have a cart that the trainers carry their supplies on. If we can lift it on that, we can push it."

"Ben, you're a genius!" Alice let out a laugh despite the grave situation. Having that much water would help their hydration and allow her to be out longer to search for Dylan. "Like I said - strength in numbers. We'll find your family. I'll make sure we look for them too."

***

Jake slowed his horse as they closed in on the ranch where he found the horses. His gaze immediately went to the barn where he found the old man. The thought of ending his own life made the hair on the back of his neck raise. It would take extreme desperation to want to resort to such a drastic, permanent solution to problems that were temporary - or were they? The way things had transpired over the past week, the current situation was starting to evolve into the new way they would have to live. No cars or trucks, electronics, or the usual things that spoiled them.

Jake nudged the side of the horse and trotted down the driveway. The weather was cool, the breeze cool and crisp, exposing them to fresh mountain air that he took in, breathing it deep into his chest. Becky caught up to him, the clop of the hooves on her horse moving rhythmically with his. Glancing over her shoulder, she smiled at Colin who was lying back, enjoying the ride.

"I think Colin got off easy," Becky said, a hint of playfulness in her tone.

"Yeah? He's lined up just right that when my horse takes a shit it could very well land on him." Jake laughed but knew it wouldn't happen. The way the travois was hooked up in a V shape meant the horse's waste would miss the passengers riding along behind them.

"Hey!" Colin through his hand up and shook his head. "I'd much rather be up on the horse, thank you very much!"

"Where'd you learn to handle a horse so well?" Becky gripped the reins and looked to her side.

"I grew up on a farm. I was riding horses from day one. It's been a while since I've actually been on one but it's like riding a bike. You don't forget how to handle them."

Becky nodded. "A real life cowboy decided to leave home and become a pilot, huh?"

Jake shook his head, his eyesight training right back to the barn. He didn't want to go back inside but there was probably supplies they could use. Seeing the dead man again wasn't something he wanted to go through again. He had killed a man, encountered the numerous casualties on the airplane, but for some reason, this was bugging him even more than everything else. The despair was likely what was bugging him the most. The man chose to end his life. A man who was established with a ranch and a way of life. Jake wanted more explanation that he wouldn't get.

"Joining the military tends to get you away. I never thought I wanted to be a pilot. And someone out there thought I'd be great at flying jets. It just sort of fell in my lap."

Becky smiled again. "I can relate to that. I never wanted to be a flight attendant either. It's funny how life doesn't turn out quite how you imagined it when you were a kid. What did young Jake want to be? What was your dream job when you were a little boy?"

"The usual. A cop or firefighter." The small talk was nice but they were close enough now to the house and barn that Jake needed to focus. Looking over his shoulder again, he allowed the others to catch up. "Be careful going inside. I'm not sure if the place is completely abandoned. Grab the obvious stuff - food, clothing, guns and anything that can be used as a weapon. Move fast - I feel like we are being watched everywhere we go."

The horses were a blessing and a curse. The longer they stayed in one place, the easier it'd be to get spotted or get trapped. Jake figured he was a glutton for punishment - he went straight to the barn, sliding the wooden door open slowly. Colin was at an angle where he could see inside and Jake heard him gasp when the sunbeams provided enough light to get a good view.

"Son of a... Is that who you were telling us about?"

Jake ducked his head and closed his eyes. "Yeah. That's him." Scrounging for supplies felt wrong but he didn't have time to have a struggle with his own conscience. Times of survival meant times of compassion being thrown out the window - it was another adjustment Jake was struggling to make.

There were several cabinets on the far wall that he didn't see in the dark. Opening them all, he found a hammer, a box of nails, and a small leather toolbox. Without a car they wouldn't be useful but when thinking of weapons, they could make use of them somehow. Setting them on the travois next to Colin, Jake took a long pull of water and looked up over at the house. Becky and Larry were busy going through it and a few of the other men were checking on a storage shed on the back lot.

"I sure hope they came up with more than I did."

"A hammer is a multi-use object," Colin replied, holding it up. "You found the horses. At this point in time, it's equivalent to striking gold."

"Now that we're alone for the first time since before the crash, level with me Colin."

"What do you mean?"

Jake leaned against the wall of the barn and folded his arms over his chest. The sky was darkening to the west over the nearby mountain range and rumbles of thunder echoed. Rain would be nice but they had to make sure the horses didn't spook and run off.

"What do you think is going on? Do you think we'll make it home?"

Colin adjusted his weight and sat up, looking Jake in the eye. "What other option do we have?"

"I know. I'm trying not to get discouraged and I'll damn sure not let my doubts be known around the others. I just wanted to see what you thought."

"What I think?" Colin pointed at his chest and sat back against the blankets underneath him. "I think every step down that highway is a step closer. One foot in front of the other, man. One foot in front of the other. If we don't do that, we're as good as dead. Either we end up like that guy in there or someone gets us if we don't keep marching forward." Colin pointed in the shed.

"You're right." Jake nodded. "I know we'll get there."

"As for what all this actually is..." Colin spread his hands and continued, "I have no damn clue, Jake.

Until we actually run across a sane person with some sense of reality, we can speculate all day and it'll just drive us crazy. And let's face it - we've seen enough crazy that we don't need anyone else losing their minds."

Colin's assessment made Jake laugh. "I'm glad you're here, Colin. Without you, I probably would need to be thrown in a padded room already."

"The feeling is mutual."

"Let's get everyone gathered up. There's a storm coming and we should probably pin these horses up. The last thing we need is for them to run off."

CHAPTER TWENTY-SEVEN

Sophie felt like everything was moving in slow motion. How could this have happened? Just when she thought that things were progressing forward and they would make it back to Texas, a hitch in their plan sent them into a tailspin, hindering her from getting back to her family. Keeping Danny from getting home to his. She understood the trek south would take months but at least they were moving in the right direction. And now, a creepy man stepped in, laughing in their face. How dare they want to get back to familiar ground.

The man doctored up Danny with the first aid kit and closed the plastic box. Clapping his hands together, his toothy grin exposed rotted teeth and Sophie's first assumption was that he was a meth addict. If that was a safe observation, it would explain the man's behavior and his immediate disregard for living a clean and legal life.

"What's your name?" Sophie asked, breaking the silence of the dark room. Maybe if they could find out more information about each other, she could play the sympathy card and he'd let them go. It was a far stretch but she had to try.

The man glanced at her from the corner of his eye and didn't answer. Standing, he patted the dust from his pants and put the plastic box back where he got it.

"It's not like we can go to the police. I'm just curious."

"Lee. My name is Lee. I'd ask you your names but I already know."

"How?" Sophie looked over at Danny who was awake but not responding. She made eye contact with him and the sadness in his expression hurt her heart. He was probably feeling exactly like she was - both in shock that something like this could happen, solidifying that life as they knew it was over.

"You're Sophie and this gentleman is Daniel." Lee held up their bags. "I went through your stuff. Found your student IDs. You both were in school back in Boston?"

"If you saw our ID's you already know the answer to that question." Sophie leaned against the wall and kicked her legs out in front of her. It felt good to stretch out. Her body was stiff and a hot yoga class would feel amazing to work the kinks out. But her yoga classes were gone like everything else. Now her fate rested in the hands of Lee, who already made it perfectly clear what his intentions of her were. *Replenishing the population.* The thought made her shiver.

Lee smirked. "Smart ass millennial rich kid. You think you're better than me because you are getting college educated?"

"No, I didn't say that." She looked at Danny again, wishing he'd chime in but he laid in the same position, his face swollen from the beating. Maybe he was mad at Sophie. Maybe he was completely out of it.

"Let me ask you this, college girl. What good is that education gonna do you now? The world is burning. And you're stuck here with me. What good is it gonna do you?"

Sophie stammered on her words. She had no answer for him. Her heart raced as Lee scooted closer to her, so close that she could smell his body odor. Lifting her chin with his index finger, he looked her right in the eye, his brow set in a hard line. The rise and fall of her chest quickened as adrenaline shot through her. Was this it? Was this how she was going to lose her innocence? She felt the warmth in the corner of her eye as a few tears fell down her cheeks. He wiped them away with his thumb and smiled, his stale breath as nauseating as his body odor.

"Are you… are you going to rape me?" Sophie had no idea where the question came from but it was too late to take it back.

Lee's eyes widened and he took his hand away from her face. "We can't stay here much longer. And I hope you eventually realize that sex is the only way we are going to save this planet. I guess I'm crazy for thinking someone who went to college in Boston would understand the situation. This will prevent the end of the world."

For a moment, Sophie saw the pain in Lee's eyes. Was his mission really to save humanity or was it a ploy to get her into bed? Either way, it wouldn't work. "If you truly believe that, Lee, you'll let me be with Danny. If that's the real reason, what's the difference in me getting pregnant by you or getting pregnant by him?" She pointed to Danny whose face showed no emotion, just a blank stare that made Sophie's skin crawl.

Lee looked up the stairs toward the exit of the cellar. He put his index finger over his mouth to silence her. Whispering, he said, "We need to go. My brother is up there and he'll help. This house is dangerous."

"You didn't answer me, Lee."

"When we get to our destination, you'll know. Until then, I need you to be quiet. We need to get out of this cellar."

Lee helped get Danny off the floor and took them up the stairs. Danny staggered and almost fell down the steps but with Lee and Sophie on either side, they prevented the tumble. When they got to ground level, they were met by a man that was identical to Lee, right up to the rotting teeth and crazed look. The woman was there too, waiting beside him.

"This is Ray, my twin brother."

Sophie didn't say anything. Ray didn't either. He held a shotgun and pointed it at them. "Come with us. You did good, Lee. She's perfect."

A knot settled in the pit of Sophie's stomach. This was really happening and there wasn't a thing she could do about it. She felt the cold metal of the gun push into the small of her back, reminding her that she had lost control of everything. Her heart skipped a beat when she felt Danny's hand take hers, his fingers intertwining in hers. He glanced at her and pursed his lips - it was a small gesture but a big indication that he was very well aware of what was going on. It was an act - better to not appear as a threat so their captors would keep him alive. The thought of Danny losing his mind scared the hell out of her. It meant she was alone in this. But now it meant he was very well still there and if they ever got to be alone again, she couldn't wait to hear what he had up his sleeve.

It took everything Sophie had to not yell out in joy. They were being marched off to God knew where but she still had a small flicker of hope deep inside that they would make it out of this situation alive. All it took was a plan - it was better than rolling over and dying.

***

Jake stood on the wrap-around porch of the vacant ranch house and watched the storm clouds come in. The weather had been tolerable since the crash with the temperatures never getting too hot - the only problem was the humidity that made it feel hotter than it was but being from Dallas made him used to it. They were able to lift Colin's pallet onto the porch as well and Jake propped him at an angle where he could also watch the weather. The rest of the group was spread out and resting, everyone quiet and exhausted from everything that was happening.

"The sky sure is beautiful, isn't it?" Colin lifted his head and watched the same clouds that Jake was.

"It is. Nothing better than mountain thunderstorms. The echo of the thunder seems to last forever."

"You think it's severe?"

Jake shook his head and ate a package of peanuts. "Nah. It's nothing compared to our big Texas storms. We got the horses penned up in time just in case they get spooked. I set up some buckets to catch the rain water too."

"Where'd you find buckets at?"

Jake pointed toward the barn. "In there when I was looking for weapons. We can refill a lot of our empty bottles. At least we'll know the water isn't contaminated. I wasn't sure about the water back at the lake."

"That's good thinking, Jake. That would've never crossed my mind."

"I have good ideas sometimes. With the way our luck has been going, this storm is coming straight at us but will turn right when it gets here."

Colin laughed and rested his head back on the blanket. "Luck seems to have taken a turn. You stumbled across horses and we found some guns. That's equivalent to winning the lottery back before all of this started happening."

Jake sat on the first step of the porch and finished the peanuts. Becky was sitting with a young girl, helping braid her hair. "We have witnessed some crazy shit since the plane crash. I killed a man. And a man killed himself right there in the barn. But I guess I still have faith in humanity. There's still some good out there, even if it's not much." Rain began to fall, soaking into the ground. The wind picked up, swirling the nearby trees. Thunder in the distance rumbled, echoing off of the mountains. At that moment, Mother Nature was beautiful.

"Of course there's good out there. If there wasn't, what the hell is the point of all of this?" Colin spread his hands and motioned toward everyone. "You're right. We're gonna run across a lot more evil on our way back home. But good always trumps evil, right?"

"I hope so."

The lightning got closer and a bright flash was immediately followed by a loud clap of thunder. Jake scooted back under the awning of the porch and closed his eyes. If he imagined hard enough, he could feel Alice next to him. He could hear Sophie and Dylan laughing as they played in the rain. It was like previous camping trips where they had to rush back to the campsite during a hike to beat the weather. He'd give anything to go back to those days.

The weather never got more severe than heavy rain and eventually turned into a nice rain shower. It seemed to have lifted everyone's spirits, including Jake's, and by the time the cloudburst had passed over them, he felt rejuvenated and ready to take on anything. The group gathered in the living room of the house where they took inventory of the supplies they had gathered from the shed, barn, basement, and the house.

"There was a gun cabinet up in the master bedroom." Larry lay four guns on the floor, along with two rifles and one shotgun.

Most of the tension Jake felt about being able to protect themselves had subsided. He found hammers and a knife and along with what Larry had come across, they were set for a while. Along with having horses, the target over their heads was bigger now. They had a good supply of food, adequate transportation, and now an arsenal of protection that would look appealing to almost anyone.

"We'll have to be smart with ammunition. There seems to be a lot there but we have no way of getting to more unless we loot some more, which we really don't have time for." He hesitated to say the rest with the children around but they'd have to learn how to protect themselves as well. "If someone is after you or anyone else in this group, shoot to kill. Shoot at center mass or their head. Since we have to ration bullets like we're having to ration food, it's what we'll have to do to make it." The image of the man he shot and killed flashed in his memory - even though Becky was in immediate danger, pulling the trigger and taking a life was still tough.

"Who all gets a gun?" Larry asked.

"All of us on horses. Colin should get one on the travois. The rest of the weapons we'll keep in reserve as backup. I hope to God we are never in a situation where we will need more." It felt like they were a cult preparing for war. He had let Sophie and Dylan learn how to shoot at a young age but the thought of teaching these children felt different. Maybe because they weren't his own kids.

"You realize people are out killing others for a lot less than what we have. We're gonna be the group that people either will want to join or want to take over." Colin cringed as he spoke. He was the voice of reason and the anchor that Jake needed. He spoke exactly what Jake was feeling but didn't want to say.

"You're right. We have to be vigilant and ready for anything." Jake pulled the handgun he had already used from his waistband and checked the magazine. With the exception of the bullet he shot at the lake, it was full. "The longer we sit around waiting, the more daylight we're burning. Let's get the horses gathered up and get moving."

"Do you really think we're gonna run into that much trouble out there?" Becky asked.

"I don't know what to think but it's better to be prepared than not, right?" Jake tried to hand her a gun but she didn't take it. "Take it. I'd feel better if you had one."

"I've never even held a gun, Jake. I'm more dangerous with it than I am without it."

"Then stick close to someone who does have one. I'm serious when I say that we will be targets."

"I know." Becky nodded. "I just don't wanna believe it. Like denying it will make it all go away."

"Ignoring it will just put us in more danger." Jake took a step toward the door. "Let's get out there with everyone else. I really wanna get home to my family. I'm sure you do too. Standing around here isn't helping us cover any ground."

CHAPTER TWENTY-EIGHT

Tom helped Ben lug the cooler full of water down the block. The water sloshed inside and it was a sound Alice loved to hear - it meant she could drink enough water to nourish her dehydrated body. Taking small sips periodically was not helping her system and now it was like hitting a gold mine. Her euphoria over finding Ben and the water faded when she thought about Dylan. He wasn't at home and he wasn't at school. Where else could he be?

Tom, Randi, and Ben all walked in silence. Alice noted the location of the sun. The heat of the day was starting to kick in but she couldn't stop. She needed daylight to help look for her son. When night time hit, the danger increased and she wanted to be back at her home where the walls of the house provided a small bit of security though it was easy to break in.

"Ben, do you know where Dylan could be?" Alice's voice shook and she didn't even attempt to hide how upset she was. The thought of any of her family being in danger or dead made her physically ill, especially since Dylan should've been the easiest one to find.

"Other than school we used to hang out at the pizza place by the freeway."

Alice took a deep breath and stopped. Attempting to gather her thoughts, she counted to three so she wouldn't lose her cool again. "What about friend's houses? Doesn't he have some friends in the neighborhood?"

Ben leaned on the water cooler and arched his eyebrow. "He was…" Ben hesitated, stopping himself in mid-sentence.

"He was what? Please, Ben… Now's not the time to worry about getting him in trouble. He was what?"

"He was seeing a girl. I can't remember her name but she didn't live far from the school. He used to…" He stopped himself again, looking at Tom and Randi, then down to the ground. "He used to go to her house at lunch. He never stayed on campus once they started going out."

Alice let out a deep sigh and closed her eyes. Her gawky little Dylan was seeing a girl? She thought she knew everything about him and never once would she have thought he was up to that. And now her sweet little boy was missing, somewhere out there in the destruction and disaster playing out in front of them.

"Show me where she lives, Ben." Glancing at her brother and Randi, she pointed to the water cooler. "It's probably best we don't lug this thing everywhere we go. Are you two okay with going back to the house with it?" It wasn't appropriate to think about all of the times Tom had screwed her and the family over. She had to trust that he'd take the water back home and wait.

"Yeah, we can do that. You sure you don't want us to come along?"

Alice shook her head and smoothed her hand down her ponytail. There was strength in numbers but it was also best to not have to depend on them. It would invite trouble. "I'm sure. Just take this back to the house and though I'm not sure it'll help much, lock the doors behind you. I'm going to look for Dylan and be back soon. Ben will stay with me since he knows where Dylan likes to go."

"Whatever you need, sis. We're here to help."

Tom got behind the cooler and pushed the cart as Randi guided it down the sidewalk. Alice turned her focus to Dylan. Relying on a fifteen-year-old kid was unsettling but who better to help than someone that apparently knew her kid better than she did.

"Let's get going, Ben. Her house is close to the school?"

"Yes, ma'am. I'm sorry you didn't know about his girlfriend."

Alice let out a quick laugh and bit her bottom lip. "Don't worry about it, Ben. That is so trivial in comparison to what we're dealing with now. I just hope to God he's there. I need to find him. I need him home."

"I'm sure he's okay, Mrs. Shepherd."

"Call me Alice. Mrs. Shepherd makes me feel like an old lady."

Alice tried to recall the morning before all of this happened. Jake was attempting to make plans where they could both have a day off together, hoping to pawn Dylan off on a friend so they could have the house alone. It made her smile - Jake's desperate attempt to have some adult time was adorable and she'd give anything to go back to that day and redo it all. Knowing what she knew now, she'd have never let either of them leave the house. At least they'd all be together.

"What are you thinking about Mrs.... I mean, Alice?" Ben kicked a rock down the street and it rolled about ten feet before hitting the edge of a yard and stopping.

"The day this all started. Dylan had to be at school early for soccer. My husband had a flight."

"Seems like heaven looking back on it," Ben replied. "I had a fight with my dad right before I left for school that day. Had I known it was the last time I'd see him, I'd have never said the things I did." Ben's voice shook and he ducked his head. "He probably thought I hated him."

Alice grabbed Ben's arm and stopped walking. "We're going to find your family. Just like I'm going to find mine. You'll get to tell your dad you're sorry for whatever it was you were fighting about. Don't get down on yourself for this."

Ben sniffed and wiped his hand on his face. "Yes, ma'am."

They walked in silence after that and Alice continued to try and think up clues from that morning. Jake had told Dylan to catch a ride with someone after school because neither of them would be able to get him. Who was it he had mentioned? She thought the name might have started with an R but couldn't recall.

"Ben, do you boys have a friend on the team whose name starts with an R?"

"Yeah, a couple. There's Randy and Ricky."

"Ricky!" It hit her like a wall of bricks had toppled over on her. "Dylan was supposed to catch a ride with Ricky after school. Does he live near here?"

"Kind of. Not as close to where his girlfriend lives."

Alice nodded. "Okay. We go to Dylan's girlfriend's house first and if he's not there, we will go try to find Ricky." There was still so much unknown but at least they had a more set game plan than just meandering around the neighborhood, turning over random rocks like they were searching for a lost puppy. "We're gonna find him," Alice said aloud. It was to convince both her and Ben. She had to keep convincing herself that it was all going to work out.

***

After the storm passed the temperature cooled down to the point where Jake felt like he needed a jacket. The mountain air was humid but definitely tolerable, which helped the mood. Everyone gathered up the supplies they had found, he secured Colin back in the travois, and they started down the highway again. Jake had felt paranoid the entire time they were out there but now even more than before. Having all of the supplies and weapons were great but the worry of what it would bring on was enough that he needed eyes in the back of his head.

The clop of the hooves was the loudest thing they could hear. Trees barely moved with the slight breeze and everyone had fallen silent. The kids were asleep on the travois that Becky's horse was pulling and the adults all seemed exhausted as well. If it wasn't for the fact that there were children riding along, he'd speed up the pace. It was still faster than being on foot but his patience was practically non-existent. He needed to know how his family was. The speculation of everything happening was driving him insane, to the point that he didn't even want to stop to rest. If his body allowed him to, he'd keep going until he made it back to Dallas.

The winding road and hilly terrain were probably adding more time on as well. The quickest way to get between two points was a straight line but they were in no shape to take things off road with Colin's injuries and the travois. Jake wasn't even sure if the horses were trained for mountain trails, though he assumed they probably were.

The hills also made it hard to see what was coming in front of them. With steep inclines and downhill jaunts, they could easily walk right into a crossfire where someone was waiting on them. Rethinking their strategy, Jake stopped his horses and turned to face everyone.

"I think someone needs to be a scout up front to watch for people. And that someone should probably be me."

"Are you crazy?" Colin sat up and shielded his eyes from the sun with his hand. "That's like committing suicide."

"Isn't it better for one of us than all of us? And it won't be a suicide mission. I can take a couple of guns. If you hear gunfire, turn and go the other way. Right now we'd all walk right up on someone. How is that going to get us home?"

"How is it gonna get you home, Jake? Haven't you been talking this whole time about how you need to check on your wife and kids?" Becky scooted her horse up a couple of steps. "We're a team. I don't think we need to split up."

Jake wiped the back of his neck with his palm and looked in the direction they were traveling. "Anyone else got a better idea? I don't see any other way."

"How many people have we actually ran into? That were alive?" Larry chimed in, his tone abrupt. "It's been like a ghost town everyone we've gone with the exception of that man you killed back at the lake. What are the chances we'll actually run into someone else?"

"Even if there's a small chance, I'm not liking it. The fact that there haven't been many people around makes me think they've formed a group. And once they see what we have, it's open season on us." Jake clenched his jaw and gripped the leather reins. "We can go two at a time if you want but we've only got four horses so we'd have to condense the supplies."

He started to say something else but a loud echo of gunfire rang out. When he finally realized what happened, Becky was off her horse, kneeling next to Larry who had been shot in the head, his glazed eyes staring up at the sky. Another gunshot pierced his eardrums and it took another few seconds for him to realize that his worst fear was coming to life - they were under attack, just like he had predicted, only he was hoping for more time to make a plan.

Grabbing Becky, he pulled her on his horse and grabbed the reins of her horse, motioning for them to ride east - there was a canyon they could go down in so whoever was shooting at them wouldn't have a good vantage point to continue to pick them off.

Aside from Larry, everyone was accounted for. The children crouched down near the river that cut through the canyon and Colin was with them. Jake edged up toward the top, staying low, gripping the shotgun so tight that his knuckles ached. The gunfire had stopped, likely due to the lack of ammunition like he was facing.

He searched in every direction - a pair of binoculars would've been helpful to catch whoever the culprit was. His gaze stopped on the highway where they were just a few moments before. Larry's body lay still, flat on the asphalt with a small puddle of blood beside him. He was speaking and then he was gone, just like that. Jake had told himself not to get too attached to anyone but seeing Larry dead made him sick to his stomach. Another casualty to tally up - another death that Jake would blame on himself.

He was having no success scouting who it was. They were hiding just as well as his group so he crawled back down to the river, keeping watch over his shoulder as he did.

"Larry's dead," Becky said, her voice quivering. "Did you see anything?"

"No. And now we're stuck here."

Jake scanned the canyon floor. They were exposed where they were. All it took was a few minutes of not paying attention and they would be surrounded in all directions.

"We need to all move over there." He pointed to a cove of trees. "We can hide there until we figure out what the hell we're gonna do."

The group moved to the trees and Jake checked on everyone. The kids were quiet, their eyes wide in fear from everything they had witnessed. They'd be scarred for life after this. The adults gathered near Colin's travois and Jake waited to speak, hoping one of them had a good idea.

"The longer we sit here and wait, the worse it gets," Colin finally spoke up. "They just came outta nowhere."

"We weren't ready." Jake took a swig of water and paced. "Either the person who shot Larry is a hell of a sniper or they're closer than we think. With all of the hills and trees, there's no way to tell."

"We can just wait them out, can't we? We've still got plenty of food and water," Becky motioned toward the stack of supplies. "If we go out there they'll kill us."

"And what if they have more than we do? What if their plan is to wait us out? I can't stand here and allow more bloodshed." Jake peered out of the trees, jumping when he saw two men walking along the top of the canyon rim. "Holy shit…" Whispering, he clutched the shotgun again. "There are two men up there."

"What? You can see them?" Becky's eyes widened. "What are they doing?"

"Pacing. Waiting. Both holding shotguns like this one." Jake closed his eyes and tried to catch his breath. "They don't know that we are armed yet. The second we start shooting, we better make damn sure we aim to kill or we're in trouble." He tossed Becky a gun. "I know you are nervous with guns but without Larry, I need your help." He also gave Colin a gun, just in case someone snuck behind them. Tossing a rifle to another man in the group, it meant three of them were mobile enough to get out of the trees and aim correctly.

"I'm not sure how many are out there," Jake said. "I only saw two but just like we were gonna do, they could be scouts."

"I'm not ready for this…" Becky said as tears ran down her face. "I don't know if I can do it."

"Think about your family, Becky. Think about getting home to them. If we don't do this, you'll never see any of them again." Jake was partly telling her and partly telling himself. "We can't wait much longer. They're gonna close in on us and then we'll be trapped. Are y'all with me?"

"We're ready."

"On my count, we'll go." Jake gripped the cold metal of the shotgun, taking a deep breath before he began to count.

CHAPTER TWENTY-NINE

"His girlfriend lives in that house right there!"

Ben pointed to a nice, two-story brick home with a picket fence around the yard. Just like the majority of houses in the neighborhood, the windows were busted out and the front door was hanging wide open. It wasn't a good sign but Alice ran toward it anyway. Ben was right behind her, matching her step for step.

"Dylan! Dylan are you inside here?"

She went through the threshold, the only light cascading in from the windows through half open blinds. The place had been looted just like her own home. Cabinets were open, the refrigerator was empty, and all of the pantries had nothing left inside but empty boxes. Stopping in the middle of the floor, Alice tried hard not to lose her composure again. Ben came down the stairs, his eyes downcast.

"They're not up there either."

"Does this place have a basement?"

Alice didn't wait for Ben to answer. She ran through the house, checking other doors until she found one that had a dark staircase. The hair on the back of her neck stood up but hope was restored when a small light flashed several feet below.

"Dylan? Dylan are you down there?" Her voice echoed against the cement walls and though she couldn't see, she took the steps down. It occurred to her halfway down that it could be someone out to hurt her but she was already committed to getting down there. "Dylan?"

"Mom? Mom, is that you?"

She'd recognize that voice anywhere. It was Dylan, and as she reached the dirt floor, the light from the lantern was brighter, giving her a much better look at who was down inside the basement. The thick musty smell was welcomed - anything was welcomed since she knew her child was okay. Pulling him in for a hug, she ran her fingers through his hair and kissed the top of his head.

"Have you been down here this whole time?"

"Mom…" He whispered, his voice trailing off. "Mom, it's Katy." He pointed to the corner, flashing the lantern in that direction. There were streaks in the dirt on his face where tears had fallen. "She was hurt. I… she's dead, mom. Katy is dead."

Alice took the lantern from Dylan and slowly approached the lifeless body in the corner. It was a young girl, about Dylan's age, with a large gash right at her hairline. There was no blood on her and her eyes were halfway closed like she was in REM sleep. Her skin was pale and when Alice checked for a pulse, rigor mortis had already set in, confirming what Dylan had said. The girl was dead.

"What happened, Dylan?"

Alice noticed Ben had joined them in the basement, all three of them gathering around Katy. She didn't know the girl but her heart ached for her son. She had meant a lot to him and now she was gone.

"It all started so fast. We were at school and everyone was telling us to run. Her house was the closest to the school so we started running this way. Something hit her on the head, mom. It knocked her out. I had to carry her." Dylan paused as more tears fell and he wiped his face with his shirt collar. "We were in the living room and I tried to clean her up. I tried to doctor her wound. She was bleeding so much. I thought we were safe and then I heard people breaking in. They were up to no good. So I took Katy down here and locked the door, hoping no one would think to look down here. And then... and then she stopped breathing. I tried CPR. I tried everything, Mom."

Alice pulled him in, hugging him tighter than she ever had before. "I'm so sorry, Dylan. I'm so sorry."

He quivered in her grasp, his body shaking as he buried his face in her shoulder. His arm tears soaked through her scrubs. "What is happening? Why are we stuck here like this? Why didn't help come?"

"I don't think anyone knows, Dylan. We're trying to get that figured out. I wanted to come find you. I'm so glad we're together now." She pulled the water bottle from her bag and handed it to him. "I bet you're thirsty. Drink all of it. We have a big water cooler back at the house full of water, thanks to Ben. Tom and Randi are there and we should probably all go back. We need to stick together."

"Uncle Tom?"

"Yeah, Uncle Tom and his new wife Randi."

"What about her?" Dylan pointed toward Katy. "What do we do about her?"

"She's fine where she is, Dylan. No one will mess with her down here. No one can even see her."

"I don't want to just leave her here."

"We will come back and give her a proper burial when we can, Dylan. I promise. But we need to get back home. We need to be with family. We need to be at the house since that's where dad and Sophie will first go when they get back to Dallas."

"Is dad there?" He wiped the tears from his face, drinking the rest of the water.

His question was like a punch in the gut. "No. It's just us right now, but we'll find both him and Sophie. We found you. I know we'll find them, too. Come on. Let's get out of here. I bet you're starving."

Dylan led them up the stairs with the lantern. Though it wasn't all resolved, finding Dylan was a huge stroke of good news for Alice. Now they had to hope luck would be on their side to get Jake and Sophie back home safely as well. Once they were all reunited, they could attempt to find some normalcy in the midst of the chaos happening all around them.

***

"One... two... THREE!"

Jake didn't hesitate as they all ran out, shooting immediately. He made sure to take careful aim so they wouldn't waste bullets and he slowed himself, training right on the first man. Pulling the trigger, he hit the man in the leg, making him fall. The second man fell with him and he couldn't tell if he had been hit, or if he was just taking cover.

Hiding behind a large rock, Jake kept the gun up, ready to fire. He saw the top of the hat one of the men was wearing and fired, hitting him, sending him backward. There was enough blood to confirm that he was either dead or he would be soon. The second man shot at him, splintering pieces of rock, hitting him close to the eye. It took him a second to blink away the dust and to be able to see clear again, but as he gained his composure, he heard gunshots from Becky and the other man who had stepped in to help.

Staying down in the canyon wasn't going to help them. It was providing good cover but to fully know how many people they were dealing with, Jake needed to see how many were up there. The last thing they needed was to run out of ammunition and be stuck. He didn't have time to tell the others of his plan. If they all stayed together the man on the canyon rim could pick them all off together.

Running toward the horse trail they had taken down, Jake ran up the hill, his legs burning, his lungs aching. He felt the weight of the handgun in his pocket along with the shotgun in his hand. Double checking to make sure it was loaded, he slid a shell inside, ready to shoot at whoever came at him. The worry about going up to the rim was getting caught in friendly fire but it was a sacrifice he needed to make to get these men off of them.

Sliding behind a large oak tree, Jake saw the man he had shot, dead from the gunshot wound to his head. The other man was crouched down and lying low on the ground. Aiming, Jake shot him in the leg, making sure the injury would only hinder him and not kill him. He needed answers and hopefully, the man would be honest.

Walking up to him, Jake kicked his gun out of his reach and aimed the shotgun right at his chest. The man rolled on his side and looked up at him, holding his hands up at his chest. It felt like a movie scene from an old western, and Jake could feel at any moment that someone was going to come up behind him and kill him.

"You son of a bitch… you shot me!" The man's words came out in short pants and sweat gathered on his brow.

"Just like you shot someone in my group and killed him."

"What do you want?"

"I wanna know how many more are coming." Jake stayed even keel, hoping he wasn't wearing his nervousness out in the open. Deep inside, he couldn't get his heart to stop racing.

"How many more of what?"

The man was playing stupid. He knew exactly what Jake was referring to. He grit his teeth and said, "How many more people gunning to kill us?"

"I'd say the entire world. You have horses and guns. And you're broadcasting your supplies for all to see."

Jake rested his index finger on the trigger. It was still hard to believe that mankind was resorting to this sort of behavior. The world they lived in was civilized and it didn't take long for everyone to revert right back to killing each other for survival. He wasn't innocent - there were two men he had killed now, and possibly a third happening soon.

"You didn't answer my question. How much more in your group?" Jake pointed the shotgun closer, his arms aching from holding it up.

"Lots more. We just came looking and found you. We were gonna take the news back to everyone. Just because you stopped us don't mean they won't find out. They'll come looking when they realize we never made it back to the camp. Your ass is dead. You'll be lying belly up like your friend in days."

Jake clenched the shotgun, hearing footsteps coming closer. Noticing in his peripheral vision that it was Becky, the tension relaxed but he didn't take the gun off of the man. "Where is your camp at?"

"That I won't ever tell you."

Jake edged closer, pushing the metal of the barrel into the man's forehead. "Where is it?"

"I won't tell. You'll just have to kill me."

"Jake?" Becky spoke up but he had tunnel vision, not even looking her way.

"We could use you as a hostage when they come for us. You're not worth anything if I kill you."

"They won't give a damn. I'm just another mouth they have to feed. Keeping me alive will make me just another mouth you'll have to feed."

"Jake. Jake, back up!" Becky yelled, finally pulling him from his trance.

Doing as she asked, another loud gunshot rang out and the warm splatter of blood splashed on Jake's face. Opening his eyes, he saw the man was dead from a gunshot wound to his chest. Becky still had the gun aimed, a small plume of smoke escaping from the barrel.

"He was reaching for something. You couldn't see it but I could from where I was standing."

Jake knelt beside the body and pulled a small caliber pistol from the man's pocket. "Thanks, Becky. I guess you're a better shot than you thought, huh?"

"Desperate times call for desperate measures."

Standing, Jake searched each body, pulling a few more guns and an ammunition belt from each of them. Tossing Becky one of them, he slung the other one over his shoulder and took a deep breath, looking toward the horizon.

"We need to keep moving. I don't know if he was telling the truth or not, but there are more out there. The faster we get out of the area, the better."

"I'll get everyone ready." Becky started toward the trail back down into the canyon but Jake grabbed her arm, stopping her. "I'll be the front scout from now on. We'll have someone else stay back in the rear. Next time, we'll be ready. No one is going to march in here and take what we worked for."

Becky nodded and smiled. "I know. I trust you, Jake. We're gonna make it through this."

He watched as she went down into the canyon to get the group ready to move. Taking another deep breath, Jake closed his eyes to prepare himself for what was to come. They had come this far and survived. He wasn't going to let anything else get in their way, even if it meant killing more people. It was a new world with new laws. Kill or be killed. Anything less than surviving was unacceptable.

They still had many miles to go, but the next time Jake would be willing to stop and rest would be back home in Dallas, with his family safely by his side.

BOOK TWO COMING SOON!

Acknowledgments:

I would like to thank all of you readers out there! Without you, none of this would even be worth it, so thank you! I would also like to thank my mother, Patti Tate and my sister, Lizzy Gryder for their continued support of my writing! You guys are amazing!

Contact Information:

If you have time, please leave a review on the product page! Any feedback is always appreciated and helps me grow as a writer! I also love getting emails and messages from people, and I always write back – all opinions welcome! Below are different ways to contact me and get updates on new projects and books:

Join my mailing list to get updates on new releases! No spam will be sent!
http://eepurl.com/byKpRb

Email:
JTateAuthor@yahoo.com

Facebook:
https://www.facebook.com/RustyBucketPublishing

Twitter:
@JTateAuthor

Blog:
http://jessiettu.blogspot.com/

Looking for more post-apocalyptic thrillers? Check out TORNADO WARNING – THE DAMAGED CLIMATE SERIES BOOK ONE:

http://amzn.to/25BFtWW
In the blink of an eye, the small Texas town of Harper Springs is flattened by the worst tornadic system to ever hit the area. Homes are demolished, trees are uprooted, and people are left for dead.

Taking cover in a cellar with his son, Ryan Gibson narrowly escapes the storm and gets separated from his wife. He hopes that help will come fast – his child is severely injured and the crippling weather pattern rages on, making them pawns in Mother Nature's game.

Weeks pass with no sign of another human being. Tornadoes continue to hammer away at the already ravished land. Ryan wonders why they have been forgotten. Basic survival skills set in – their food rations get smaller, their water intake less, and their limited resources will soon be gone. With his son's fading health and his wife still missing, he will have to make a decision soon – leave their shelter and risk death, or stay patient and hold out hope that a rescue team is on the way.

A harsh truth will soon be revealed – the tranquil way of life in Harper Springs will never be the same.